I Ma

D0052138

THERE'S NO MYSTERY WHY CRITICS LOVE BILL PRONZINI AND "THE NAMELESS DETECTIVE"

"NO ONE IS BETTER AT FINDING LINKS BETWEEN TRICKY HOMICIDES THAN 'NAMELESS' AND NO ONE IS MORE POETIC IN RELATING THE DETAILS OF A CASE."
—*Booklist*

"THE READER'S INVOLVEMENT WITH 'NAMELESS' AND HIS PROBLEMS CONTINUES TO INCREASE IN INTENSITY, MAKING [THE SERIES] SUCCEED ON AN EMOTIONAL LEVEL RARE IN THE FIELD."
—*Ellery Queen's Mystery Magazine*

"PRONZINI'S LOVING DESCRIPTIONS OF THE BAY AREA AND ITS ECCENTRIC DENIZENS MAKE THIS SERIES DELIGHTFUL READING."
—*Publishers Weekly*

"PRONZINI IS A MAGNIFICENT ENTERTAINER OF THE FIRST RANK. HIS 'NAMELESS DETECTIVE' SERIES IS NOW ONE OF THE THREE OR FOUR MOST IMPORTANT SERIES BEING WRITTEN—WRY, MELODRAMATIC, COLORFUL, CONTEMPORARY."
—*Cedar Rapids Gazette*

"PRONZINI IS THE LOGICAL CLAIMANT TO THE CROWN OF PRIVATE-EYEDOM."
—*The Norfolk Virginian-Pilot*

JACKPOT

A *"Nameless Detective"* Mystery

BILL PRONZINI

A DELL BOOK

Published by
Dell Publishing
a division of
Bantam Doubleday Dell Publishing Group, Inc.
666 Fifth Avenue
New York, New York 10103

ISBN: 0-440-20821-1

Reprinted by arrangement with Delacorte Press

Printed in the United States of America
Published simultaneously in Canada

January 1991

10 9 8 7 6 5 4 3 2 1

RAD

For Brian DeFiore

MOST DAYS, I'M ALL RIGHT. Close to my old self again.

It has been almost two months since the end of the ordeal at Deer Run. The first few weeks were the hardest. People flocking around wherever I went, asking endless questions— the media, old friends and casual acquaintances, strangers who felt they were entitled to probe into my personal life and private hell by right of public domain. Voyeurs, many of them, and not all well-meaning. I craved human contact, but I did not crave the poking and prodding attention, as if I were some sort of curious specimen on display in a zoo cage. Anonymity was what I needed—that, and Kerry and the comfort and routine of my work.

If it were not for Kerry and Eberhardt, things might have been much worse. They shielded me whenever they could; they gave me stability and normalcy and understanding and love. For the ninety-seven days I was away, chained like an animal to the wall of an isolated mountain cabin, they kept the faith . . . as if those ninety-seven days were nothing more than an extended vacation or business trip. As if they had known all along that I would come home again. My flat and everything in it just as it had always been, waiting. My car put away in storage. My business and personal affairs kept in order. So that when I did come home, it required little surface effort to step back into the mainstream of my life.

The old saw is true: Time heals. It blurs the past, too; today's news becomes tomorrow's recent history and next week's half-forgotten memory. Days go by now without anyone reminding me of the thing I went through. There are the nightmares, of course, but there have always been nightmares and there will always be nightmares. They are part of the job, part of the lives of men like me.

But there are still days when I wake up on edge, with little patterns of dread lurking like goblins in the corners of my mind. Days or parts of days when I can't work, can't concentrate, can't stand to be alone or to be cooped up in an enclosed space even if others are present. Sometimes, on those days, I call Kerry and she comes to be with me, to walk with me on crowded streets or in the park or on Ocean Beach where I can feel the soothing closeness of the Pacific. Other times I want no one to talk to, not even Kerry, so I go alone to walk or sit or just drive. And slowly, gradually, as time wears on, the goblin shapes vanish, and the edginess vanishes, and I am no longer afraid.

Most days, I'm all right. Close to my old self again.

Most days.

Chapter 1

WHEN I GOT HOME that Friday evening, there were two messages on my answering machine.

The first was from a Hollywood TV producer named Bruce Littlejohn, who had been pestering me off and on for weeks. "Yo, guy, Bruce here. It's heating up, baby, and I mean burn-your-fingers hot. You wouldn't believe who I been talking to. Just one of the biggies on the little screen, that's all, and I do mean a *biggie*. He loved the concept. What I mean, it melted his chocolate bar. No shit, I think we got him in the bag. I'm winging up this aft to see some sugar daddies, talk numbers. How about you and me have breakie tomorrow ayem? Nine-ish, Stanford Court. Think I can get you a consultancy on the flick but we need to rap, get our signals straight. Extra maple syrup on your waffles, you know what I mean? Nine-ish tomorrow, don't forget. Be good until. *Ciao*, kid."

Hollywoodspeak. Mostly as indecipherable to us laymen as a coded CIA message. What it boils down to, I thought, is that they're all as crazy as stoned monkeys down there.

The second message was from Kerry. "Hi, it's me. Five-thirty now and I just tried calling your office but Eb said you'd already left. Can you come over a little early tonight, six-thirty instead of seven? There's somebody I'd like you to talk to—business, not social. Okay? Love you."

Love you too, I thought.

I reset the machine, went into the kitchen and took a bottle of lite beer out of the refrigerator. One beer a day—that was my limit now. I had lost more than forty pounds in that cabin at Deer Run and I was determined to keep it off. The reason had nothing to do with vanity or even health; losing the weight had allowed me to survive those three hellish months, and my mind had translated the weight loss into something both symbolic and visceral. I *had* to keep the pounds off; the slow mending process, as fragile as it still was, depended on it. So I consumed my one beer a day, I ate sparingly and limited my intake of fats and carbohydrates, and I followed a somewhat less rigorous daily exercise program than the one I had developed in the cabin. And I would keep doing these things as long as I was physically capable of it.

In the bedroom again I put on a clean shirt. Through the window I could see a cold wind swirling leaves and a scrap of paper into the misty overcast sky. Late May in San Francisco and it was already topcoat weather. Tourists come here this time of year with nothing but spring and summer clothing in their suitcases and then register loud complaints, as if they were victims of a conspiracy instead of their own shoddy planning. If San Francisco had weather like L.A., the city would be inundated not only with tourists but with sun-worshiping transplants from east of the Rockies—and then where would natives like me be? The city was changing too rapidly and too negatively as it was. Drugs and drug dealers had the poorer sections in a stranglehold. The politicians had mismanaged all aspects of local government until there was a huge debt that had brought on a cutback in public services. Yuppies and Asians and money-grubbing developers were changing the faces of the old neighborhoods, a few for the better, too many for the worse, and all irreparably. Sometimes I felt I no longer knew the city, that it was no longer mine even though I had lived in it for more than half a century. That it was metamorphosing into an alien entity, and that maybe its new existence would be as vulnerable to destruction as a butterfly's after it emerges from its cocoon. But at least the weather was the same; there was nothing the drug dealers or the pols or the tourists or the developers could do to change that. Fog and chill winds invaded San Francisco from late May until September and always would, and I for one was glad of it.

I finished my beer, got my topcoat, went out and picked up my car and drove to Diamond Heights. When I turned down Kerry's street I felt my hands turn slick around the wheel, the stirrings of apprehension. It was here, on this street, that I had been kidnapped at gunpoint; shoved into the back of a car, handcuffed, chloroformed, and driven away for ninety-seven days. Since I had been back the sweaty apprehension gripped me nearly every time I came here, as if my subconscious harbored fears that it would happen again, or that I might somehow be thrust back in time and forced to relive it. On one of the bad days, I could not come here at all. The one time I had tried it I had had an anxiety attack so severe, it was almost crippling.

My watch said that it was just six-thirty when I let myself into Kerry's building. I thought that if she had company, I had better ring the bell instead of using my key, and I did that when I got up to her apartment. She came and opened the door.

I kissed her. Said against her ear, "Who have you got here?"

"One of the secretaries from the agency." By agency, she meant Bates and Carpenter, the ad firm where she worked as a senior copywriter. "Her name's Allyn Burnett."

"What's her trouble?"

"I'll let her tell you," Kerry said. "I don't know if there's anything you can do for her, but she does have reason for concern. I think so, anyway."

I nodded, and went on into the living room. The woman sitting on the couch near the fireplace looked to be in her midtwenties. Blond, thin, and hipless in a tan wool dress, plainfeatured; but for all of her plainness, there was that little-girl quality about her that stirs protective instincts in some men.

She wore a solemn expression now, but you sensed that when she smiled, it would be like a light going on to reveal a warm, pleasant room. She would not lack for male attention, I thought.

We exchanged names and small smiles, the way strangers do, and I sat down in one of the chairs opposite. Kerry was a businesswoman and she knew that it was always easier for two people to establish a business relationship one-on-one; she said to me, "I'll get some coffee," and disappeared into the kitchen.

Allyn Burnett cleared her throat. "I read about you in the papers," she said. "About . . . well, you know. And Ms. Wade says you're the best private detective in the city."

"She's biased. And you shouldn't believe everything you read in the papers."

Small, wan smile. There was a little silence; then she said, with emotion thickening her voice, "It's about my brother. David. He . . . a week ago he . . . took his own life. With pills . . . an overdose of pills."

Old story, sad story. "I'm sorry," I said.

"Yes. But it doesn't make any sense, you see. No sense at all."

"What doesn't?"

"That he would commit suicide."

"Well, people on drugs—"

"No, he *wasn't* on drugs."

That was an old, sad story too: the faith and denial of a loved one. "You said he took an overdose of pills . . ."

"Sleeping pills. He never took those things before, never."

"So he bought them with the intention of taking his own life?"

"That's how it seems, yes."

"Do you doubt it?"

"Doubt what?"

"That your brother actually did commit suicide. Do you suspect foul play?"

"No, it isn't that. I can't imagine anyone wanting to harm David. And the police . . . they say it couldn't have been anything but suicide. The circumstances . . ." She shook her head and looked into the cold fireplace.

I said gently, "Then just what is it that's bothering you, Ms. Burnett? Why would you want a detective?"

She sat without answering for a time. It was not really the fireplace she was staring at; it was at something long ago and far away. I waited, listening to Kerry in the kitchen making homey sounds with crockery. Outside the picture window, wisps of fog chased each other across the balcony and the wind rattled glass and made cold purling sounds in the gray dusk.

Allyn said abruptly, as if my questions had just registered, "He had no reason to want to die. No real reason. He was so young, so happy—he had a good job, he and Karen Salter were planning to get married in September . . . it just doesn't make any sense that he would kill himself."

"Did he leave a note?"

"Yes. But all it said was that it was best for everyone if he . . . that Karen and I should forgive him . . ."

Her voice broke on the last few words and I thought she was going to go weepy on me. If she had, I would have sat there like a lump, feeling awkward and helpless; crying women have that effect on me. But she didn't break down. A couple of hiccoughing sobs escaped her and then she caught her breath and leaned forward with her mouth and throat working, as if she were trying to snatch the sobs out of the air and swallow them again. She put one hand up to her face, fingers splayed, and sat there like that: little girl lost.

I wanted to tell her that she was grasping at straws, wasting her time and mine. I wanted to say that in very few cases of suicide was anything sinister or even particularly unusual involved. I wanted to remind her that the suicide rate among young people today was at an all-time high; that kids who seemed to have every reason for living, who seemed carefree and happy on the surface, could in fact be seething bundles of neuroses underneath. Dissatisfaction with their lives, disillusionment with modern society, pressures, fears, private demons—all those and more could and did drive a young person to suicide even more easily than an older person.

But I didn't say any of that. All I said was, "Do you know of anything unusual that happened to him recently? Any trouble he might have gotten himself into?" I have never particularly wanted to be either a father or a father figure, but there are times when my latent paternal instincts get the best of me.

She said, "No trouble, no. But the money . . . it must be the money. Only that doesn't make any sense either."

"Money?"

"Two hundred thousand dollars. David won it two weeks before he . . . died."

The amount surprised me. "How did he win that much? One of the lottery games?"

"No. In Reno. He and a friend went up for the weekend and David . . . it was one of those super-jackpots you read about."

"Progressive slot machine?"

"Yes. Something called Megabucks."

"What did he do with the money?"

"Paid some bills. Bought a new car for himself, a Corvette. Bought expensive presents for Karen and me. And then . . . this is the crazy part . . . then he *lost* the rest of it. And more—enough so that he had to sell back the Corvette and return the presents and go around trying to borrow money. I gave him a thousand dollars, all I had in my savings, but it wasn't even close to being enough."

"Lost the money how? Gambling?"

"That's what he said. He bet it on sports events with those places in Reno and Las Vegas . . . what do you call them?"

"Sports books."

"Yes, sports books."

"So he was a heavy gambler?"

"No. No, he wasn't. That's what's so crazy about it. He never gambled much—never. He went to Reno and Lake Tahoe several times a year, but it was mostly to see the shows. He never won or lost more than a hundred dollars on any trip."

"Are you sure of that? Sometimes compulsive gamblers cover up the extent of their losses."

"Then he would've had a lot of debts, wouldn't he? He didn't. Karen or I would have known if he had."

"Well, it could be that the big jackpot changed him—gave him the gambling fever. It wouldn't be the first time a major windfall has done that to somebody."

"That's what everyone says. But David was my brother, I knew him better than anyone. He just wasn't like that."

"Then why would he make large bets on sports events?"

". . . What if he didn't?"

"You mean he might have lost the money some other way?"

"It's possible, isn't it?"

"Anything's possible," I said. "But gambling is the only way I can think of for somebody to lose a large sum of money in a few days." Which wasn't true. There were other ways, illegal and highly unpleasant ways. But I did not want to go into that with her.

"It just doesn't make any sense," she said. "Money never mattered that much to David. What he cared about was sports. And going places, doing things, having fun."

"The more money you have, the more places you can go and the more fun you can have. Theoretically, anyhow."

She shook her head and said, "He wasn't materialistic."

"All right. When did you last see him?"

"Two days before he died."

"How did he seem then?"

"Fine." But then she shook her head again. "No, that's not so. He always put on a happy face, no matter how he was feeling inside. But I could tell when something was bothering him. He was upset about something, I sensed that, but he wasn't depressed. He didn't act like someone thinking about suicide."

She thought she knew him so well. Only he was the type who always put on a happy face to hide his true feelings. And if a person is thinking about suicide, and wants to hide his intention from his loved ones, naturally he'll act as normal as possible. But grieving relatives aren't always capable of sorting out contradictions and looking reasonably at facts. Grief itself is an irrational emotion.

I said, "Was it just that one time he struck you as upset about something? Or did you notice it before then?"

"He was like that a couple of days earlier, too, when he asked me to return the necklace he'd bought and to borrow my savings. That was when he said he'd lost all his jackpot winnings and more with the sports books."

"He told his fiancée the same thing?"

"Yes. She finds it just as hard to believe."

"What about his friend, the one who was in Reno with him? Did you ask him about it?"

"Jerry Polhemus. He and David used to share an apartment, before David moved in with Karen last year. Yes, I asked him. At the funeral. He couldn't tell me anything . . . didn't have much to say at all." She paused, frowning. "It was odd, though, the way Jerry acted that day."

"Odd in what way?"

"He seemed . . . I don't know, angry about something. Almost as if he weren't . . ."

"Weren't what?"

"Weren't sorry David was dead."

"Why wouldn't he be, if they were close friends?"

"I don't know. Maybe I'm wrong. I was so upset that day . . ."

"Had he and your brother had some kind of falling out?"

"Not that I know of."

"You didn't talk to him about it? Then or since?"

"No. I haven't seen him since."

I allowed another little silence to build. She looked so forlorn, sitting there. And I had a soft schedule at present, with more than a little extra time on my hands. And I needed to work as much and as often as possible. . . .

"Well," I said finally, "I suppose I could talk to Jerry Polhemus for you. See what else I can find out."

"Would you?" Relief brightened her voice.

"I'll do what I can. But don't expect too much of me.

Detectives aren't miracle workers." Nor clinical psychologists, I thought.

"I know. It's enough to have you try."

It wasn't and we both knew it. Still another little silence descended. Then Kerry came in—she'd been listening in the kitchen, if I knew her—and distributed coffee and gave me an approving glance before she went over to sit beside Allyn.

There was some more talk, not much. I took down Allyn's address and telephone number, the addresses of Jerry Polhemus and Karen Salter, and such other information as I thought I might need. Allyn asked me if I wanted a retainer—they get that word off TV—and I said no, not until I had drawn up a contract for her to sign. She thanked me again, and we shook hands, gravely, and Kerry showed her out while I sat there sipping my lukewarm coffee and wondering why I had never learned how to say no.

When Kerry came back she plunked herself down in my lap and said, "That was nice of you, offering to help Allyn."

"Yeah."

"Well, it was. There really isn't much you can do, is there."

"I doubt it. But I've always been a sucker for stray cats and lost waifs, as if you didn't know. How much does she make at the agency?"

"Three-fifty a week."

"Uh-huh. And the rest of her family's poor as church mice."

"Her mother and father are dead too. All she's got left now is an aunt in Los Altos."

"Christ. I'll be lucky if I make expenses."

Kerry kissed me, ardently. "You're a nice man, you know that?"

"Yeah. And you know where nice guys finish."

"In my bed, if they're lucky."

"I thought we were going out to dinner."

"We are. After dinner you get your nice-guy reward."

"So what are we waiting for? Go get your coat."

She went and got her coat. On the way downstairs I said, "That Hollywood producer called again today."

"What did he have to say this time?"

"Fortunately I wasn't home. He left a message. Things are getting burn-your-fingers hot, he said. He talked to one of the biggies on the little screen, he said, and the concept melted the guy's chocolate bar. Once we get our signals straight, he said, there'll be some extra maple syrup on my waffles."

Kerry shook her head. "They're all crazy down there," she said.

"Yup. He wants me to have breakie with him tomorrow morning."

"Breakfast? Are you going to?"

"Probably not. In the first place, he's a lunatic. And in the second place, I don't want him or anybody else making a movie about what happened last winter."

"Didn't he say it would be your life story?"

"Yeah, sure. But my life story is dull. What happened up at Deer Run isn't dull."

"Well, you'd have the final say about what goes into it, wouldn't you?"

"Supposedly. You think I should see him?"

"Not if you don't want to. I know how you feel about what happened."

No, you don't, babe, I thought. But I smiled at her and said jokingly, because I did not want things to turn serious between us tonight, "The last time I saw Brucie he drank five shots of Wild Turkey for lunch. I wonder what he drinks for breakie."

"Booze is better than cocaine or heroin," she said.

"Marginally. But that's about the only positive thing you can say about him."

"He's produced a couple of movies, hasn't he? He can't be a *complete* idiot."

"His big hit was called *Shoplifter: A Mother's Tragedy*. You think it takes a Rhodes scholar to make a TV movie about shoplifting?"

"I never saw it. Maybe it was good. Who's to say he couldn't make a good, honest movie about *you*?"

"Nobody'd watch it."

"Sure they would. You'd be immortalized on TV."

"Immortalized on TV is a contradiction in terms."

"Says you. Who do you suppose the 'biggie' is?"

"The guy with the melted chocolate bar? No idea. You know how much prime-time TV I watch."

We were outside now, climbing uphill into the teeth of the wind. Halfway to where my car was parked, Kerry said, "I wonder if it's Brian Keith."

"Who?"

"Brian Keith. The 'biggie.' You look a little like him, except that he's fair and you're dark."

"And he's Irish, with a name like Brian Keith, and I'm Italian. How about they get an Italian to impersonate me?"

"Ben Gazzara," she said.

"Dom DeLuise," I said.

She was horrified. "My God, what a thought!"

"It's *all* nonsense, that's the point. Bruce Littlejohn isn't going to get financing to make a TV movie about me, with Brian Keith or Dom DeLuise or Rin Tin Tin or Howdy Doody. Anyday now somebody will realize what an airhead he is and put him away for observation."

"Don't bet on it. If they put away all the crazies in Hollywood, there wouldn't be anybody left to make movies."

Now we were at the car. I unlocked the passenger side, went around and got in under the wheel. "I just figured it out," I said.

"Figured what out?"

"Why you want me to see Brucie tomorrow. Why you want him to make a movie about me. You're a closet groupie."

"I'm what!"

"A closet Hollywood groupie. You think Bruce Littlejohn is your ticket to La-La Land and audiences with the stars."

She glared at me. "Shut up and drive," she said.

I shut up and drove, smiling a little, enjoying myself. This was one of my good days. Even Allyn Burnett's dead brother hadn't changed that.

Chapter 2

I TRULY DID NOT WANT to go downtown on Saturday morning
to meet Bruce Littlejohn for "breakie." Unfortunately I spent
Friday night at Kerry's. She was awake at seven, had me awake
not long afterward, went and fixed me coffee, and made sure I
was aware of the time. At a quarter to eight she said, gently,
that I ought to get ready if I was going to make it down to the
Stanford Court by nine.

I said, "But I don't *want* to have breakfast with an asshole
from Hollywood."

"He might actually have good news for you."

"Yeah, sure."

"Aren't you just a little curious?"

"No."

"I am," she said, and she gave me one of her wistful looks.

I would rather do battle with a slobbering, attack-trained
Doberman than a woman's wistful looks; I'd have a better
chance of coming up winners. I sighed, I grumbled. And then
I got out of bed and showered and dressed and went off to
have maple syrup poured on my waffles. Figuratively speaking,
I hoped.

It was nine-fifteen by the time I walked into the Stanford

Court, but that didn't matter because Littlejohn was also fifteen minutes late. We ran into each other in the middle of the lobby.

He was a short, round, middle-aged guy who wore flashy clothes made for somebody half his age and a couple of pounds of gold jewelry, most of it around his neck. This morning he had on lemon-yellow trousers, a ruffled pink shirt open at the throat, a paisley neck scarf, and a mod-type off-white jacket with tight sleeves that ended halfway up his forearms. All of the clothing was wrinkled and baggy, whether on purpose or not I had no idea. His hair was even bushier than I remembered it, and so black he might have dyed it with shoe polish. At his best he looked like one of the Three Stooges in a Mack Sennett two-reeler. Today he was not at his best. Today his eyes were blood-filled and sunken deep inside puffy hollows, his face had a swollen look, his appendages trembled, and he walked the way a man might if he were barefoot on a bed of hot coals. Hangover with a capital *H*.

The Stanford Court is a very ritzy, conservative Nob Hill hotel, even more exclusive than the Mark Hopkins and the Fairmont nearby. Well-dressed citizens, most of them past fifty, stared warily at Littlejohn as if they thought he might suddenly become violent. They stared at me, too, when he threw one arm around my shoulders and used his other hand to squeeze mine like a grocery shopper squeezing a peach to see if it was ripe. He also breathed on me, which made it difficult for me not to throw up on him. He had a breath like a goat with pyorrhea.

"Oh, baby," he said in rueful tones, "I got a head big as a watermelon. Goddamn booze. Sometimes I think I should have kept on doing coke, never mind what happened to guys like Belushi. At least you don't wake up with a head like the Goodyear blimp and a taste in your mouth like some dog took a dump on your tongue."

An aristocratic lady in furs heard that, gasped delicately, and then cut him up with a glare like a laser beam. He didn't even know she existed. I tried offering her a small, apologetic smile, but she curled her lip at me. Guilt by association.

"It was worth it, though, kid," Littlejohn said. He had hold of my arm now—the way Kerry holds it when we're walking together—and was steering me toward the restaurant. "I got a couple of sugar daddies lined up. *Mucho* bucks. Last night it was fast serves and hot volleys; now the ball's in their court. But the linesman's on our side and we'll get the call, I feel it in my gut. You know what I mean?"

"Sure," I said. I had no idea what the hell he was talking about.

The restaurant wasn't crowded, but it took a few minutes for us to get a table. I think that was because there was a discreet discussion among the staff as to the advisability of seating somebody who looked like one of the Three Stooges with a hangover. Two different employees asked him if he was a guest of the hotel, as if they couldn't believe the management had been so lax. When we finally did get a table, it was at the rear and well removed from any of the other patrons.

A cherubic blond waitress appeared, looking as wary as the people out in the lobby. She couldn't keep her eyes off Littlejohn; she may have thought she was hallucinating. At length she asked him, "Black coffee for you, sir?"

He pulled a face. "Christ, no. Tell you what I want, sweetmeat. Three cinnamon buns, the frosted kind. Big ones. Six bananas, cut up in a bowl, no milk or cream. And a couple of bottles of Amstel lager."

She just looked at him. So did I. Pretty soon she said, tentatively, "Are you making some kind of joke?"

"Do I look like I'm joking? I'm in pain, sweetie."

"Three cinnamon buns, six bananas, and . . . two bottles of beer?"

"Amstel lager. Right."

"All just for you? For *breakfast*?"

"Right, right. Give my man here whatever he wants."

She shifted her gaze to me, not without reluctance. I eased her mind some by ordering coffee, orange juice, and an English muffin. She wrote that down, stared some more at Littlejohn, and went away looking dazed.

Littlejohn leaned toward me, as if he were about to impart a great truth. "Glucose," he said.

"Uh . . . pardon?"

"Glucose, baby. That's the secret."

"Of what?"

"Life. Yours and mine—everybody's. We're like cars and glucose is our high octane unleaded. Capeesh?"

"Glucose," I said, nodding.

"Too much booze, see, that sends the old corpus into a glucose depression. So the first thing you got to do the morning after, you got to build your glucose level back up. That's what the cinnamon buns are for. Lots of sugar, see?"

"Lots of sugar."

"Right. The bananas, they're for serotonin and norep. Norep, that's short for norepinephrine. The booze knocks down your serotonin and boosts up your norep. Adrenaline is what puts 'em back in balance, so you got to give the old adrenals a kick in the ass to get them producing. Gorilla fruit is the ass-kicker."

"Ass-kicker," I said.

"Right. And the beer, that's how you rebalance your screwed-up electrolytes. Beer's loaded with sodium and potassium, right? And what it *also* does, it manufactures urine. *That* washes all the alcohol poisons out of your system." He leaned back and spread his hands. "You see how the whole thing works?"

"Sure," I said. I had no idea what the hell he was talking about.

He nodded vigorously, winced, and nodded again much less vigorously. "Sure. I got the poop from this med student wanted to write screenplays. Lousy screenplays but he sure as hell knows his chemistry. Works like a charm. Eat those buns and bananas, drink the beer, go take a leak, and *voilà!* you're a new man."

This was going to be a long breakie, I thought. This was probably going to be the longest breakie of my life.

Littlejohn didn't want to talk business until his serotonin was down and his norep was up and his adrenals had been kicked in the ass; so we sat there and waited for the waitress, and after she came I sat there and watched Littlejohn hunch over his cinnamon buns and bananas and beer like a gaudy vulture over a road kill. The spectacle was such that I had no appetite for my English muffin and managed to get only half the orange juice down. After he was done eating he belched, not too loud, and went off to take the leak that would make him a new man. When he came back the new man looked as hungover as the old one, except that it was grinning. He sat down again, leaned toward me, and imparted his big news in the same great-truth tone he had used to tell me about glucose.

"Eldorp," he said.

At first I thought he'd belched again. I just stared at him. But it wasn't a belch; it was a name. "Frankie Eldorp," he said.

I said, "Who?"

"Frankie *Eldorp*, kid."

"Who's Frankie Eldorp?"

"You're putting me on, right? Joke, right?"

"No joke. I never heard of Frankie Eldorp."

"You never heard of the hottest face on the little screen?"

"No."

Littlejohn stared at me as if I might be an alien life form masquerading as a human. "Star of *The Destructor*. Don't tell me you never watched *The Destructor*."

"I don't watch much TV," I said.

"Geez," he said, awed.

It developed that *The Destructor* had been the number-one-rated show a couple of years back, about a guy who went around murdering lawbreakers in the name of truth, justice, and the American way. Frankie Eldorp had been its star. And it was Frankie Eldorp's chocolate bar that had been melted by the possibility of portraying me, a real-life private eye, in a TV movie based on my life.

That was the good news, according to Littlejohn. The bad news was that Frankie Eldorp was twenty-seven years old, stood five six, and weighed a hundred and thirty pounds fully armed. He also had petulant lips and a scraggly blond beard. Littlejohn showed me a publicity photo in which Eldorp bristled with prop Uzis and handguns.

"He's so hot he sizzles," Littlejohn said. "Steak on the grill, baby. The young chicks are apeshit over him."

"That figures," I said.

"Yeah. He plays older, too, don't worry about that. He did Father O'Mara in that flick last year, the one about the defrocked priest knocks up this black woman from the Detroit ghetto and they take off for Canada in a Winnebago. You remember that one, right?"

"One of my all-time favorites," I said. "Does he play taller and fatter, too?"

"Huh?"

"Frankie Eldorp. Does he play taller than five six and fatter than one-thirty?"

"Huh?"

"All those guns in his photo," I said, and now there was an edge to my voice. An edge in me, too, of a sudden. "Is he going to carry a gun when he plays me? Shoot people with it?"

"Well, hey, there's a certain amount of action—"

"I don't carry a gun," I said. "I don't shoot people." *I wanted to shoot somebody this past winter, real bad, but not anymore. Never again. Those were crazy days. Terrible days.*

"Sure, sure, we'll downplay that," Littlejohn said. "But what we're talking about here is *TV*, you know what I'm saying? Private eyes on TV, they got to carry guns—"

"Why?"

"Why? They just do, that's all. They always have, sweetheart. It's what the public expects."

"Lots of shooting, then. Heavy on the violence."

"*Action.* Like I said, kid, it's the name of the—"

"Car chases, helicopter chases, all that bullshit."

He spread his hands and said like a father trying to explain the facts of life to his not very bright child, "We're talking prime-time crime here. Capeesh? I mean, you're a private eye; we're not doing comedy or social drama, nothing light and nothing heavy, just boffo entertainment. You do a crime thing, you got to have action. And Frankie Eldorp's your top action actor, it's his trademark. He likes guns, he likes to do stunts, we got to take advantage of his talents to get the Nielsen numbers—"

"That's enough," I said. The edge was sharpening in me. I shoved my chair back and got on my feet.

"Hey," Littlejohn said, "hey, where you going?"

"To work," I said. "I've got a client and a job to do."

"Don't get your balls in an uproar, for chrissakes. We can work this out so you're happy, Frankie's happy, everybody—"

"No we can't. There's nothing to work out. I don't want any part of it."

"You will when you hear the numbers, kid. I haven't told you the numbers yet." He jumped up, caught my arm, breathed his goat's breath in my face. But he was no longer an amusing Hollywood crackbrain; he was a silly, uncaring, jerkoff exploiter and I did not want him touching me. I shoved his hand away as he said, "Fifty thousand for the story rights. Fifty K, right? And another twenty K for the consultancy, plus a slice of the profit pie. Two points, maybe three, how about that? Huh? Is that maple syrup on the old waffles?"

Numbers, just numbers; and foolish words like lines of dialogue in a bad film about somebody trying to convince somebody else to make a bad film. I shook my head at him, started away.

"No, wait, baby—"

"Good-bye, baby."

I left him standing there among all the staring customers. And took myself straight out of the hotel and slowly downhill to where I had parked my car.

There was just no way to make somebody like him understand. He floated on the surface of existence, in a boat made of money and make-believe. How could I make him understand that it was my life we had been discussing, my *life*, and that I could not turn it over to him? Nor any part of it—all the things that had shaped it, good and bad, and made me who and what I am. If I gave my life to him and Frankie Eldorp, they would distort it, cheapen and trivialize it, and in the end negate it: turn me into a chunk of meaningless prime-time boffo entertainment viewed by millions for two hours between Miller Lite and Mitsubishi commercials and promptly forgotten the instant it was offscreen. The real me would be forgotten soon enough after I was gone, but at least my life would stand as I had lived it in the real world, not as some minor-league Stallone had interpreted it in a phony world of glitter and painless death.

A man's life has little enough dignity. If he is any kind of man, he owes it to himself to preserve what little there is.

Chapter 3

JERRY POLHEMUS lived on Ninth Avenue in the inner Sunset, a few blocks from Golden Gate Park. His building had three units, one per floor, which meant that they were good-sized flats rather than apartments. He occupied the second floor, with at least two Asian families crowded together above him —there were a bunch of different Vietnamese or Laotian names on that mailbox in the vestibule—and a Hungarian couple below. One of the city's typically heterogenous neighborhood residences.

I pushed the button under Polhemus's mailbox—four times. Nobody home. Almost eleven of a Saturday morning, and the weather was a little better today; the sun seemed to be threatening to shine through the gray, though if it did make an appearance, it probably wouldn't stay around long. No weekend slugabed, Polhemus. Places to go and things to do.

I turned out of the vestibule, onto the sidewalk. And a voice high above me said in broken English, as if God were just learning the language, "You look for Jerry?"

I stopped and turned and tilted my head upward. A middle-aged Vietnamese or Laotian woman was leaning out of a third-floor window. In one hand was a dust mop that she was shaking vigorously; the wind caught the dust from it and swirled it around her head in a gray nimbus.

"Yes, I am."

"I hear bell," she said. "Very loud."

"Do you know where I might find him?"

"Work. Saturday morning, work."

"Where?"

"Carpet-clean place. You know?"

"Yes, ma'am. Which one?"

"Irving Street, not far. Over Nineteen Avenue."

"Can you tell me the name?"

She quit shaking the dust mop and shook her head instead, just as vigorously. "Irving Street, over Nineteen Avenue."

"Thanks."

"Okay," she said, and pulled her head back in and slammed the window shut for no particular reason that I could figure. Maybe she just liked to slam windows.

I drove downhill to Irving, found a place to park, hunted up a public telephone booth, and looked in the Yellow Pages under "Carpets & Rugs—Cleaning and Repairing." There was only one place on Irving: Basic Carpet Cleaners, "Put Your Rugs and Carpets in Caring Hands," Saturdays 9:00–1:00. And the street number located it a couple of blocks west of 19th Avenue.

When I walked into Basic Carpet Cleaners fifteen minutes later, a scowling fat guy in a suit and tie confronted me across a wide, bare counter. Prominent on the wall behind him was a sign that lied shamelessly, SERVICE WITH A SMILE.

"Yes?" he said.

"Does Jerry Polhemus work here?"

"He does. Are you here about a carpet or rug?"

"No. It's a personal matter."

That deepened his scowl. "Jerry has work to do."

"I won't take up much of his time."

"Is it important?"

"The person I represent thinks so."

"Represent? What do you mean, represent?"

The edginess Bruce Littlejohn had instilled in me was gone

now, dissipated by routine activity. But there was enough of a residue left to lower my tolerance level to the point of perversity. So I smiled at the fat guy. Didn't say anything, just smiled. It made him nervous; he was the sort who would always become nervous when people smiled at him for no reason, because he would think they had ulterior and probably nefarious motives.

At length he said, "Jerry's in the warehouse. You'll have to use the alley entrance."

There was a closed door in the wall behind him that I would have bet led directly into the warehouse. I smiled at him some more, for ten seconds or so, until he began to twitch; then I said, "Thanks. I'll be sure to mention you in my report," and turned for the door.

Behind me he said, "Report? What report?" And I went out, paused on the sidewalk, and smiled at him one last time through the glass.

I walked around to the alley and down it to Basic's backside. The warehouse doors were open, the opening filled with a van that had the company name and slogan painted on it. Inside the warehouse, two young guys in coveralls were working at a big steam-cleaning machine. The thing made plenty of noise, so there was no point in my trying to make myself heard above it. I squeezed inside past the van, maneuvered around stacked, tagged, and various-sized rolls of floor covering, and stopped near where the two guys were working.

They both frowned at me. One of them shut off the machine and the other said, "Help you?" but not as if the prospect pleased him. This was one hell of a cheerful place of business. You could find more good humor in an undertaking parlor.

"I'm looking for Jerry Polhemus."

"That's me. What do you want?"

"We talk in private?"

"Why? What about?"

"David Burnett."

The name rocked him a little—much more than it should have. That surprised *me*. So did the sudden nervous tic on his jaw, the flicker of something in his eyes that might have been fear. He was quick to get his defenses up, though. And quick to tell the co-worker that he'd be right back, then to lead me out into the alley.

The first thing he said there was, "You a cop?"

"Now why would you think that?"

"You look like one."

"I'm a private investigator," I said.

". . . No shit?"

"You want to see my license?"

Headshake. "Who you working for?"

"David Burnett's sister."

"Allyn? Why'd she hire a detective?"

"She wants to know what drove her brother to suicide."

"I don't know anything about it," Polhemus said. "Christ, I told her that at the funeral."

I let him stew a little while I looked him over. Mid-twenties. Short, stocky without being fat. Good-looking in a weak, characterless way. Brown hair and a bushy brown mustache that seemed longer on one side than the other and gave his face a slightly lopsided appearance. His eyes were bright, nervous, like a bird's eyes. Scared about something, I thought, and trying like hell to hide the fact.

I said, "He ever mention suicide to you? Give you any indication he was thinking about taking his own life?"

"Hell no. Why should he?"

"So you were surprised when you heard the news?"

"Sure I was. Wouldn't you be surprised if your best friend offed himself?"

That much was truth, I thought. Or half-truth, because he was also holding something back. You get so you can feel it when people lie or half lie to you.

"Burnett strike you as troubled the week before his death?"

"No. But I didn't see much of him that week."

"He told his sister he lost all the money he won in Reno, and more besides. Gambled it away with the sports books. That what he told you?"

"Yeah. Yeah, that's what he said."

"What did you think?"

"Think?"

"Didn't you find it odd?"

Now his fear was beginning to show through the camouflage he'd thrown up. He seemed to realize it, and shoved his hands into the pockets of his coveralls as if he were afraid they might start to shake and really give him away. He wet his lips before he said, "What you mean, odd?"

"His sister says he never gambled for high stakes. So why all of a sudden would he lay down big bets with the sports books?"

"Greed, why else."

"Got a taste of big money and wanted more."

"Yeah. Dave was a greedy bastard."

"Bastard? I thought he was your best friend."

"Sure he was. So?"

"Then why call him a greedy bastard?"

"Because he was. You don't have any pals who're greedy?"

"A couple. But I wouldn't refer to them as bastards if they'd killed themselves last week."

No answer. He was literally biting his tongue.

I said, "You and Dave have some kind of falling out?"

"No. What makes you think that?"

"Over money, maybe? The money he won up in Reno?"

"I told you, no."

"You were with him when he hit the Megabucks jackpot."

"So what?"

"One of the big casinos, was it?"

"Yeah. One of the big casinos."

"Which one?"

"Coliseum Club. What difference does that make?"

"Lot of fanfare in places like the Coliseum Club when there's a big jackpot payoff," I said. "Plenty of glory for the winner. The guy he happens to be with, though, gets zip."

"That's for fuckin' sure."

"But Dave was your buddy. He probably gave you a cut of his winnings—a small slice of the pie, at least a few crumbs. That how it was, Jerry?"

"None of your business."

"Or maybe he didn't give you anything at all. Maybe that's why you called him a greedy bastard."

"I said it's none of your goddamn business!" His voice had taken on a shrill edge.

"And then he blew the whole wad," I said. "And ran up a debt besides. He borrowed money from his sister to help pay it off. He hit you up for a loan too?"

"No."

"Would you have given him money if he had?"

"I don't have any to loan out."

"Uh-huh. So what do you think? You think he killed himself because he was in deep and couldn't raise enough to pay off the sports books? Or did he have some other reason?"

"I told you, I don't know!"

"Seems out of character for a happy-go-lucky guy to knock himself off just because he loses money gambling, gets himself in debt. You'd think his philosophy would be easy come, easy go. Unless money meant a lot to him?"

"Everybody likes bucks."

"Some more than others. How about you?"

"Yeah, so?"

"What would you do if you got your hands on two hundred thousand bucks? How would you spend it?"

I had worked him into a pretty good state: fear, confusion, anger. He couldn't seem to keep his feet still; shuffled them around like a kid with a full bladder. But you can push somebody just so far. Then he either pushes back or breaks and runs.

Polhemus was the kind that broke and ran. "That's enough bullshit questions," he said. "You're not a cop, you're nobody, I don't have to talk to you."

"Why not, unless you've got something to hide?"

"Leave me the hell alone," he said. "You hear? You bother me again and I'll call the cops on *you*."

There was no force or conviction behind the threat; it was nothing more than a lame exit line. He swung away from me and hustled himself back inside the warehouse.

Lies and half-truths, I thought as I walked around to where I had parked the car. Polhemus's responses had been loaded with one or the other. But why? And why was he so frightened? It was possible that he had somehow managed to get hold of a portion of David Burnett's jackpot winnings, and was covering up the fact—but then why would Burnett have lied to his sister about the sports books, sold back the car and presents he'd bought, borrowed a thousand dollars from her? I couldn't see where a theft by Polhemus would explain Burnett's suicide, either.

Puzzling.

Maybe it wasn't such a simple, clear-cut tragedy after all.

Chapter 4

RUSSIAN HILL is one of the city's oldest residential neighborhoods; and if you believe research studies, like the one some outfit did in the early seventies, it is also the choicest urban area in the country. Steep hills, odd little cul-de-sacs, sweeping bay views, easy access to downtown, the Financial District, and North Beach—and extortionate rents and condo purchase prices that nowadays keep out the riffraff. You can still find a few struggling writers, would-be artists studying at the Art Institute, aging hippies still living in their sixties dreamworld, but the high rents have forced them to share quarters in clusters and will eventually force them out altogether. Mostly, now, the Hill's residents are Old Money and white-collar New Money, those young go-getters who would toss a glass of vintage Napa Valley chardonnay in your face if you called them Yuppies. The wealthy types might know—and tell you if they do—that in the 1890s the Hill was a mecca for the influential San Francisco literary crowd: Ambrose Bierce, Frank Norris, George Sterling. But they probably don't know—and wouldn't tell you if they did—that it was the site of the city's first public hanging, back in the Gold Rush days. Or that their home or garden may have been built atop the graves of some murdered Russian sailors; according to legend, that was how the Hill got its name.

The apartment David Burnett had shared with Karen Salter was on Russian Hill, not far from the old renovated firehouse on Green Street. But it was not in one of the fancy dowager buildings or shiny new high rises; it was in a structure that had probably been built between 1906 and 1910, since most of the original buildings on the Hill were destroyed in the big quake, and been denied a face-lift ever since. It was also situated above a dry cleaners, and surrounded by enough taller structures so that its windows would offer no particularly desirable view; and judging from the size of the building, the apartment itself wouldn't be very large. All of these things would help keep the rent down to an affordable level. If Karen Salter had that rara avis, a fair-minded landlord, she might actually be one of the few Hill residents who was getting a bargain.

Street parking on Russian Hill is always difficult; on Saturdays it is virtually impossible to find a legal space. So, because the world is a perverse place and sometimes the perversity works in your favor, I found a slot fifty feet uphill of the dry cleaners. Some idiot behind me didn't want to let me park. He kept blowing the horn in his Porsche while I jockeyed into the space, and when the traffic going the other way thinned he roared around me and shouted out his window, "Stupid schmuck!" There had been a time, not so long ago, when I let people like him—the real stupid schmucks—prod me into an angry response. No more. I have a higher boiling point now. Much higher.

The entrance to Karen Salter's apartment was a recessed doorway between the dry cleaners and the building next door. The mailbox still had both their names on it—K. Salter, D. Burnett—which told me something about K. Salter. I rang the bell. And was about to ring it again when a female voice said through the squawk box, "Yes? Who is it?"

I identified myself and told her why I was there, mentioning Allyn Burnett's name. The voice said, "Oh, yes, just a second," and I waited for ten before the lock-release buzzer sounded.

Inside was a flight of stairs, at the top of which was a door. The door opened when I was halfway up and a young woman looked out, but it was dark in the stairwell and I couldn't see her clearly until I got up to where she was. Twenty-six or -seven, attractive in a pug-nosed, gamin sort of way. Dark hair cut short and rumpled now, as if she hadn't bothered to comb it this morning. Nor had she applied makeup of any kind, not even to cover the dark half-circles that formed cups for her eyes. Her small, round body was encased in blue jeans and an old Cal sweatshirt, both of which were splotched with paint and varnish stains. She also wore one rubber glove—the other was in the gloved hand, along with a drippy paintbrush. Waves of smell came off her and the brush: paint stripper, one of the stronger varieties.

She let me have a brief impersonal smile and her ungloved hand. "Allyn called this morning. She said she'd hired a detective and that you might stop by to see me."

"I hope I haven't come at a bad time."

"No, no. I'm refinishing a table. You don't mind if I keep working while we talk? The gunk I'm using dries fast and if it gets hard I'll have to start all over again. I've got the window open back there, so the smell isn't too bad."

"Sure, that's fine."

She led me through a narrow, cluttered living room whose walls were dominated by an odd combination of art deco and sports posters, into a small room that had been outfitted as an office: desk with a home computer and printer on it, filing cabinet, bookcase containing computer books and tapes. But there were frivolous male touches here too: a basketball on top of the bookcase, a jockstrap that had been turned into a hanger for a potted fern.

A plastic dropcloth covered most of the carpet, and in the middle of it was a small, twenties-vintage smoking table glistening with a thick application of the paint stripper. Strip-Ease, it was called; there was a gallon can next to the table, along with a little pan of the stuff. The window sash was up, as she'd said, letting in cold puffs of wind, but the smell of the paint stripper was strong in the room anyway. What it reminded me of was a mixture of alcohol and nail polish remover. Spend enough time sniffing it, and it would make you light-headed—maybe even a little spacey.

Karen invited me to sit down in the desk chair, the only chair in the room, but I said, "Thanks, I'll stand," and went over next to the window.

Down on her knees, she began slathering Strip-Ease on the table legs. "Do you really think you can find out what made David kill himself?" she asked. Emotion underlay the words, even though she spoke matter-of-factly. She had her grief in check, it seemed, but not enough time had passed yet for it to begin to fade. Or for her to eliminate the reminders of him from her living space. Or for her to begin sleeping well again. The refinishing work was a kind of therapy, I thought—a productive way to keep herself busy on an empty Saturday.

I said, "Well, I'm going to try."

"It means a lot to Allyn, I guess."

"Doesn't it to you?"

"Knowing won't bring him back," she said. A trace of bitterness had come into her voice. People who take their own lives don't realize what it does to their loved ones, how much hurt and anger and resentment it engenders. Karen Salter was *angry* at David Burnett for leaving her the way he had, and she had every right to be. Suicide is the ultimate form of desertion.

"No, it won't," I said. "But it's better than not knowing. It might help you cope with it."

"I am coping with it. I'll be all right. I'm a strong person, even if David wasn't."

"Why do you think he did it?"

"The money, of course. That damned money."

"Winning so much and then losing it all, you mean."

"If he hadn't won it in the first place," she said, "he'd still be alive."

"Was it like him to gamble so heavily?"

"No." She paused. "But it wasn't like him to kill himself, either." Her anger was closer to the surface now. I could hear it in her voice and see it in the hard, determined way she kept dipping the brush in the pan of paint stripper and slapping the stuff on the table legs, so that it splattered over the plastic cloth.

"He must have been pretty excited about the jackpot," I said.

"At first he was. He was bubbling over when he got back and told me about it."

"He didn't call to tell you, from Reno?"

"No."

"Didn't that strike you as odd?"

"Not really. He said he was too shaken up after it happened. I would have been, too, I guess, if I liked to gamble."

I wouldn't, I thought. If I won two hundred thousand dollars, I wouldn't be too excited to call Kerry. I'd call her first thing. Especially if we were planning to be married in a few months.

But then, I wasn't in my mid-twenties. Sometimes I wonder if I was ever that young.

I asked, "Did David tell you he was making large bets with the sports books?"

"Not until after he'd already done it."

"How upset was he?"

"As upset as David ever got. He didn't show negative feelings. Or positive ones very often. He kept everything locked up inside. He was a very private person."

"So you had no inkling he was thinking about suicide?"

"My God, no." The bitterness was sharp in her voice again. She savaged the tabletop for a few seconds, as if the scraping tool were a weapon and the table a victim. David, symbolically, I thought. "At least he didn't do it here. At least he had that much feeling for me. If I'd come home and found him . . . God, I don't know what I would have done."

"Where did he do it?"

She looked up. "Don't you know?"

"No. Allyn didn't tell me."

"In a motel," she said, and slashed at the tabletop again. "He rented a room in a cheap motel. Wasn't that thoughtful of him?"

I let a few seconds pass before I said, "I talked to Jerry Polhemus a while ago. About his relationship with David and David's death. He wasn't very cooperative. In fact, he seemed nervous, afraid of something."

"Afraid? Why would Jerry be afraid?"

"That's the question."

"I can't imagine."

"Have you seen him or spoken to him since the funeral?"

"No."

"How did he act that day?"

"Cold, not very sympathetic, but that's Jerry for you."

"How well do you know him?"

Wryly, "Not as well as he'd like."

"Oh?"

"He tried to hit on me once," she said, "after I started going out with David. I should have told David, I guess, but I didn't. I wouldn't be surprised if he called me one of these days and tried to hit on me again."

"You don't like him much, do you?"

"No. If he does call . . . well, that doesn't matter. I'll handle him."

"You have any other reasons for disliking him?"

"Lots of them. He's immature, for one. I went with David and him to a Giants game once. Jerry drank too much beer and started yelling things like 'Dodgers give blowjobs' at the top of his voice. A man with little kids told him to shut up and he threatened to punch the man out."

Blowjobs, I thought. When I was young, most girls didn't know what blowjobs *were*, much less use the term in polite conversation. Or was I just being naive? I wondered again if I had ever really been twenty-five.

"I don't trust him, either," Karen said. "He's a sneak."

"How do you mean?"

"He just is. Trying to hit on me behind David's back. I don't think he cares about anybody but himself."

"How did he and David get along?"

"Oh, as far as David was concerned, Jerry couldn't do anything wrong. They were always going to baseball and football games or off to Tahoe and Reno—you know, the way guys do."

I nodded. "How did he feel about David's big jackpot?"

"I don't know. David didn't say. But I'll bet he was jealous. Anyway, David must have felt sorry for him because he gave Jerry ten thousand dollars out of his winnings."

"Did he now. Jerry didn't mention that to me."

"Well, David said it was the least he could do for a friend who'd been with him at the time. He was always so generous . . ." She let the sentence trail off, and her mouth set tight again. She picked up the scraping tool again and worked on the tabletop, where the Strip-Ease had loosened the old varnish.

"Would you have any idea what Jerry did with the ten thousand dollars?"

"No. But if he hasn't spent it yet, it'll all be gone before the end of the year. That's the way Jerry is."

"David didn't try to get it back from him, did he? To pay off his gambling debt?"

"I don't know. Maybe he did. I know he borrowed money from Allyn and tried to borrow from others he knew. He asked me to try to get him a loan at the bank where I work but he just didn't have any collateral."

"How large a loan did he want?"

"Thirty-five thousand dollars."

"He lost that much in addition to his jackpot winnings?"

"I suppose he must have. He could be such a fool."

I watched her work for a time. The smell of the paint stripper was giving me a headache. I sat on my haunches, finally, so the cold wind from the window could wash over the back of my neck. Then I asked, "Are all of his belongings still here?"

"What?" She had turned inside herself, to commune with her grief and anger. "I'm sorry, I didn't—"

"David's belongings," I said. "Are they all still here?"

"Oh. Yes. I haven't had a chance to . . . Allyn said she'd come over and help me box them up, but . . . I really should do it pretty soon. Maybe tomorrow."

"Have you gone through them?"

"You mean to see if there was anything that might help explain his suicide?"

"Yes."

"I looked," she said. "Allyn asked me to, and the police. But I didn't find anything."

"Do you mind if I look?"

"No, go ahead. There isn't much. David didn't have much, really."

"Will you show me where to start?"

"The bottom two drawers in the desk there were his," she said.

I poked around in the two drawers. Souvenir-type junk, mostly: football and baseball programs and pennants, drink tokens from three different gambling casinos, a big yellow-and-red button that proclaimed the 49ers world champions of Super Bowl XVI. There was a folder full of bank statements and canceled checks; I shuffled through the checks, but none of them told me anything. The balances listed on the most recent statements, dated last month, were $39.54 in his checking account and $168.23 in his savings account. I hunted around for a checkbook or savings passbook. No checkbook or passbook.

I asked Karen if she had them. She said, "No, Allyn does. There wasn't much in either one—not even enough left to help pay for his funeral."

"Did he put all of his winnings into those two accounts?"

"He didn't put any of it into them."

"Any particular reason why not?"

"I don't know. He didn't say."

"Did he open a new account?"

"If he did, I didn't find a record of it."

"That's a little strange, isn't it?"

She shrugged. "He might have thrown the new passbook away when he drew the money out to gamble with."

She may not have thought it was strange, but I did. Why would he open a new account if he intended to place large bets with the Vegas and Reno sports books? Even if he hadn't

decided beforehand to do some high rolling, why bother with
a new account? Why not just funnel the jackpot winnings
through his existing accounts?

I asked, "Did he show you the check he got from the Coliseum Club?"

"No. I asked to see it but he said he'd authorized the casino
to send it straight to his bank."

"But he couldn't have," I said. "There'd be a record if he'd
had it sent to one of his old accounts, and you can't open a
new account long-distance over the weekend."

She was frowning now. "No, of course you can't. I should
have thought of that before. But why would he lie to me?"

I said, "To cover the fact that he took his winnings in cash,
maybe."

"Cash? But that's not—"

"Not very smart, no."

"I can't imagine why he'd do such a thing."

"Neither can I," I said. "On big casino payoffs, the IRS
demands its cut right off the top—so there's no tax advantage
to taking cash. Was David irresponsible where money was concerned? I mean in the sense of wanting a lot of cash around."

"No, never. He didn't seem to care that much about
money."

"Did he have a safe-deposit box?"

"Not that I ever knew about. I didn't find any record of
one."

"If he did take the money in cash, where might he have
kept it?"

"Not here. I'm sure of that."

"Anywhere else you can think of?"

"No. No."

"Would he have entrusted Jerry Polhemus with it?"

"God, no. David wasn't that foolish. He knew how Jerry
was about money."

I said, "I'd like to look through the rest of his things.
Where would they be?"

"In the bedroom. I'll show you."

Without taking off her gloves, she led me into the bedroom. This was entirely her domain, everything feminine but without frills, done in whites and yellows. If David Burnett had put his stamp on it, left any little pieces of himself behind, she had removed them from sight.

"The nightstand by the window was his," she said. "And the bottom two drawers in the dresser. The rest of his stuff is in the closet." She started out.

"Don't you want to stay while I look?"

"No, it's all right. I want to get the table stripped so I can sand it down."

That wasn't it at all. She did not want to be present while I went through more of his things; she just wasn't ready yet to deal with his leavings, even in the role of spectator. She wouldn't be, I thought, until her anger had spent itself and she was ready to get on with her life.

I went to the nightstand first. Nothing in there but a paperback sports biography and a Prince Albert tin containing half a dozen joints. Allyn Burnett had told me that her brother wasn't on drugs. So maybe she was wrong. Or maybe she and her brother didn't feel that smoking a little grass now and then constituted drug use; a lot of people don't. Or maybe these joints belonged to Karen Salter and she smoked dope and David never had.

I moved over to the dresser. On its top, next to Karen's jewelry box, was a silver photograph-size frame that had been turned facedown. I picked it up. Head-and-shoulders color photo of a smiling young man with shaggy blond hair and bright blue eyes, signed on the bottom in a bold but childish hand: *To Kittyhawk, Love and Kisses, David*. Kittyhawk. Some sort of pet name. I put the photograph back as I had found it, facedown, and bent to the bottom two drawers.

Shirts, sweaters, underwear, socks—all neatly folded. Her doing, I thought; he wouldn't have been that neat. Nothing hidden under or between or inside any of the items.

The closet was big, not quite a walk-in. His things were bunched on the left: half a dozen pairs of trousers, two sports jackets, a flowered vest, some pullovers and sports-type jerseys, a 49ers jacket and a Giants windbreaker. I went through pockets, found nothing of any interest until I got to the wind-breaker. A thin piece of paper was tucked into one of the slash pockets. I fished it out—ordinary memo paper torn off a pad —and read what was on it.

Manny. 2789 De Haro St.

The handwriting was the same as on the photograph. I held on to the paper while I rummaged through the rest of his clothing, looked at the man's shoes and sneakers on the closet floor, poked among the things piled on the single shelf above. Nothing. I shut the closet door and went back into the room where Karen Salter was.

She was kneeling before the smoking table with her head bowed, in a posture that was almost one of prayer—as if the table had become an altar. Her eyes were shut, I saw as I moved over to the window. Again I felt like an intruder, not just on her living space but on her grief: they were both places I had no right to be. We were strangers; and grief, like love-making, is too personal to be shared properly with someone you hardly know.

When I cleared my throat she jerked upright and blinked at me. "Oh," she said, "I—"

"It's all right. I understand."

Her eyes were moist; she brushed at them with her forearm. "What did you find?"

"Nothing except this." I handed her the piece of paper. "Mean anything to you?"

She looked at it for several seconds before she said, "No, I don't think so."

"You don't know anyone named Manny?"

"No."

"Did David ever mention anyone by that name?"

"Not that I remember."

"What about the address? Ring any bells?"

"De Haro Street . . . no. That's industrial, isn't it?"

"Some of it is. Not all. Where did David work?"

"Halpern Sporting Goods, downtown. On Grant."

"All right," I said. "Is there anything else you can tell me that might help? Names of David's other friends, someone he might have confided in?"

"Jerry was the only person he was close to, except for Allyn and me. He knew a lot of people but . . ." She was silent for a few beats; then she said, "It was a small funeral," which was not a non sequitur at all.

I asked her about his co-workers, favorite hangouts, but she had nothing more to tell me. She was working on the table again when I left—dull strokes with the scraper. Looking inward as she had been earlier, holding his memory against her pain.

Chapter 5

POTRERO HILL, on the eastern rim of the city, used to be a low-income, blue-collar neighborhood. To a large degree it's still blue collar, but the Yuppies have changed the face of it in the past couple of decades. They've moved in in droves, bought up and restored hundreds of the old Victorians and two-flat houses that cling to the hill's steep sides; and where the Yups go, so go the entrepreneurs who cater to them. Nowadays, the venerable Victorian ladies with their new coats of paint stand cheek by jowl with real estate offices, travel agencies, fashionable boutiques, trendy nightclubs and wine bars, and nouvelle cuisine restaurants.

The gentrification of Potrero Hill is the main reason the face of the flatlands that fan out below is also changing. Once that area was heavily industrial. Southern Pacific tracks crisscross it; not far away is what's left of San Francisco's port business at Central Basin, Islais Creek, and India Basin. The area is still the home of small manufacturing companies, drayage warehouses, industrial supply houses, the Greyhound and Sam Trans bus yards, and Anchor Brewing Company, the city's last brewer of quality beer. But mixed in among them are dozens of outfits, some entrenched in fancy new or reno-

vated buildings, that cater to San Francisco's burgeoning inte-
rior-design trade: designer showrooms, antique furniture coop-
eratives, import/export companies, graphic arts studios, and
the Butterfield & Butterfield auction warehouse. There are
also numerous upscale lunchrooms and taverns, and clusters of
private housing that are slowly being taken over by less affluent urban professionals who can't afford the prices that have
grown as steep as the streets on Potrero Hill above.

I expected 2789 De Haro to be one of the private houses,
but I was wrong. It was a weathered warehouse-type structure
set behind a chain link fence that had some kind of climbing
plant growing thickly over it, so that from the street you
couldn't see much of the building or the grounds. A metal
sign wired to one half of a pair of closed gates read:

    EKHERN MFG. CO.
    Industrial Solenoid Valves

I parked and walked back to the gates. There was none of
the climbing plant on them; through the links I could see a
deserted blacktopped area, a loading dock, and two closed
metal roller doors into the building. Nobody was around.
Closed Saturdays, maybe. But there was no padlock at the
joining of the gate halves, and when I pulled up on the bar
that held them together, one half swung open.

I walked in, shutting the gate behind me. No sounds came
from the warehouse or anywhere else on the grounds; my
shoes made little flat, hollow sounds as I crossed to a set of
cement stairs that gave access to the loading dock. I climbed
those, followed an extension of the dock around to the east
side of the building.

A car was nosed up in front of what looked to be an office at
the far end. Cadillac—dark gray and shiny new, with nobody
inside. I went on down to the office. One door, with a sign on
it similar to the one on the gate; one long window with vene-
tian blinds pulled down on the inside. I tried the door.
Locked. I leaned over to see if I could get a squint past the
blinds, but they were drawn tight.

I was thinking about knocking on the door when a voice
behind me said, "Looking for something, soldier?"

It startled me, brought me half around in a crouch. Since Deer Run, I have been overly sensitive to sudden noises, unexpected movements. The man standing ten feet away on the dock walked soft for a big guy; he hadn't made a sound coming along. He was a couple of inches over six feet, wide at the shoulders and hips, with brown hair cut long and in puffy wings so that he seemed not to have any ears. Wearing a chocolate-brown business suit and a plaid shirt open at the throat.

He stood still, hands down at his sides, watching me out of eyes that did not blink. Pale eyes, without expression. His whole face was expressionless, almost a blank, like one of the half-formed pod creatures in *Invasion of the Body Snatchers*. One good look at him was enough to make me edgy again, to put a coldness on the back of my neck. Hardcase. Not one of the swaggering macho types that frequent bars on the weekends, looking for ways to prove their manhood. The genuine article.

"Man asked you a question, soldier."

Another voice, behind me again. This time I was not startled. I turned and backed up two steps, doing it slow, until my back was against the building wall and I could see the other man. Shorter, leaner, with blond hair that grew light on top and streaky dark at the temples; dressed in a tan suit and a blue sport shirt. Same blank expression. Same mold. He was a soft walker, too: if he had come out of the office door, I would have heard it click open.

The blond one said, "Well, soldier?"

"I'm looking for Manny."

"Manny who?"

"I don't know his last name."

"Nobody here named Manny," the dark one said.

"I thought there might be."

"What made you think that?"

"Somebody I know had his name and this address."

"Who would that be?"

"David Burnett."

The blond one said, "We don't know anybody named

David Burnett. Or anybody named Manny. You must have the wrong address."

"Maybe."

"No maybes about it."

"We're closed today," the dark one said. "Closed weekends. Couldn't you tell that from out front?"

"The gate was open—"

"No, the gate was closed. It just wasn't locked."

"Then you should lock it if you don't want anybody to walk in."

"That's right," the blond one said, "we should lock it. Usually we do. Today we forgot. We won't forget again."

"What's your name, soldier?" the dark one asked.

I told him.

"What do you do for a living?"

"I'm a private investigator."

"That so?" the blond one said, but not as if he cared. "What would a private investigator want to come here for?"

"I told you, I'm looking for Manny."

"What for?"

"I want to ask him a few questions."

"What about?"

"His relationship with David Burnett."

"Why?"

"Burnett killed himself last week. His sister wants to know the reason."

"That's too bad," the dark one said. "We'd help you out if we could but we can't. You must have got the wrong address."

The blond one said, "Tell you what, though. You give us your business card and we'll keep it on file, just in case we hear anything about somebody named Manny. You got a card, don't you?"

I took my wallet out, slow, and removed one of my business cards. The blond guy made no move to come and get it; neither did the dark one. There was anger in me now, like a low, pulsing heat, but it would be foolish to act on it, or even to let any of it show. They were tougher than I could ever be and twenty-five years younger to boot; and I was technically trespassing on private property. I pushed away from the wall and walked to where the blond one stood and gave him the card.

He looked it over, nodded once, put it away in his shirt pocket. Then he said, "Sorry we couldn't help you, soldier. You have a nice day for yourself. And don't forget to close the gate on your way out. We wouldn't want anybody else to come wandering in by accident before we get it locked."

Without saying anything, I went past him and down the steps and across the blacktop. I looked back once, halfway to the gate. The dark one was walking along the dock, so that he could watch me all the way out. The blond one had disappeared.

In the car, I sat for a while to let the anger and tension ease out of me. Then I started the engine and drove over to 16th and out Potrero to Army—on my way to Noe Valley.

I kept thinking: Hired muscle, but not the garden variety. The Mob variety.

San Francisco has never been a hotbed of organized-crime activity; there is none of the Family networking you find in East Coast cities. Mob operations in California are so poorly organized, in fact, thanks to internal disagreements back in the sixties, that they have a reputation as "the Mickey Mouse Mafia." Still, the city had produced people like Jimmy "The Weasel" Fratianno, a Mob underboss linked to illegal gambling, extortion, and pornographic film distribution. And over the years there have been instances of organized-crime ties to prostitution and union corruption. So it wouldn't be all that unusual to find a Mob front operation here.

But how would David Burnett have got himself mixed up with those people? Sure, there was the money he'd purportedly lost with the Reno and Vegas sports books, the debt he'd run up. The Mob *does* have a strong power base in Nevada; he might have picked one of their booking outfits. Or, for that matter, he might have hooked into an illegal gambling setup right here in San Francisco. But the problem with either possibility was, I couldn't see the Mob taking a thirty-five-thousand-dollar marker from a kid who had no collateral and a job in a sporting goods store—not even after he'd blown more than a hundred grand in cash. They'd have known who and what he was; anybody who makes big-money bets with them and then wants to lay down more gets himself checked out thoroughly.

The Mob and David Burnett . . . it just didn't add up. So maybe I was wrong. Maybe Ekhern Mfg. Co. was just what it seemed to be—a solenoid valve company—and maybe those two back there were something other than what they seemed to be. Maybe I was building sand castles here, the kind populated by armed enforcers and guys who put severed horses' heads in other guys' beds.

Maybe.

One way or another, I was going to find out.

Chapter 6

EBERHARDT WAS HOME when I got to his old two-story house in Noe Valley, just below Twin Peaks: working with the power tools in his garage workshop. He had always been good with his hands, always enjoyed making furniture and things. He'd let the hobby slide after Dana divorced him several years ago, and I was glad to see that he'd taken it up again. Another positive effect Bobbie Jean was having on his life, I thought.

She was there too—not in the garage, inside the house somewhere. Her car was parked out front. The garage door was up, so I walked straight in there from the street and waited for Eb to finish fashioning an ogee molding with his band saw. From the cut pieces spread out over his workbench, he appeared to be making a table of some kind.

As I watched him, it struck me again how leaned-down and gray he'd gotten. At least ten pounds thinner and a shade or two grayer than last December. The weight loss might have been the result of his relationship with Bobbie Jean, but I could not help feeling that it and the added gray were in fact the result of what had happened to me. Kerry had been thinner when I came back from Deer Run, though she had since put the lost poundage back on. Those three dead months had

been an ordeal for them, too. Not knowing what had become
of me, worrying, spending time and effort and money trying to
find out. Eberhardt had worked day and night, Kerry told me,
hounding SFPD's Missing Persons Bureau, following small
dead-end leads and exploring empty possibilities on his own
and with the help of two other detectives he'd hired. Frustration, psychic drain . . . and yet through it all he'd lent support to Kerry and somehow managed to deal with day-to-day
agency business as well. When I'd tried to thank him, back in
March, he'd turned gruff and growled something about paying
back past favors. Sure he was. The first thing he'd said to me
when I walked back into his life was "Jesus, I never thought
I'd see you again," and he'd fought like hell to keep me from
seeing the wetness in his eyes.

And what was his reward for caring so much? A flatter belly,
loose jowls, and some more dead hair follicles. It wasn't my
fault, but there was a feeling of guilt in me just the same.
Guilt and love and pain and gratitude. I had never felt closer
to him and to Kerry than I did now. And I had never felt more
alone.

It was a small relief when he finally shut off the saw; the
whine and screech of the blade was like an abrasive on my
nerve ends. He wiped his forehead with the back of one hand,
getting sawdust on his gray forelock, and said cheerfully, "So
what brings you by today, *paisan*?" He was in a good mood, all
bright-eyed and bushy-tailed, which meant that he had gotten
laid last night. You can usually tell when he's had his ashes
hauled. Some men wear their hearts on their sleeves; Eberhardt wears his gonads there too.

"I need you to do something for me, Eb."

"Don't tell me you're working? When are you gonna learn
to take it easy on weekends?"

"Probably never."

"Drop dead of a heart attack one of these days," he said.
"All right, which case?"

"You don't know about it yet. A thing I took on last night—
favor to one of the secretaries at Kerry's agency."

"You and your favors. Well?"

I told him about it. He was not particularly interested until I got to the part about Ekhern Manufacturing Company; then I had his full attention.

"What the hell?" he said. "The Mob?"

"I'm not kidding. If you'd seen those two, you'd be thinking the same thing."

"Then for Christ's sake why did you give them your card? You want trouble with people like that?"

"I didn't have a choice. Besides, it's not going to come to anything rough."

"Depends on what's going on. And whether or not you keep poking your snout in."

"It's my snout, Eb."

"Ahh," he said. "I suppose you want me to find out if there's anything official on this Ekhern outfit?"

"I'd do it myself, but you've got more pull than I have— friends who'll tell you what they won't tell me."

"Uh-huh."

"Another thing I need is the name of the inspector who investigated David Burnett's suicide. I want to ask him a few questions." I paused. "Maybe you can set up a meet."

"Now I'm your social secretary."

"Indulge me, Eb, all right?"

"Ahh," he said again. Then he said, "Come on inside while I phone. Bobbie Jean's making cornbread."

I could smell the cornbread as soon as he opened the inside door. It made my mouth water; I had not eaten anything all day, unless you counted coffee and the half a glass of orange juice with Bruce Littlejohn. We went through the utility porch into the kitchen, where Bobbie Jean was bustling about and the cornbread smell was overpowering. There was a fresh, steaming pan of it on top of the stove.

Eberhardt said, "Look who's here, hon," and patted Bobbie Jean on the fanny for my benefit. She paid no attention to the pat, also for my benefit, and came over and kissed me on the cheek. Eberhardt went upstairs to make his call. I went and smelled the cornbread close up.

"Go ahead, take a piece," Bobbie Jean said.

I took a piece. Nobody makes cornbread like a southerner; I don't know why that should be true but it is. A northerner makes it, it's just cornbread; a southerner uses exactly the same ingredients and it's a culinary art form. I made myself eat slowly, to savor the taste and because one piece was all I was going to allow myself.

Bobbie Jean stood watching me, smiling. She was a couple of years shy of fifty, tallish and slender in a pair of blue chambray pants and a dark red sweatshirt. The first time I'd met her, the same December night I was abducted, she had worn her brown hair in a shag cut; since then she had had it permed, a style that better complimented her lean, angular features and made her look younger. Eberhardt had met her during the course of a routine skip-trace—she worked as a secretary to a San Rafael real estate agent—and in December they had been dating casually for several weeks. Now they were a "hot item," as Eberhardt put it. Translation: They were sleeping together. I was glad for both of them. I liked Bobbie Jean much more than any of Eb's recent string of lady friends; she had a wry, sometimes bawdy sense of humor and a frank way of speaking, and she could handle him even better than Dana could, back in the days when their marriage was a good one. Kerry liked her too. She and Bobbie Jean had become fast friends.

I finished the cornbread and said, "Good." Eloquent praise is not one of my long suits. But Bobbie Jean didn't seem to mind. She said, "Well, it's my mother's recipe, so I can't take any real credit for it. But don't tell Eb that. He thinks I'm in a class with Julia Child."

"Better watch out or he'll chain you to the stove."

She sighed. "He keeps trying to do just that."

"Oh?"

"He's asked me to marry him four times now," she said. "Didn't he tell you?"

"No."

"Probably because I keep saying no. But just between you and me and the stove . . . I think I'm weakening."

"I thought you were a card-carrying member of the I Hate Marriage Club." Like Kerry, dammit, I thought.

"I am. Or was. He looks at me with puppy eyes and tells me how much he needs me . . . oh hell, I don't know. It gets harder and harder to turn him down."

"He'll keep right on asking, you know."

"I know. Mr. Persistence."

"He's a good man, Bobbie Jean."

"I know that too. I wish I'd met him thirty years ago, before either of the two jerks I said 'I do' to."

She'd married the first jerk when she was eighteen, in her native South Carolina; he had taken her to Texas so he could fulfill his ambition of working on the Galveston docks, and she had divorced him a year later. (He'd been good-looking and a terrific bed partner, she had confided to Kerry, "but he had a brain the size of a lima bean. Did you ever try to hold a conversation with a lima bean?") The second jerk was an electronics engineer who had transported her from Texas to Silicon Valley, where he had fathered her two daughters. She'd divorced *him* after twenty not-so-blissful years, when she discovered he was actively bisexual and had been for most of their married life. With a track record like that, it was little wonder that she was gun-shy where marriage was concerned.

Bobbie Jean said, "I'm not the first woman Eb's proposed to since his divorce. You know that. I guess that's the biggest thing holding me back. Is it me he wants, or any old body to take care of him and warm his bed?"

I asked her what she thought—an old trick to avoid answering a difficult question.

"I think he cares for me, but that he's also tired of living alone. The trouble is, I think I feel the same way."

We talked for another twenty minutes, though not any more about the marriage issue, before Eberhardt finally reappeared. He motioned me out into the garage.

"Well, you called it," he said when we were alone. "Ekhern Manufacturing is a suspected Mob front, all right. Probably a low-level clearinghouse. I didn't get that from anybody at the Hall, either. I was referred to the feds and I got it from the head of the Organized Crime Strike Force here. He wanted to know why I was interested so I told him. *He* wasn't interested after that. But he didn't mind talking a little."

"If the Strike Force knows about Ekhern, why don't they shut it down?"

"Why do you think? No legal cause. Besides, they're after bigger fish."

"Who runs Ekhern for the Mob?"

"Guy named Garza, Frank Garza. One of the new breed. He's got an MBA, for Christ's sake."

"I believe it."

"The suspected owner, though, is one Arthur Welker. Mob underboss, came out of Chicago about ten years ago. Garza worked for him back there."

"This guy Welker doesn't operate here, does he?"

"No. Northern Nevada. He lives at Tahoe."

"Then he's hooked into the gambling business?"

"Right. He owns pieces of two casino-hotels."

"Which ones?"

"Coliseum Club in Reno, Nevornia in Stateline."

"Uh-huh. The Coliseum Club was where David Burnett won his big jackpot."

"Which means what?"

"Good question."

"Hell," Eberhardt said, "the Mob's got its claws in more than a couple Nevada casinos. But the gambling is strictly legit, you know that. No way would Welker come down on a citizen for winning *any* amount of money. They love it up there when a big hit happens. Brings new suckers in in droves."

"Sure. But there's got to be a connection somewhere. You find out who Manny is?"

He shook his head. "Nobody by that name works for Ekhern."

"Maybe for Welker in Nevada, then."

"Could be. His file's thin here. He pretty much confines his operations to the other side of the state line."

"Okay," I said. "Who was in charge of the Burnett suicide?"

"Harry Craddock."

"I don't think I know him."

"He's fairly new. Good man."

"You talk to him?"

"No. He's working the four-to-midnight this week. Go down to the Hall from here, you ought to be able to catch him when he comes on duty."

"I'll do that."

"Just take it easy, huh?" he said.

"With Craddock?"

"You know what I mean. Word is that Welker's rough goods."

"I'll walk soft. Thanks, Eb."

I headed out to my car. But he wasn't done with me yet; he tagged along and said as I opened the door, "So what did you and Bobbie Jean talk about while I was upstairs?"

"Why?"

"I'm just curious. Well?"

"You," I said.

"Yeah, I thought so. She tell you I asked her to marry me?"

"Four times, she said. Mr. Persistence."

"You don't approve, huh?"

"Sure I approve. If you really love her."

"What the hell kind of crack is that? Would I ask her if I didn't love her?"

"You asked Wanda."

That made him mad. His affair with Wanda Jaworski of Macy's footwear department had been a disaster, mainly because he hadn't been able to see past her gargantuan chest to a mind of the same lima bean proportions as Bobbie Jean's first husband. "Always throwing Wanda in my face," he said. "I made a mistake, all right? You never made a mistake?"

"Lots of them. But never one like Wanda."

"Get out of here," he said, glaring. "Go play games with the goddamn Mob."

"Does this mean I don't get to be best man if Bobbie Jean finally says yes?"

"You don't even get an invitation," he said, and put his back to me and stalked off in a huff.

I watched him into the garage, thinking: I hope you do love her, Eb. Because she's right for you, because she loves *you*. And because in my own way, so do I.

Chapter 7

INSPECTOR HARRY CRADDOCK was a heavyset black guy in his mid-thirties, very serious about his work, very intense. He smoked long, thin cigarillos with plastic mouthpieces and had trouble keeping his hands and body still, standing or sitting. Classic type A personality. If he didn't fall victim to a coronary or a perforated ulcer, he would probably make captain before he was fifty and chief or deputy chief before mandatory retirement. You only had to spend five minutes with him to know that he was a first-rate cop.

When I first approached him he allowed as how he'd heard of me, being noncommittal as to what it was he'd heard, and said he could give me fifteen minutes. We went to his desk in the squad room. Things were relatively quiet here for a Saturday afternoon; we were able to converse in more or less normal tones.

I told him why I was interested in David Burnett's death, keeping it brief. When I was done he said, "Well, if you think it was anything but suicide, you can forget it. Kid killed himself and no mistake."

"In a motel, wasn't it?"

He nodded. "Place called the Bay Vista, off the Bayshore

north of Candlestick. Used to be a hot-sheet motel, but it changed hands a few years ago. Fairly respectable place now."

"He checked in alone?"

"Right. About seven the night he died."

"Night clerk remember him?"

"Said Burnett didn't say much, acted withdrawn."

"Who found the body?"

"Maid. Past noon the next day, when she went in to clean. Door was double-locked; she had to use both her keys. Both windows locked too."

"What time did he die?"

"Coroner says sometime around midnight."

"Is it possible he had a visitor between seven and midnight?"

"Anything's possible," Craddock said. "But nobody saw one, and there was nothing in the room to indicate one."

"I understand he left a note."

"Handwritten. Burnett's handwriting."

"What did it say, do you remember?"

"Two lines: 'This way is better for everybody. Karen, Allyn, please forgive me.' "

"Cause of death was an overdose of sleeping pills?"

"Nembutal. Compounded by alcohol. We found an empty pint of bourbon anchoring the note. Dutch courage. When he got drunk enough he took the pills—almost a full bottle."

"You know where he got them?"

"Off a small-time drug dealer named Niko," Craddock said. "Burnett bought grass from him a few times."

"What did Niko have to say?"

"Oh, we had a nice little talk." Craddock grinned and I grinned back at him. "He sold Burnett the Nembutal two days before the kid checked into the Bay Vista."

"Did Niko ever sell him any other drugs?"

"Just grass. He said it was the first time Burnett had ever asked for anything else."

"What about Burnett's motive?"

"For doing himself in?" Craddock shrugged. "Never know

what goes on in people's heads, but in this case it seems clear-cut enough."

"Losing all his jackpot winnings and running up a big debt besides."

"Right."

"You find out which sports books he made his bets with?"

"Nobody seems to know. He was secretive about it."

"You might have run checks," I said mildly.

"That's right, we could have. But why? Kid committed suicide, that's definite. And there are dozens of sports books in Nevada. And I've got a caseload that would break a camel's back."

"I'm not blaming you," I said. "It's just that a hundred and fifty thousand bucks, give or take a few thousand, is a hell of a pile to wager on horses, boxing matches, and baseball games."

"Been known to happen."

"Sure. But Burnett had no history of heavy gambling."

"So he caught the fever," Craddock said. "Hitting a Mega-bucks jackpot for two hundred grand can do that to a man—make him want to parlay a small fortune into a big one."

"The friend Burnett was with when he hit the jackpot, Jerry Polhemus—you talk to him?"

"Briefly. Why?"

"I spent a few minutes with him this morning. He didn't seem to like it when I brought up Burnett's name. Acted nervous, scared."

"Of what?"

"My investigation, maybe. I had the feeling he was covering up something."

"Such as?"

"No idea yet."

"I didn't get that kind of hit off him," Craddock said. He lit another cigarillo, glanced at his watch; my fifteen minutes were almost up. "Your best friend kills himself, it makes you think about your own mortality. Could be he just doesn't like the idea of you opening up old wounds, and you misread him."

"Maybe," I said. "You check him out?"

"No reason to. He was up at Lake Tahoe the night Burnett died."

I told him about Ekhern Manufacturing, the Mob angle, the name Manny. He thought it over, but it didn't impress him. "So Ekhern's a clearinghouse," he said. "The kid picked a Mob-owned sports book to make his bets with, and paid off his losses here. Either that, or he lied about Vegas and Reno and dropped his pile with an illegal book in the city, one with Mob ties."

"I thought of that too. But why would they take his marker for thirty-five grand—a kid like him, with no way to raise the money?"

"Somebody screwed up, maybe."

"Maybe. Here's something else: I think he may have taken his jackpot payoff in cash."

"You kidding?"

"No. He told his fiancée he authorized the Coliseum Club to send a payoff check directly to his bank. But there's no record of a deposit to his checking or savings accounts. Or anything to indicate that he had a secret account somewhere."

Craddock had grown fidgety. He looked at his watch again. "Why the hell would he take cash?"

"People do stupid things," I said. "Or maybe he had a good reason, one that has nothing to do with gambling. Maybe he didn't blow all his winnings on sports events after all."

"What did he do with the money then?"

"How about a large drug buy?"

"Oh come on, man. There's no evidence Burnett was into that kind of scene. I told you what Niko said about him."

"Yeah."

"What were you thinking? He didn't kill himself, he was murdered in some kind of Mob drug burn? Well, you can forget it. He committed suicide—period. I'd stake my badge on that."

I didn't pursue it any further. He was right—it was an off-the-wall theory. Instead I said, "Okay, just one more question. Was Burnett ever in trouble with the law?"

"Picked up once for drunk driving three years ago. First

offense, damn judge gave him a slap on the wrist." Craddock scowled as he said that; he didn't like judges who were lenient with drunk drivers, even first offenders. For that matter, neither did I. "That's all. Considering what it's like on the streets these days, he was just your average city kid—maybe a little above average."

"Sure. Except that he won and lost a small fortune and then killed himself a few months before he was supposed to get married."

"Compared to most of the stuff that crosses my desk," Craddock said, "that's so tame it doesn't even make me raise an eyebrow."

"I guess you're right."

But I was far from satisfied.

UNTIL RECENT YEARS, when some dealerships moved to the Auto Center out on 16th Street, Van Ness Avenue was *the* place San Franciscans went to buy a new or used car. A dozen or so lots and showrooms still line the busy avenue, from near the Opera House north toward Lombard Street. One of them was Benoit Chevrolet, where David Burnett had bought a brand-new Corvette three weeks ago. His sister had told me that when I called her from the lobby of the Hall of Justice.

It was a few minutes shy of five o'clock when I walked into the Benoit showroom. At five on the nose I was sitting in a glass-walled cubicle with an assistant manager named Kamroff. He wasn't the salesman who had first waited on Burnett, but he'd been in on the second round of dealings. And he was not averse to talking about it. Most car salesmen suffer from diarrhea of the mouth; Kamroff was no exception.

"Things like that don't happen much," he said. "Not here, they don't. Young guy comes waltzing in off the street, plunks down fifty thousand bucks for a new 'Vette, drives it for a week, puts a couple hundred miles on it, and then brings it back and says he wants a full refund."

"Did he pay the fifty thousand in cash?" I asked.

"Yes, sir. Stacks of fifties and hundreds in a Giants tote bag. Can you believe it?"

"He say why he was paying cash?"

"Told Lloyd Adams he won the money in Reno, big slot-machine payoff. Well, why not? It's none of our business where they get the money to buy a car."

"So then he brought the Corvette back a week later."

"That's right," Kamroff said. "Says something came up, big emergency, he's got to have the fifty thousand back."

"What sort of emergency, did he say?"

"No. But he was all worked up over it. Even more worked up when I explained the facts of life to him. We couldn't have refunded the full purchase price if we'd wanted to. You can't sell a car as new when it's got mileage on it—that's a state law. You have to market it as used, which means a price reduction even if it *is* brand-new and only has a couple hundred miles on it. I did what I could to oblige Mr. Burnett, got most of his outlay back to him; we try to please our customers, even the wacky ones. He didn't like it, but that's life. You take the good with the bad."

"Did he ask for the refund in cash?"

"At first he did. We convinced him to take a cashier's check."

"Can you tell me whether he cashed it or signed it over to someone?"

"Cashed it."

"For currency or another cashier's check?"

"Currency. The bank manager mentioned it when I spoke to him the next day."

So David Burnett had taken both his jackpot winnings and his refund in cash. Which meant what? Why would he want to risk carrying around all that green?

MY OFFICE was only a few blocks from Benoit Chevrolet, on O'Farrell Street, so I made that my next stop. For one thing, I needed to prepare an agency contract for Allyn Burnett to sign. And for another, I wanted to get hold of Joe DeFalco—*Chronicle* reporter, poker buddy, and expert on gambling and related matters. There were a couple more theories I wanted to explore, one reasonable and the other off-the-wall.

Eberhardt had closed up last night and for a change he had remembered to switch on the answering machine. No messages, though. I called DeFalco's home number. His wife said he was out on some sort of assignment but that he was due home by six. I asked her to have him call when he showed up.

I used my old portable to fill out one of the standard contract forms. Then I took a look at Saturday's mail, which consisted of two bills and a catalogue of "the latest in professional and security control devices" from some company in Kentucky. Eberhardt was always after me to upscale the agency, outfit ourselves with modern technological advancements that would, he claimed, make our job easier. So I opened the catalogue and paged through it.

Miniature cameras and "camera systems." Mini-stethoscopes. A variety of bugs and bug monitors. A thing to detect whether or not somebody you were shaking hands with was wearing a covert listening device. Bulletproof briefcases and tote bags made of something called "ballistic polypropylene" that was guaranteed to have five times the strength of steel in stopping slugs fired at point-blank range. Some gunk you could spray on letters to turn the envelopes translucent, thus allowing you to read the contents without muss or fuss. But the gunk wasn't the best little privacy-invader offered in the catalogue. No siree. That honor belonged to a glittering gem of advanced technology called the Night Penetrator.

What the Night Penetrator did was to electro-optically amplify starlight or other ambient light into phosphor green images that literally let you see in the dark. With this cameralike baby, you could read license plates in unlighted garages, peer into shadowy corners; and if you happened to have a voyeuristic bent, why, you could even look through your neighbor's bedroom window when you suspected he might be humping his wife or girlfriend. It came with an optional hand-held image intensifier, and an infrared spot for greater clarity, and a tripod, *and* a pistol grip. The Night Penetrator cost a paltry four thousand dollars, and you could get all the accessories for another twelve hundred. And the best part about it was that it was government-approved and perfectly legal to own.

I threw the catalogue into the wastebasket. Alienation, fear, paranoia, distrust, deceit—that was what life was all about nowadays. Every man for himself and to hell with anybody else and *his* right to privacy. I couldn't live that way, wouldn't live that way. Caring too much could be a curse, but it was far better than caring too little. Far better, too, that the meek should inherit the earth than the paranoids and hard-core paramilitary "patriots" with hideout guns in their clothing and Night Penetrators tucked into the trunks of their cars. . . .

The telephone bell put an end to my brooding. Joe DeFalco.

I said, "Joe, I've got some questions about gambling. Can I pick your brain?"

"Go ahead, shoot."

"Is there an illegal gambling and booking operation in the city, one with Mob ties, that's set up to handle six-figure bets?"

He took some time to think it over before he said, "Officially, the answer is no."

"How about unofficially?"

"I wouldn't want to be quoted."

"That's a laugh, coming from a newshound. Don't worry, I don't reveal my sources."

"Then the answer is yes. But the ties are loose."

"Man named Manny wouldn't happen to run it, would he?"

"No. Manny who?"

"That's what I'm trying to find out."

"Nobody named Manny connected with it that I know of."

"How about Frank Garza? Or Arthur Welker?"

"Nope."

"Either of those names mean anything to you?"

"Garza, no. Welker's a Nevada underboss—Reno and Tahoe."

"Know much about him?"

"Not much. He keeps a low profile."

"Okay," I said. "Do me a favor?"

"Depends."

"You've got sources. Find out if one David Burnett made any big bets with the local combine—upwards of a hundred grand—within the last month. If so, see if you can set up a meet with somebody who knows the details."

"Why?" DeFalco asked. "Who's Burnett?"

"Nobody you'd know."

"If what you're working on has news value, I want first crack at it. Guaranteed."

"You'll get it. Guaranteed."

"Give me a day or two," he said. "Anything else?"

"Yeah. What can you tell me about the Megabucks progressive slots in Nevada?"

"Multicasino computer network, operated by an outfit called International Game Technology. More than fifty casinos in fifteen cities hooked into it."

"Legitimate, I suppose?"

"Oh, yeah. Strictly."

"Big payoffs?"

"Potentially huge. Depends on how many silver dollars or tokens you feed in before you hit the jackpot. Some guy lined up four sevens at the Cal-Neva in Reno a couple of years ago and took down six point nine million. Biggest jackpot in gaming history."

"I don't suppose there's any way for an individual to rig one of those slots?"

"Christ, no. Some hacker might be able to devise a jackpot program, but he'd have to go through too many safeguards to get it into the system. In the old days, when you had the reel slots, there were plenty of ways to gaffe a machine. Hell, some manufacturers did it themselves, on order from their customers to keep payoffs down. That's where the term 'one-arm bandit' comes from."

"Uh-huh." So much for off-the-wall theory no. 2.

"First slot machine was invented right here in San Francisco," DeFalco said, "just over a hundred years ago. Bet you didn't know that."

"No, I didn't."

"In 1887. Guy named Charley Fey, had a machine shop on Howard Street. Called his first slot the Liberty Bell. It had three reels—horseshoes, spades, diamonds, hearts, and bells. Took a nickel, paid off up to twenty nickels if you lined up three bells. He rented them out to a bunch of saloons on Market, the Embarcadero, and the Barbary Coast. Fey had a lock on the slot machine business for twenty years, until a Chicago manufacturer, Herbert Mills, invented the first iron-cased slot—"

"Joe, you're wasting all of that on me. You know so much about gambling, why don't you write a book?"

"I *am* writing one," he said. "Comprehensive history of gambling in the U.S. I'll have it done this year."

"Good for you. Send me a copy when it's published."

"Like hell I will. You cheap bastard, you can go out and buy a copy just like all my other friends."

After we'd rung off, I tucked the contract into an envelope and locked up the office. Jerry Polhemus was the person I wanted to talk to now. He was the vault: he had at least some of the answers hidden away inside himself. Find a way to unlock him and I'd have them too. But when I got to his building on Ninth Avenue, he wasn't home. Or if he was, he was not answering his bell.

Allyn Burnett lived in Glen Park, not far from Diamond Heights; I made her apartment building my last stop on the way to Kerry's. She was still home, and she signed the contract and gave me a check to cover the first two days of my employment. But she didn't have any answers to the questions I asked her. Her brother had never mentioned the names Manny or Arthur Welker, or Ekhern Manufacturing. No, as far as she knew he had never gambled exclusively at the Coliseum Club in Reno or the Nevornia in Stateline; he'd said something to her once about liking to club-hop because he felt it changed his luck. And she was amazed when I told her that he'd evidently taken his jackpot winnings in cash; she had "absolutely no clue" why he would have done such a thing.

Dead end for Saturday.

Tomorrow I would try to connect with Jerry Polhemus again—and see if I could crack him wide open.

Chapter 8

ON SUNDAY MORNINGS I like to stay in bed late. Read the paper with my coffee, the only day I bother with it; one day out of seven is all the current events I can stand. Read a book or a pulp magazine, watch an old movie on TV or on tape. It's especially nice if Kerry is there, too, because Sunday morning is a good time for making love or just sharing space. And it's best of all when we're in her bed because it and the room always smell clean and fresh, scented with her perfume. My bed has a vague musty smell, even with clean sheets, that I have never been able to identify. The effluvium of fifty-seven years of hard living, maybe.

This should have been a fine Sunday morning, because it started off in Kerry's bed. But it didn't turn out that way. At nine-thirty she got a call from Jim Carpenter, one of her bosses, who wanted her to come down to the agency for some kind of emergency meeting on one of her accounts. Even when you're a senior copywriter, you don't say no to the boss; so she went. There had been a time when I was jealous of Jim Carpenter, because he was handsome and suave and well-mannered and an impeccable dresser—all the things I'm not—and because I knew he had a letch for Kerry and had made more than one sophisticated pass at her. I wasn't jealous anymore, though. If she had wanted Jim Carpenter, she could have had him at any time during the three months I was chained to that cabin wall—for comfort and strength, if for no other reason. But she hadn't wanted him or any other man; she had remained faithful to me. I'm damned if I know what a woman like her sees in a man like me, but I am eternally grateful for her love. Now more than ever.

After she left, I tried to finish reading the paper. Then I tried watching a creaky Bowery Boys comedy on TV: silly stuff at the best of times, but I like the Bowery Boys and Laurel and Hardy and Abbott and Costello and the Marx Brothers and all the other old comedy teams because their humor reflects a simpler, more innocent time. Slapstick antics had no appeal for me this morning, however. Nothing did, with Kerry gone and things on my mind.

At ten-thirty I abandoned the bed for a shower. At eleven I left the apartment with half a cantaloupe and a glass of orange juice nestling in my stomach. And at eleven-twenty I parked my car just up the street from Jerry Polhemus's apartment building on Ninth Avenue.

There was a two-car garage under the building, right of usage probably going to the tenants who had been there the longest. One of the doors was up and parked in front of the opening, trunk lid raised, was a dark-red Mercury Cougar of recent vintage. The license plate read JERSCAT, which I translated to mean "Jerry's Cat." Polhemus was nowhere to be seen, nor was anybody else who might be a resident of the building.

I got out into an icy wind that smelled of fog and salt-damp. The fog had rolled in thickly this morning, was blowing overhead in scudding tatters; the day felt like one in the middle of January. Hunched inside my overcoat, I wandered around to the rear of the Cougar.

An old leather suitcase was wedged inside the trunk, opposite the spare tire. I looked at it for a couple of seconds and then walked inside the garage by two paces. No other car occupied it at the moment. At the far right, beyond a cluttered storage area, a passageway led to the rear of the building. From back that way, I heard the sound of footsteps on wood—somebody descending a flight of stairs. Utility stairs, probably, that would lead up through some kind of airshaft and provide a second means of access to all three flats.

The footsteps were Jerry Polhemus's. After a few seconds he came hurrying out of the passageway, dressed in Levi jeans and an air force bomber jacket, lugging a small duffel bag and a suitcase that matched the one in the Cougar's trunk. He stopped short when he saw me standing there and let the suitcase down hard, as if it might have slipped out of his grasp. Even in the half-light inside the garage, I could see the look of sudden fear that pinched his features.

He said, with the shrill edge to his voice, "What the hell are you doing here?"

"That's not a very friendly greeting, Jerry."

He had nothing to say to that. I waited a couple of seconds for him to pick up the suitcase or to come my way without it, but he didn't do either one. So I moved ahead to where he was.

"Going on a trip?" I asked him.

"That's my business, not yours."

"Depends on why you're going. Wouldn't have anything to do with me, would it?"

"Hell, no."

"Come on, I'm the one who reopened the can of worms."

"I don't know what you're talking about."

"David Burnett's suicide."

"I told you, man, I don't know anything about that—"

"Sure you do, Jerry. You know a lot of things you don't seem to want to talk about. The ten thousand dollars Dave gave you from his jackpot winnings, for instance. How come you didn't mention that yesterday?"

"None of your goddamn business."

"Then there's the fact he took his winnings in cash. How come he did that, Jerry?"

He did some rabbit-gnawing at his lower lip. Didn't say anything.

"And then there's the Mob," I said. "Dave was mixed up with those people and I think maybe you are too."

That one rocked him pretty good. His head jerked, his eyes bulged; fear-sweat put a sheen on his cheeks. In convulsive movements he leaned down to take hold of the suitcase, then straightened again.

"Get out of my way," he said.

"Not until you give me some straight answers."

"Get out of my way!"

I'd panicked him more than I intended. When I didn't move he swung the duffel bag at my head—swung it hard enough and with such suddenness that it caught me flat-footed and staggered me sideways. He hit me again, the son of a bitch, on the side of the head with greater force, and that blow sent me reeling into the storage area shelves. I went down hard, half cockeyed with pain, boxes and other objects tumbling around me. I got my arms up just in time to prevent a bicycle wheel from opening up my scalp, maybe concussing me; a sharp edge ripped through three layers of clothing and gashed my forearm.

By the time I pulled my legs under me and blinked my eyes back into focus, Polhemus had thrown the suitcase and duffel bag into the Cougar's trunk and was rushing for the driver's door. There was a rage in me that bordered on bloodlust; in that moment I wanted to hurt him, too, I wanted to hurt him *bad*. I lunged to my feet, into a stumbling run that brought me to the driver's side of the car just as he scrambled inside and slammed the door.

He might have tried to lock it, except that the window was halfway down; instead he threw himself across the bucket seat on the passenger side and clawed at the dash. I dragged the door open, leaned in, got a grip on his jacket with my left hand. I would have hit him with my right but he'd had enough time to open the glove compartment and paw inside, spilling out cassettes for the car's tape deck; he twisted around with something in his hand—a gun, a damn Saturday night special—at the same time I yanked on his jacket. He shoved the gun into my face so that I was looking straight down the bore, began screaming at me in a voice as high-pitched as a terrified child's.

"Get away from me, get away from me, I'll blow your fuckin' head off!"

There was a frozen segment of time—three or four seconds —during which I came close to doing something crazy, because I still wanted to hurt him and I didn't care that he had a gun or that his hand was shaking and the thing might go off even if he had no intention of using it. Reason came back with a jolting sensation that was almost physical. I let go of his arm then, the way you'd let go of something hot, and withdrew from the car so abruptly, I whacked my head against the window frame and gave myself another instant of double vision.

Polhemus lifted up on the driver's seat, still pointing the Saturday night special at me, his hand still shaking and his eyes still wild with his fear. "Back up, get away from the car!" he said in that shrill child's voice.

I backed up. Ten feet down the sidewalk, fifteen. I was shaking too, now.

He switched the revolver to his left hand, started the Cougar's engine, gunned it. Then he rolled his window up, not taking his eyes off me; locked the door, reached over to lock the other door, and threw the transmission into gear. Without looking upstreet or down, he popped the clutch and sent the car yawing out of the driveway, tires laying down forty or fifty feet of burned rubber; almost sideswiped an oncoming van and two parked cars before he had the Cougar under control. He made a skidding turn uphill on Noriega and was gone except for the fading noise of his engine and squealing tires.

I stood there on the sidewalk, arms flat against my sides. There were people around now, white and Asian faces peering out of windows, from doorways, from inside the garage. Voices lifted and fell—phantoms muttering gibberish in the fog. It was another few seconds before I could move. I walked to my car and got inside and sat waiting for the shaking to quit.

I would have hurt him, I thought. If he hadn't had the gun, I would have hurt him worse than he hurt me.

That frightened me more than the Saturday night special had. During those long weeks shackled in the mountain cabin, I had developed a capacity for violence: I had been prepared, eager, to kill my abductor when I found him. But I hadn't done it, when the moment of confrontation finally came, because of his motives and because of circumstances, and so by not killing him I believed that I had rid myself once and for all of the *desire* to commit mayhem. Now I knew that I hadn't, not quite. It was as if a new element had been added to my makeup—one comprised of equal parts of steel, which made me stronger, and atavism, which made me weaker. As long as I was aware of it and took pains to avoid situations like the one with Polhemus just past, I ought to be able to control it. And maybe expunge it completely in time. But what if I was thrust into another desperate situation, as unexpected as this one, and I was unable to hold myself in check?

It was ten minutes before the shaking stopped and I felt able to drive. The neighborhood was quiet again, the white and Asian faces gone. No one had called the police, or else patrol cars would have responded by this time. It didn't surprise me. This was a large city, and in large cities people do not like to get involved. A brief fight, somebody waving a gun, a car racing off with shrieking tires . . . no big deal. Happens all the time, that sort of minor disturbance. It takes blood to make citizens holler cop nowadays. Or somebody stealing something that belongs to them; then they set up a howl you can hear for blocks. Everything else is just spectacle, annoyance, or both.

I drove to my flat in Pacific Heights, because I did not want Kerry to see me like this. Not that I had suffered much in the way of physical damage. Bruise on my left temple, at the hairline, that you couldn't see unless you looked closely; tears in the sleeves of my overcoat, sport jacket, and shirt; and the gash on my forearm. I put some iodine on the cut, changed my shirt and jacket, and sat in the front room with a beer.

To keep from thinking about what I might have done to Jerry Polhemus, and what he might have done to me, I tried to get a handle on what had put him on the run. It wasn't just me he was afraid of. The Mob? Must be, the way he'd reacted when I mentioned the name. But why? What was *his* connection with organized crime?

Find him, I thought, find the answers.

Sure. But where do I go looking? Where would a scared kid like him run to?

KERRY WAS HOME when I returned to her place at three o'clock. I didn't tell her about the incident with Polhemus. It would only have upset her, worried her. She was concerned enough about me as it was.

My problem. One more thing to overcome, one more wound to heal, before I was whole again.

Chapter 9

MONDAY was one of the bad days.

I woke up tense, sweaty, with the room close around me. Residual effect of the skirmish with Polhemus—I knew that, but knowing it did not help me deal with it emotionally. The claustrophobic feeling was worse in the bathroom, and worse yet in the shower; I stayed in the stall less than a minute, went back into the bedroom to towel off. Too quiet in there: I switched on the radio, turned it up loud. Even though it was cool in the room, I was sweating again. I hauled up the window sash, stood naked in front of another day's worth of the late-spring fog. Sucked in cold air and listened to the sounds of the city until I began to feel a little better.

I dressed quickly, with the window still open and the radio still up loud. The bedside clock said that it was almost eight. Kerry wouldn't have left for work yet. If I called her, she would come right over, stay close to me, make it easier for me to weather this latest small crisis.

But I didn't call her. Not this time, nor the last couple of times. I had been enough of a burden to her the past several months . . . a burden much of the time I had known her, in one way and another. She didn't mind, *said* she didn't anyway, but I minded. I loved that woman; I did not want her to be hurt any more. Besides, she had her own profession, her own needs. She had made enough sacrifices for me.

It was better outside, in the cold, damp wind, with the pulse of the city beating steadily in my ears. I sat in the car for a time, letting the engine warm, sitting perfectly still as I had on Ninth Avenue yesterday. When I was sure I was fit for the road I put the transmission in gear and began to drive.

Going nowhere, just driving. Down to the Marina, out to Fort Point under the Golden Gate Bridge, through the Presidio and Sea Cliff, up El Camino del Mar, past the Palace of the Legion of Honor and in among the misty greens and fairways of Lincoln Park and down past the Cliff House and then along the Great Highway. Driving slow, careful. Watching the traffic patterns, looking at the people, letting my life glance against other lives so I would not feel alone.

When I got to Sloat I pulled off into the parking area above the beach and walked over to the zoo. But that was a mistake; the zoo was not a good place for me today, with so many of the animals in cages, and I didn't stay long. I went back across the Great Highway and down onto the beach. Walked along near the water for close to a mile before I turned back. Cold and blustery here, whitecaps on the ocean, heavy surf pounding at the dirty sand. Not many people around; a man walking his dog, a pair of young gay men strolling hand in hand, a few runners. But there was life in the pounding rhythms of the sea, the constant squawking of the gulls that wheeled above it. The ocean is a living thing; it teems with life, seen and unseen. There is danger in it, yes, and violence, but there is no evil. It is pure and clean. And if you respect it, it bears you no malice. It can even be your friend—an immense, comforting friend.

A myth that the ocean symbolizes loneliness. For me it symbolizes freedom.

Much of the tension was gone by the time I returned to the car; the hovering fear-shapes were gone too. My mind was coming to ease. I sat and watched the sea and the gulls and the people.

It was one o'clock, nearly six hours after my day began, before I felt well enough to start living again.

WHEN I CHECKED IN with Eberhardt at the office, he said that Joe DeFalco had called. "But you don't need to call him back. He said to tell you he talked to his sources and the local gamblers never heard of David Burnett."

Another theory shot down. Which meant that Burnett *had* lost the money and run up a debt with the Vegas and Reno sports books.

Or did it?

THE WAREHOUSE DOORS at the rear of Basic Carpet Cleaners were open and the same delivery van I had seen on Saturday—or its twin—was parked in the opening. When I came up I saw Jerry Polhemus's co-worker struggling to load a long, heavy roll of carpet into the rear of the van. He was doing it alone; there was nobody else around.

I moved in past him and said, "Let me help you with that." He gave me a look but didn't object. So I hoisted up one end and together we muscled the carpet inside the van.

He said, "Thanks," a little warily, and shut the doors. He was a tall, wiry redhead around Polhemus's age. He wore a disgruntled look along with his white uniform overalls, as if his day so far hadn't been much better than mine. The name *Kevin* was stitched above one pocket of the overalls.

I said, "Remember me? I was here on Saturday."

"Yeah, I remember. Jerry's not here."

"So I see. Didn't come in today?"

"Didn't come in, didn't call, nothing. I got to do his work and mine too."

"Well, he didn't decide to stay home," I said. "I just stopped by his place. Any idea where he might have gone?"

"No. How would I know?"

"I thought the two of you might be friends."

"We get along. Why? Who're you, anyway?"

"Didn't Jerry tell you Saturday?"

"No. He didn't say nothing."

"I'm a friend of Dave Burnett's sister. You happen to know him? Jerry's pal Dave?"

"Dude who offed himself? Yeah, I knew him. Not too well. Went to a couple of ball games with him and Jerry."

"Jerry talk much about the suicide?"

"Not to me. I don't want to hear about it. Stuff like that . . . man. You know what I mean?"

I nodded. "He tell you about being up in Reno with Dave when Dave hit his big jackpot?"

"Sure. Said Dave lost it all betting sports and that's why he took them pills. I never figured him for such a crazy dude."

"That all Jerry said?"

"I don't remember nothing else."

"Suppose Jerry wanted to get away for a few days, take a little vacation for himself. Where might he go?" Kevin started to shake his head and I said, "No, just think about it a minute."

He thought about it for ten seconds, with his face squeezed up as if thinking caused him physical pain. "Someplace out of the city, you mean?"

"Yes," I said patiently, "someplace out of the city."

"I dunno," he said. But then he pulled a face and said, "Well . . . maybe up to his folks' cabin?" as if he were asking me a question.

"Where would that be?"

"Some lake up near Tahoe."

"But not Lake Tahoe itself?"

"No, some other lake. A little one."

"Try to remember the name."

"Nah," he said. "I'm not good with names."

"What is it, a summer place? Or do his folks live there year-round?"

"His folks live in Sacramento. His old man's a foot doctor."

"They spend their summers at the lake?"

"Nah, they're old now, they go on cruises, stuff like that. Jerry's got the place to himself just about anytime he wants it." Kevin grinned. "He takes chicks there, you know? For the weekend sometimes. He—"

"Kevin! I thought I told you to deliver that Sarouk!"

We both looked in the direction of the new voice. The fat sourpuss I'd spoken to on Saturday was waddling toward us from the front of the building, scowling and muttering to himself in a way that made me think of the rhyme about the Jabberwock, how it came whiffling through the tulgey wood and burbled as it came. When he got close enough for a good look at me he scowled even harder and came to a flat-footed stop.

"You again," he said.

"Me again."

"What is it this time?"

"More information for my report." I jabbed Kevin's arm by way of thanking him and turned past the van without another glance at the sourpuss.

Behind me he said with rising inflection, "*What* report? Dammit, you come back here—"

I quit listening to him. I was listening instead to an echo inside my head: Inspector Harry Craddock's voice, telling me Jerry Polhemus had been "up at Lake Tahoe" the night David Burnett died.

CRADDOCK walked into the General Works squad room at two minutes to four. When he saw me waiting he said the same thing the fat sourpuss had: "You again."

"I won't take up more than a couple minutes of your time, Inspector. I just need the answer to one question."

He kept on walking across to his desk, which was next to a window that offered a scenic view of the freeway approach to the Bay Bridge. I went along with him. He gave me a look, sat down, and began to unwrap a cigarillo. I sat down, too, without being invited, in the metal visitor's chair I had occupied on Saturday.

"All right," he said. "What's your question?"

"You told me the other day that Jerry Polhemus was at Lake Tahoe when David Burnett killed himself. Did you mean that literally, or did you mean in the vicinity of Lake Tahoe?"

"The vicinity. Why?"

"At his folks' summer place, was he? Did he happen to give you the address?"

"That makes three questions," Craddock said.

"One question, three parts. It's triple-jointed."

That got a small chuckle out of him. He lit his cigarillo before he said, "Yes, Polhemus was at his folks' place. On Fallen Leaf Lake. He went up there for the weekend."

"By himself?"

"So he said."

"What about the address?"

"Seem to remember asking him for it. I'd have to look it up."

"Would you? I'd appreciate it."

"Mind telling me why you want it?"

I explained, briefly, about my skirmish with Polhemus yesterday. "He's running scared," I said. "I want to know why."

"And you think he went up to Fallen Leaf Lake."

"Sometimes people run to familiar places. If they're not running too hard."

"Uh-huh," Craddock said. "You plan to drive that far on a maybe?"

"I don't have anything better to do."

He ruminated for ten seconds or so, studying the end of his cigarillo. Then he said, "Tell you what. I'll give you the address if you don't forget where it came from. I want to know right away if you find out anything that I ought to know."

"Sure thing. I'm not one to play games."

"Everybody plays games," he said. "The ones I get along with are the ones who play by the rules."

There was a computer terminal at one side of his desk, but this kind of information wasn't important enough to have been logged in; it would be in Craddock's notes and those would be in a paper file. He got to his feet, said, "I'll be right back," and went away.

I looked at the computer. Everybody uses them these days —except me and those like me. Throwbacks, the hopelessly old-fashioned. Eberhardt wanted to buy a small one for the agency, and so far I had resisted on the old-dogs-and-new-tricks principle. But maybe someday I would weaken for his sake, if he promised to do all the work on the thing himself. A computer, to me, was like a Zippo to a Cro-Magnon.

I shifted my gaze to the window and watched the early rush-hour traffic pile up on the bridge approach. It was a little clearer out now, with a cold pale sun shining through tears in the cloud cover. That was about the way it was inside me now too: a little clearer, with a cold pale light shining through the clouds.

Craddock came back. "Eight thousand and six Fallen Leaf Lake Road," he said.

"Got it. Thanks."

"Just remember," he said as I stood. "Winning and losing don't matter. It's how you play the game."

KERRY SAID, "Lake Tahoe? Are you sure it's such a good idea to drive up there alone?"

"Why shouldn't it be?"

"You know why."

"Kerry," I said, "I'll be okay."

"What if you have an anxiety attack?"

"I haven't had one in over a week," I lied.

She was silent for a time. Finally she said, "Will you call me when you get up there?"

"Every night I'm away, if you want."

"I want." She moved closer to me—we were on the couch in my flat—and touched my cheek with the tips of her fingers. Her eyes were shiny. "I couldn't stand it if I lost you again."

I thought of Karen Salter on the floor in her apartment, slashing at the tabletop, the anger and grief naked on her face. And shook the thought away and put my arms around Kerry, held her tight.

"You won't," I said.

Chapter **10**

THE DRIVE FROM SAN FRANCISCO to Lake Tahoe takes about three and a half hours. When I left the city at nine on Tuesday morning, the fog was so thick you could have spread it on toast. When I got over by Vallejo, there was no more fog and the sky was a scrubbed blue. By the time I reached Sacramento the temperature had climbed to an unseasonable eighty; a hot wind sweated me until I was up into the Sierras beyond Placerville. Then the air cooled and stayed cool until I crossed Echo Summit, where old snow lay in patches and pockets and it was almost chilly, and began to drop down the east slopes toward Tahoe. Then it got warm again at the lower elevations, though there was a mountain breeze to remind you that it was still spring—and when I pulled into the town of South Lake Tahoe at a quarter to one, the temperature was in the mid-seventies. Screwy, localized weather. But that was California for you, at just about any time of the year.

Despite what I'd said to Kerry, I had been a little leery of the drive starting out. It was the first long drive I had undertaken since my return from Deer Run. And the Sierras were where I had been held captive, though close to fifty miles south of Highway 50; the Sacramento area where I had done the bulk of my hunting for the man who had kidnapped me. I felt fine that morning, but how would I feel when I came back into the same general area of my ordeal?

Well, I still felt fine. I had not even had a bad twinge anywhere along the way. The human mind is as much an enigma to its individual owners as it is to the medical profession; it simply refuses to behave in a predictable fashion. Show me a person who says he knows his own mind and means it, and I'll show you a case of self-delusion.

At the wye junction where Highway 50 meets Highway 89, I turned into a service station for gas and the use of a public telephone; my car phone has limited range. I called Kerry at Bates and Carpenter and relieved her mind.

The third road into the wye junction is Lake Tahoe Boulevard, the town's main drag; I went east along there from the service station. Even though it was a weekday, there was plenty of traffic—though not nearly as much as there would be in July and August. Every third vehicle seemed to be a gamblers-special bus bringing day-trippers and overnighters to the Stateline casinos from all over the Bay Area and as far away as Oregon and Idaho.

The lake stretched out placidly on my left: twenty-two miles long and ten miles wide, set in a huge mountain-rimmed bowl six thousand feet above sea level. Scattered pleasure boats and paddle-wheel excursion boats moved over its surface like waterbugs on a pond. Pretty setting, Tahoe, but it used to be a lot prettier. Tourism and gambling and overdevelopment and now something called eutrophication had marred and cheapened its beauty.

Kerry and I had watched a PBS special on the area a few weeks back. Depressing program. The Tahoe Basin, which had once catered to small numbers of residents and vacationers, now had a year-round population of 50,000 and a yearly summer influx of 12 million tourists and part-time residents. On still late-summer days when the traffic is bumper-to-bumper, the smog gets so bad it's almost urban. And where the lake had once been uniformly clean and blue, shallow fringes now turn a sickly green in spring and algae slimes the shoreline, a result of this thing called eutrophication—nutrient pollution. So many trees and shrubs were cleared off during a century of human development that natural nutrients from decomposing plants and animals, normally caught by the roots of vegetation, have washed into the lake. Sewage, too, and leaching and runoff from tons of nitrogen fertilizers used on golf courses and lawns, all of which feeds the algae. The prediction is that in another forty years Tahoe will be more green than blue. And meanwhile, a long-term battle between developers and environmentalists continues to rage in both California and Nevada—the lake is split by the states' boundary—with some recent compromise agreements but no satisfactory long-term resolution in sight.

It had been a couple of years since my last visit to Tahoe, when Kerry and I had driven up one weekend to see a show at Harrah's. Superficially, nothing much had changed in South Lake Tahoe since then. The Chamber of Commerce was still in the same place on the western end of Lake Tahoe Boulevard, along with most of the town's regular business establishments; the eastern end, approaching Stateline, is nothing but a two-mile string of motels—the nice, the not so nice, and the ugly—that cater to the gambling trade. A C-of-C employee sold me a map of the area for a buck and a half. Nothing comes free anymore, especially in a tourist area. I sat in the car with the map spread open over the wheel, familiarizing myself with Fallen Leaf Lake. I'd never been there before and didn't know much about it.

It was off Highway 89, a few miles west of town. Two and a half miles long, about a mile wide, with a mostly undeveloped shoreline. Well, hallelujah. Fallen Leaf Lake Road was the main access in off 89, and at that it didn't go all the way around the lake. It petered out not far beyond a lodge and campground at the south end, the only such accommodations marked on the map.

I drove back to the wye, out 89 to Fallen Leaf Lake Road. Narrow bumpy blacktop that wound in through wooded sections broken up here and there by rocky meadowland and by another campground. It was a couple of miles before I caught sight of the lake itself—a beautiful little body of water, ringed by trees and by bare-rock scarps along the west shore. Populated, yes, but unspoiled by motel complexes and fast-food restaurants and all the other products of modern society that defaced much of Lake Tahoe's shoreline. You had a feeling of wilderness here, despite the cottages that began to appear along the road. You also had a feeling that the people who owned property wanted to keep it that way. The water was the kind of bright clear blue Tahoe's used to be, unmarred by any apparent nutrient pollution. The cottages—some small and rustic, others elaborate and stone-faced—all seemed to be well maintained. There was money here but, at least visibly, none of the ostentation of wealth. Even the fancier dwellings had been constructed so that they blended into their surroundings rather than clashed with them.

The road ran close to the lake, dipping up and down, cutting sharp around trees and outcrops. Some of the cottages were set down below it, at the water's edge; others were above the road, in cleared patches among the trees. There were a few rural mailboxes, but for the most part people's names and address numbers were burned into or painted on wooden markers nailed to trees. It did not take me long to spot one that said: POLHEMUS – 8006, with an arrow pointing lakeward. Or to spot the dark red Cougar drawn up on a platform parking deck opposite.

Jackpot.

I pulled off on a slant behind the Cougar. It was the only car on the deck. A set of stairs led down from there to a small old shingled cottage with green shutters that squatted among moss-hung lodgepole and sugar pine at the lake's edge. I could see part of a deck and a short dock. The trees screened it from its neighbors on both sides, giving it a sense of complete seclusion.

I went over between the Cougar and the stairs. There was nobody on the deck or dock, at least so far as I could see. Behind me, on the road, a car rattled past; somewhere on the lake, a powerboat made an angry droning buzz, like a fly caught in a jar. Otherwise the area seemed wrapped in a cathedral hush.

The road was deserted now. I stepped back to the Cougar and tried the passenger door. Locked. I walked around to the driver's side and that door was locked too. So I couldn't tell before I braced Polhemus if the Saturday night special was still in the glove compartment or down in the cabin. I would have to be extra careful with him this time, for his sake as well as mine.

The stairs were mossy, the wood risers half rotted; I picked my way down them carefully, onto a short path that led to the cottage. There was no door on this side. The main entrance was off the deck, half hidden by a wall and the cone-heavy branches of a pine. I couldn't see it until I came up onto the deck.

The door was standing wide open.

All of the deck was visible from where I stood; there was nobody on it. Nobody on the dock, either. I went ahead to the door, not being quiet about it. Shadowy inside; drapes or blinds had been drawn across the windows. I reached in and rapped my knuckles against the door panel.

"Hello? Anybody home?"

No answer.

I stood looking into the cottage for a few seconds, at furniture shapes and shadows that didn't move. Maybe Polhemus was out on the lake somewhere. Except that as scared as he had been on Sunday, it wasn't likely he would go off and leave his front door open like this. . . .

I called out again, listened to the faint echo of my voice. Then I backed off, moved from the deck onto the dock and on out to the end.

A patched-up rowboat, sans oars, was tied there. So was a string for keeping caught fish; I hauled up the string but there were no fish on it now. I straightened again, stood scanning the water. Two boats, one moving and one stationary, both down at the south end near the marina and campground. There was nothing else to hold my attention.

I retraced my steps to the open cottage door. A feeling of

wrongness had begun to stir through me. Polhemus's car up on the parking platform, the unused rowboat, front door wide open and nobody around. Add all of that together and what did you get?

Trouble, that was what you got.

I kept staring in among the shadows. Walk in there, I thought, and it's trespassing. But I didn't seem to feel as reticent about even a minor piece of lawbreaking as I once had. And the feeling of wrongness kept itching at me, growing stronger. All right—the hell with it. I walked in far enough to feel along the inside wall with the back of my left hand. Located the light switch and knuckled it upward.

Dull orange light from a chandelier fashioned out of an antique horse collar prodded most of the shadows into corners of the beamed ceiling. Biggish living room: rattan window blinds, wicker furniture, woven Indian-type throw rugs, a stag's head mounted over a fieldstone fireplace. All very commonplace rustic. And all very empty.

I moved farther inside. Open can of beer on the table next to the wicker settee, sections of newspaper tossed over the cushions, the remains of a sandwich on a plate with a crumpled napkin. The air was close, thickened by trapped sun-warmth, and I could smell the faint, clinging odor of marijuana. There was an ashtray near the plate, and when I moved another few steps closer I saw that it contained half a dozen roach ends.

Well? I thought.

The living room opened into a darkened kitchen. I had come this far; I went the rest of the way. On the counter next to the sink were a loaf of bread and an open jar of mustard and packages of sliced bologna and American cheese that had been left out quite a while; the bologna had curled up at the edges and the cheese had darkened and turned hard. Nothing else caught my eye in there.

Behind the kitchen was a short hallway with three doors opening off it. Small bedroom, with a pair of twin beds pushed together and neatly covered with a quilt. Empty. The middle door was ajar. I gave it a nudge with my shoulder.

Bathroom. And blood on the sink, on the floor in front of it —dried blood in drops and splotches and streaks. Not a lot of it but enough to take somebody's wound out of the simple household-cut category. Polhemus?

The door to a stall shower was closed; I eased it open. As empty as the rest of the bathroom. I moved on to the third door. Another bedroom, larger than the first. Queen-size bed, slept in and unmade, with Polhemus's two suitcases and duffel bag on the floor nearby. Both suitcases were spread open, letting me see a jumble of hastily packed clothing.

All right. The place was deserted. There was that blood in the bathroom, but it did not have to have a sinister explanation. Polhemus had been here since Sunday, the way it looked, and it could be that he was out somewhere now on an errand; if I waited around long enough or came back later, there he'd be.

Sure. Except that there were bad vibes in this cabin, as subtle and clinging as the odor of smoked grass. Something had happened here, something grim and violent.

I went back into the living room. Stood looking around again. And this time little things, little pieces of wrongness, revealed themselves in there too.

The place had not been swept out in a good long while; dust covered the floor in a thin layer. On the left side of the room, nearest the door, the dust was mostly undisturbed. On the right side, there were marks all through it, including scuff marks and a long swath as if something had been dragged across the floor. The cushions on a rattan chair near the hearth were askew, and the chair itself looked out of place— kicked or shoved over there. Some kind of struggle, I thought.

I moved over that way. And in the disturbed areas by the window and near the fireplace I found more splotches and drops, so dark against the dark-wood flooring that you couldn't see them at a casual glance from a distance. I scratched up a few flakes from one of the stains, went to the nearest window and pulled an edge of the blinds away from the glass so sunlight shone on my fingernail. Yeah. More dried blood.

Well? I thought again.

When I turned from the window, something else caught my eye. Propped on the fireplace mantel were half a dozen small color snapshots, the Polaroid variety. I went to take a closer look.

Five of the photos had been taken here, out on the deck and down on the dock. The sixth looked to have been snapped in front of a gambling casino—the Nevornia Club, judging from the purple-and-gold facade visible in the background. Jerry Polhemus was in four of the shots, with his shirt off in one, and in each he was in the company of a raven-haired girl with high cheekbones and striking features. Indian, possibly. But it was the other photos that interested me most. A young blond man was prominent in those—David Burnett and no mistake—and so was a willowy redhead with overlarge breasts for her size and shape. In one of the candid shots taken down on the dock, the redhead had her arms around Burnett's neck and her tongue licking his upper lip, and he had both hands planted squarely on her behind.

Old photos, I told myself. But they weren't. The color definition was still sharp and there was only a thin speckling of dust on each print. They had not been on that mantel very long. Who keeps old photographs on display these days?

I had another vivid mental image of Karen Salter, down on her knees in the Russian Hill apartment, her grief and pain naked on her face. While she'd been making her wedding preparations and keeping her bed warm for Davey, the man whose death had so ravaged her was up here having himself a fling with a hot-looking redhead. Sowing a last few wild oats? Or was the redhead one of many?

I looked again at the photo taken in front of the Nevornia Club. All four of them were in that one, arms linked, smiles bright on their faces, Polhemus mugging some for the camera. He and Burnett and the dark-haired girl were in casual clothes; the redhead was wearing a purple blouse with gold piping and a gold skirt with purple piping—the uniform worn by female floor employees of the casino.

I took that photo down and turned it over to see if there was anything written on the back. There wasn't. I started to

return it to the mantel, changed my mind, and slipped it into
my shirt pocket instead.

Without touching anything, I made another circuit of the
kitchen, bathroom, and small bedroom. In the second bedroom I poked briefly through the contents of Polhemus's suitcases and duffel bag. The only thing I found of any interest
was a handful of extra cartridges for his Saturday night special.
There was no sign of the gun itself, not in the luggage or the
bed or the drawer in the nightstand or anywhere else in the
room.

I was sweating when I finished in there. I had been in the
cottage too long—more than twenty minutes now. I knew
more than when I'd entered, but I also knew less, and I did
not like any of it.

Out on the deck, I thought about leaving the door open as
I'd found it. But there was the possibility it might entice
somebody else to go poking around inside. I shut it finally,
using my handkerchief on the knob, and made sure it was
latched before I climbed the stairs to the parking platform.

My instincts, as I jockeyed the car around and headed back
toward Highway 89, were to go to the El Dorado County
Sheriff's Department and file a report. But what would I tell
them? That I had trespassed on private property, for no valid
reason? That I had felt bad vibes and found some dried blood
that *could* have come from a severely gashed finger or a high-
altitude nosebleed? That I had unlawfully searched the premises and removed a photograph belonging to the owner? There
was no evidence that a crime had been committed on those
premises, and without any, I did not have a legal leg to stand
on.

So?

So I was not going to the El Dorado County Sheriff's Department. I was going to the Nevornia Club over in Stateline.

Chapter 11

THE NEVORNIA was one of the newer, posh casino-hotels. Its fifteen stories vied for attention with the cluster of older high-rise resorts—Harrah's, Harvey's, High Sierra, Caesar's Tahoe —on the quarter-square-mile "glitter strip" just across the Nevada line. Nonstop gambling action and star-studded live entertainment. Gaudy neon and a steady ebb and flow of eager suckers. But for the most part it was the men like Arthur Welker who struck it rich. Evidence of that was the Nevornia's opulent gold-and-purple facade and decor, its extravagant musical shows, its profusion of boutiques and specialty shops where you could buy everything from diamond jewelry to Oriental antiques. At inflated prices, of course; the house percentage was high on those businesses too.

I left my car in the free Harrah's lot, on the California side, and walked over to the Nevornia. Even though it was a weekday afternoon, the banks of splashily neoned slots and the rows of purple-and-gold blackjack tables were getting moderately heavy play from tourists and small-timers. The craps and roulette and baccarat layouts were quiet. The high rollers were like vampires: they couldn't stand the daylight, so they only came out after dark.

I showed the photograph to a woman in a change booth, a sleepy-eyed croupier, and a blackjack dealer; none of them recognized the willowy redhead, or owned up to it if they did. But the fourth person I tried—a middle-aged woman with henna-rinsed hair and a squint in one eye, who presided over an empty pai gow poker table—netted me a small payoff.

She looked at the photo for five seconds and at me for ten, probably trying to decide if I was a pervert. Then she said, hedging, or maybe fishing a little, "You can't sit here unless you make a bet." So I made a two-dollar bet, without knowing what the hell I was doing; pai gow poker is a recent addition to the roster of Nevada casino games, put in to accommodate the ever-increasing number of Asian gamblers, and I had never played it before. I won anyway, and slid my winnings over to the henna-rinse's side of the table. That put her on my side, more or less.

"So why do you want to know about her?" she asked, nodding at the photo.

"The boy with her is my son. He's been seeing her on the sly and he won't tell me anything about her. I came up to find out for myself."

The henna-rinse laughed knowingly. "I'll just bet he didn't tell you about her."

"Why do you say that?"

"You'll find out when you meet her."

"What's her name?"

"Make your bet," she said slyly.

I put my original two bucks back on the table. This time I lost it.

She shrugged—easy come, easy go—and said, "Better luck next time." Then she said, "Her name's Wendy Oliver. Sweet Wendy."

"What shift does she work?"

"She doesn't. Not here, not anymore."

"Oh? She quit?"

"Fired," the henna-rinse said with relish. "Thrown out on her sweet little can."

"When?"

"Make your bet."

Another two bucks down. The henna-rinse and I lost this time too.

"Couple of weeks ago," she said.

"You know why?"

"With sweet Wendy, it could be just about any offense you can think of."

"But you don't know which one."

"Nope."

"Would she be working at one of the other clubs?"

"Maybe. Or maybe she's just working these days, if you know what I mean."

"Hooking?" I put my last two singles on the table. "Is she that kind?"

"She's that kind."

"I don't suppose you know where she lives?"

"Try the phone book. She's probably listed. Easier for her customers to find her that way. If you know what I mean," she said, and took those last two singles of mine for the house.

There was a concourse nearby, along which I found a bank of telephone booths. I tried the South Lake Tahoe directory first. One Oliver listed: W. Oliver, 274A Tata Lane. The Nevada directory had no listing for anybody named Oliver in this area. So it was W. Oliver on Tata Lane or I was going to have to start over again.

When I got back to my car I looked up Tata Lane on the South Lake Tahoe map. It was off Lake Tahoe Boulevard, down past the wye junction—all of three miles away. But it took me nearly twenty minutes to get there because of the traffic.

The area was a mix of small industrial companies, city offices, the Lake Tahoe Ranger Station, and private residences. Most of the residences were trailers in different parks spread out over several blocks: 274A Tata Lane was on the eastern end of a park called Sugar Pine Estates that didn't seem to have any sugar pines growing in it. The trailer bearing the number was not much to look at: gray with yellow trim, both colors faded and splotched here and there with rust spots;

small front and side yards composed of browned strips of lawn, weedy flower beds, and one diseased-looking tree. Parked under a sagging metal carport was a Toyota Tercel that had had a badly dented right rear fender panel.

I parked across the street. The sun glinted brightly off the trailer's metal surfaces; unless W. Oliver had air-conditioning, I thought, it would be like an oven inside on hot days. On the carport side was a narrow porch carpeted with dusty green Astroturf. I went up onto the porch—and the screen door opened before I got to it and a young woman leaned out in my direction. She must have seen or heard me coming.

She was the one in the photograph. Tall, slender, with dark red hair worn long and cut in wavy layers; pale skin dusted with freckles and lightly sheened with perspiration; a wide mouth and light-colored eyes, both of which were too wise and too cynical for a woman in her mid-twenties. The green halter top she wore revealed about half of each of her overdeveloped breasts. A pair of skimpy white shorts, cut tight through the crotch, also left little to the imagination. There were freckles on her chest and legs, too—lots of them.

She saw me looking and said in a voice that was part sneer, part tease, "See anything you like?"

"Well, you seem to be advertising."

"You still read the ads, huh?"

"Sure," I said. "But I haven't answered one in years."

She laughed in a mildly snotty way. I was an amusing old fart, whoever I was. "You selling something?"

"Nope."

"Neither am I. So?"

"Are you Wendy Oliver?"

"What if I am?"

I took out the snapshot and held it up between us at eye level. "I've got some questions about David Burnett."

Her whole demeanor changed. It was like watching a piece of trick photography: one second she was soft and sexy, cynical and wise and twenty-five; the next second she was tight-drawn, wary, frightened, with lines around her mouth and eyes that made her look ten to fifteen years older.

"Who are you?" she said. Her voice had changed, too; now it was full of tremolos.

"Private investigator." I put the snapshot away and let her look at the photostat of my license. It seemed to ease her anxiety some—not too much.

"How did you find me? Where'd you get that picture?"

"I just told you, I'm a detective. I get paid to find things and people."

She gnawed flecks of tangerine-colored lipstick off her lower lip. "Who hired you?"

"Burnett's sister. You know he committed suicide?"

"Yeah. I heard."

"Pretty terrible thing, wasn't it."

"Awful," she said.

"You don't sound very upset."

"It didn't just happen yesterday. Besides, Dave and me, we weren't that close."

"That's not how it looks in the photo."

"I don't care how it looks in the damn photo."

"Why did he kill himself, Wendy?"

"How should I know?"

"Money? Winning a lot, losing more?"

"I don't know anything about that," she said. But she was lying. I could see it in her eyes.

"Who told you about the suicide? Jerry Polhemus?"

"So?"

"When?"

"Day after it happened."

"In person or on the phone?"

"He called up."

"Where did he call from? San Francisco?"

"Yeah."

"Then he must have just gone home. He was at Fallen Leaf Lake the night Dave died."

"Yeah, that's right. He found out when he got back."

"Did you see him while he was up here?"

"No."

"Talk to him?"

"No. He called but . . . no."

"When was the last time you saw or talked to him?"

"I don't remember. Weeks ago."

"Not in the past couple of days?"

"No. I told you. Listen, what's the idea—"

"How about the weekend Dave won his big jackpot. You see both of them then?"

For some reason, that seemed to scare her all over again. "I don't remember. What difference does it make?"

"Must have been pretty exciting, Dave hitting a Megabucks slot for two hundred grand."

"I wouldn't know."

"Weren't you with him at the time?"

"No. Hell, no."

"I had the idea you were."

"Well, you had the wrong idea."

"But he came and told you about it afterward?"

". . . Is that what Jerry said?"

"I'm asking you."

"All right, yeah, he told me about it afterward. So what?"

I let a few seconds pass in silence. Then I said flatly, "What are you afraid of, Wendy?"

She didn't want to hear that, either. She might have pulled back inside and shut the door in my face, or she might have told me to go to hell; she didn't do either one. Something kept her standing there talking to me—the same sort of thing, maybe, that keeps a rabbit standing in thrall of a snake.

She gnawed off some more lipstick before she said, "Listen, my boyfriend'll be home any minute. He catches me talking to a strange guy, he'll kick my ass. So why don't you just leave me alone, okay?"

"Your boyfriend isn't what you're afraid of."

"No? You don't know Scott."

"Were you living with him while you were seeing Burnett?"

One, two, three beats. "Yeah. You happy now? Scott doesn't know. He finds out, he'll *really* kick my ass."

"Tell me about you and Burnett."

"Tell you what? There's nothing to tell. We saw each other a few times, had some grins together . . . that's all."

"When did you start seeing him?"

"What difference does that make?"

"Answer the question, Wendy."

"Last year. Late last year."

"How did you meet?"

"He came into the Nevornia, where I used to work. Him and Jerry. I was dealing blackjack and play was slow that day and we started talking."

"Pretty heavy gambler, was he? Big bets?"

"Not Dave. Five bucks a hand, tops."

"So the two of you got to talking. Then what?"

"Jerry's got this cabin at Fallen Leaf Lake. They were up for a long weekend and Dave asked me if I wanted to come party with them."

"And you said yes."

"Scott had a winter job in L.A.," she said, and shrugged.

"Dave tell you he was living with a girl in San Francisco? That they were planning to be married soon?"

"You kidding? Guys say that, it chills you right out. Dave was no airhead. He knew what he was doing."

"Sure he did. Good old Dave. He tell you about his fiancée later or did somebody else?"

"He told me. Didn't matter by then. He had somebody, I've got somebody—that's the way it is. We were just having some grins, I told you that."

Yeah, I thought. Grins.

I said, "Who else was at Jerry's cabin that first weekend?"

"His girl, nobody else."

"The other girl in the photo?"

"Yeah."

"What's her name?"

Five-second hesitation. "Janine. Janine Wovoka."

"You know her well?"

"No. We never met before then."

"She live here in Tahoe?"

"No."

"Where, then?"

"Reno. She lives in Reno."

"Where in Reno?"

"She never told me and I never asked."

"She tell you where she works?"

"Coliseum Club. She did then, anyway."

"Not anymore?"

"I dunno. I haven't seen her since the last time the four of us were together."

"The weekend Burnett won his big jackpot, you mean."

"I told you, I wasn't with him then!"

"Jerry was, though. How about Janine?"

"How should I know?"

"What was Janine's job at the Coliseum Club?"

"Change-girl. She was trying to get on as a dealer."

"Burnett made his big score at the Coliseum Club," I said. "But I guess that's just coincidence. Couldn't have had anything to do with Janine working there."

She didn't bite on that. She said, "How many times I have to tell you? I don't know!"

"You think maybe Janine got fired from her job?"

"Why would I think that?"

"You said she might not be working at the Coliseum Club anymore. Why not? There a reason she might have been fired?"

"I don't think she got fired. I don't know if she's still there and I don't give a shit, either."

"You were fired from *your* job, though. At the Nevornia."

". . . So?"

"Couple of weeks ago. Right before Burnett killed himself."

"So?"

"Mind telling me why?"

"Yeah, I mind. It's none of your fucking business."

"It is if it has something to do with Burnett or Polhemus or Janine Wovoka."

"Well, it doesn't."

"Same people own both the Nevornia and the Coliseum Club, did you know that? Arthur Welker, for one."

The name made her twitch. She worked on her lower lip some more; there wasn't much lipstick left on it.

"You know him?" I asked. "Arthur Welker?"

"No."

"But you do know he's got Mob connections."

She said, "You're crazy." But she knew, all right. She might be good at deception with her mouth, but she hadn't learned the trick yet of carrying it through with her eyes.

I said, "The Mob have something to do with Burnett's suicide, Wendy? That part of what's scaring you?"

She made a low sound in her throat, and I think she would either have cracked or slammed the door in my face if a car hadn't come wheeling into the driveway just then. She said, "Oh *shit*," almost moaning the words.

I turned. The just-arrived car was a battered, primer-patched, twenty-year-old Porsche, and the guy who got out of it was six feet of blond curls, tanned skin, and muscles rippling under cutoff jeans and a sleeveless net shirt. He stood glaring up at us for a few seconds, then came stalking over the porch.

I glanced back at Wendy. Her eyes pleaded with me: *Don't say anything about Dave!* When I turned my head again, it was just in time to come nose to nose with the blond kid.

"Who the hell are you, man?"

"Lakeside Maintenance," I said.

"Huh?"

"Lakeside Maintenance. We paint and repair trailers. Looks like yours could use the work, but the lady doesn't seem to think so."

He shifted his gaze to Wendy. "That right?"

"Well, what did you think?" she said. I'd given her a re-prieve and she had hold of it with both hands. "Would I mess around with an old geek like him?"

"You'd mess around with a goat if it had a big enough pecker," the blond guy said. His eyes flicked my way again. "Get out of here," he said.

"Try being polite. I'm more than twice your age."

"So what? Get off my property or I'll throw you off."

"No you won't," I said. "I'll walk off but that's the only way."

I smiled as I spoke—the kind of smile that has wolf's teeth in it. He didn't like the smile or the words but he didn't do anything about them. Maybe he wasn't as macho as he pretended to be. Or maybe there was something about me that made him think twice about trying to get tough.

I transferred the smile to Wendy, said, "Thanks for talking to me, miss," and went down off the porch and across the drive, taking my time about it. I was almost to the sidewalk when I heard her cry out behind me, not too loud and more in surprise than anything else. When I looked back, he had hold of her arm and was shoving her roughly inside the trailer. She said, "God damn you, Scott!" and he said, "Shut up, you little bitch!" and then the door banged shut behind them.

Nice kids. The kind that made me glad I'd never had any of my own.

Chapter 12

THERE WAS A TIME, not so long ago, when Reno—"The Biggest Little City in the World"—was known for two things: quickie divorces, because of a six-week residence law established in the 1930s; and gambling, which was first licensed in Nevada in the 1870s, outlawed between 1910 and the end of Prohibition, and then fully legalized. Nowadays, with the no-fault divorce law in many states, a lot more people go to Reno to take on spouses than to shed them: wedding chapels outnumber divorce lawyers by a wide margin. Gambling is still a big business, but not nearly as big as it once was; revenues are down all over Nevada because of competitive pressure from the lotteries in California and other states, legalized gambling set-ups on Indian reservations, and other factors. Light industry has burgeoned in the Washoe basin in recent years, which has led to a population explosion and a suburban sprawl typical of other small cities its size, which in turn has made Reno much more family-oriented and image-conscious. It now has its own opera company and symphony orchestra, and such wholesome tourist attractions as hot-air balloon races.

The changes are for the best, maybe, but I preferred the old Reno, when it really was the biggest little city in the world:

loud, gaudy, a little tawdry, but still loaded with excitement and allure, like a slightly tipsy middle-aged bawd flaunting her charms and telling the world to go to hell. The new Reno was going the way of too many other small cities; it had confined its bawdiness to Virginia Street and other little pockets of socially acceptable sin, exchanged its tarnished image for one of upscale respectability, and lost some of its identity as a result.

The distance between South Lake Tahoe and Reno is only about fifty miles, but it took me close to an hour and a half to cover it. Traffic wasn't bad along the southeastern shore of the lake or coming down out of the mountains, but it got heavy in Carson City and stayed heavy all the way up Highway 395 and through an endless string of traffic lights on the outskirts of Reno. It was six-thirty by the time I found a motel that still had a vacancy—a place called the Starburst off 395 between the airport and the biggest and fanciest of the local casinos, Bally's.

I called Kerry first thing, or tried to; she wasn't home yet. I left a message on her machine, telling her where I was. Then I dragged the local telephone directory out of a nightstand drawer and looked up Janine Wovoka. No listing for her or anyone named Wovoka. So much for that idea. Just for the hell of it, I looked up Arthur Welker. No listing for him, either. I would have been surprised if there was. According to the information Eberhardt had gotten from the Organized Crime Strike Force, Welker lived over at Tahoe.

I hadn't eaten since breakfast and I was hungry, so I went to a nearby "family restaurant" and waited half an hour for a tough, gravyless veal cutlet shamelessly described in the menu as "scrumptious chicken-fried steak." I could have sued them for false advertising, if not for attempted food poisoning, and won the case with no trouble at all. Instead, I settled for leaving a quarter tip. On the one hand, it wasn't the waitress's fault; on the other hand, she was slow and on the cranky side, and all restaurant employees share in the gratuities, including the cook.

It was after eight when I got into my car and pointed it

crosstown to Virginia Street, and eight-thirty by the time I found a parking place within walking distance of the casinos. You could see the neon glow a long way off; up close, the glitter and sparkle and splashes of primary color from dozens of signs large and small assaulted your eyes. Harrah's, Harold's, Fitzgeralds, Eldorado, Cal-Neva, Sundowner, Riverboat, Circus Circus, Nevada Club, Coliseum Club. Best Odds. Megabucks. Triple-Odds Craps. Progressive Slots. Video Poker. Pai Gow Poker. Progressive Keno. Reno's Best Variety 21. Fantastic Fun Machine. Free Cash Drawings. All You Can Eat Buffet. Fun, Fun, Fun. And looming across Virginia, Reno's famous gateway arch—not the plain original arch that had been put up in 1927 to signify completion of U.S. Highway 40, not the big lighted arch that had been erected on New Year's Eve of 1963 to celebrate Nevada's 1964 centennial, but a huge, garish blazing thing that had been installed in 1987 and hurled laser and fiber-optic light into the night sky as if it were heralding the second coming of the Messiah. The irony was, it heralded or celebrated or commemorated nothing at all.

The sidewalks were moderately crowded this warm night. But the gamblers and funseekers here were different than those in Stateline, less affluent, older—another of the reasons that gambling in Reno was on a decline. A couple of the older, smaller clubs, in fact—the Mapes and the Riverside—had gone out of business. Polyester and seersucker were the dominant fabrics; late forties to early sixties was the dominant age-group. People from small towns and rural environments; blue-collar men and blue-haired women. Every third person looked to be overweight. Most of the fatties were women, and most of the men with them were thin—as if the women might have been feeding off them, consuming their flesh a little at a time over a period of years. Even the younger people ran to fat. I passed one entire obese family: father, mother, two young sons; the kids eating ice cream, the father munching on popcorn, the mother hunting in her purse as if for a misplaced chocolate bar.

No, this wasn't the Reno of old, the biggest little city in the world, the mecca of divorcees and high rollers. This was a cheap year-round carnival, complete with sideshow and glitter and new forms of the old come-on. Hey, rube! Lookee here! Try your luck, win a big prize! Virginia Street in the high-tech, low-taste, knock-your-eye-out eighties.

And if I hadn't believed that walking the streets, I'd have believed it the instant I entered the Coliseum Club. Carnival kitsch not only lived here; it flourished like weeds. The motif was fake Roman—fluted pillars, busts on pedestals, big alabaster torches with electric flames, bar-girls and change-girls in togas and high gold-strapped sandals—and it was made even more ludicrous by all the bright flashing neon. A rage of whirring, clanging, babbling, shrieking noise reverberated off the walls and mirrored ceilings and swelled in your ears like a pagan beat. Roman orgy, updated and travestied, with the lust for sex replaced by the lust for easy money and fun, fun, fun.

I spent twenty minutes pushing my way among the tight-packed banks of slot machines. Row after row of men and women on stools feeding in coins, yanking handles, feeding in coins, yanking handles in a steady monotonous rhythm and with a kind of controlled frenzy. Some of them would be there for hours, for days on end, performing the same mindless ritual. And yet, paradoxically, you couldn't have hired any of them to do a job in a factory where they had to continually put a piece of metal in a slot and then pull a handle. Too boring, they would have said. You couldn't pay us enough to do a boring job like that, they would have said.

None of the change-girls was Janine Wovoka. None of the five I spoke to claimed to know Janine Wovoka, either. Finally I made my way to the central gaming area.

Most of the tables were getting heavy play; I was not going to find a dealer or croupier to talk to here. If this had been a different club and a less hectic time of day, I might have tried to buttonhole one of the pit bosses: they always know who's who and what's what. Or I might have gone over to the cashier's booth and asked to see one of the managerial staff. But I didn't want to take that sort of chance here. This was a Mob-owned club, at least in part. Nobody up in the pecking order was likely to answer questions about one of the employees.

The menials were my best bet. They're not supposed to be privy to inside information, so the higher-ups don't bother to tell them to keep their mouths shut. And most of them know more than the bosses think they do.

Behind the long rows of gaming tables was the Chariot Bar, the entrance to which was built to resemble something out of *Ben Hur*. I went in there and tried to talk to one of the three bartenders on duty. No soap; the place was full to overflowing and they were too busy mixing drinks. So I wandered out again, tried a couple of toga-clad table waitresses and didn't get anywhere with them either.

Back toward the rear was the Keno booth, and beyond that was another bar—smaller, more intimate, and not nearly as crowded. Nero's Fiddle. Only one bartender was on duty and he didn't look half as frazzled as the trio in the Chariot Bar.

I sat on an empty stool removed by two from the nearest of the other customers. When the bartender, a thin guy in his forties, came my way I ordered a draft beer. And when he brought it I said, "I'm trying to find a girl who works here or used to work here. Change-girl named Janine Wovoka."

"Who?"

"Wovoka, Janine Wovoka."

He shook his head, started to move away. I said, "Wait," and showed him the snapshot, pointing out the raven-haired woman.

"Oh," he said, "yeah. What do you want with her?"

"Conversation. See, it's my daughter I'm really trying to find and Janine's a friend of hers." I put a pleading note into my voice. "She's been missing two weeks. My daughter, I mean."

"That's too bad." He didn't sound particularly sympathetic, but then he didn't sound indifferent either. "Run off with some guy?"

"I hope that's all it is. So does Janine Wovoka still work here?"

"I don't think so. Ask Candy. She'd know."

"Candy?"

"Keno runner." He glanced past me, scanning the bar. "She's not around now but she'll be through pretty soon."

"How will I know her?"

"Name tag on her toga. Short black hair. Nice bod."

"Thanks."

"Sure. Hope you find your daughter."

There was one empty table at the rear. I took my beer over and claimed it. Mounted nearby was a Keno board; the latest game, #256, was in progress. I watched the numbers light up, and sipped my beer, and waited.

Five minutes after Game #256 closed and #257 opened, a young woman with short black hair, wearing the toga-and-sandals costume and carrying a tray of crayons and Keno odds booklets and marking sheets, appeared and began making her way among the tables. Saying "Keno? Keno?" like someone calling a lost pet.

When she got close enough so that I could see her name tag, I said, "Here, miss." And when she leaned down, "The bartender told me you know Janine Wovoka. Is that right?"

"Janine?" She frowned. "Sure, I know her. Why?"

"I'm trying to find her."

"What for?"

I gave Candy the same pitch I'd given the bartender. The results were even better; she said, "Gee, that's too bad about your daughter. I hope she's okay."

"Me too."

"Maybe I know her too. What's her name?"

"Abigail. Abigail Randisi."

"Gee, I don't know *anybody* named Abigail," she said.

"Well, I'm sure Janine does. Any idea where I can find her?"

"She doesn't work here anymore. She got canned."

"When was that?"

"Couple of weeks ago. I haven't seen her since."

"Why did she get canned?"

"I don't know. It was pretty sudden, though."

"Would you happen to know where she lives?"

"Well . . ."

Somebody called to Candy from one of the other tables—a Keno customer. She looked over there, looked back at me. "I've got to hop. I'll come back when I can, okay?"

"Please do. I'm really worried about Abigail."

She nodded, moved over to the other table, took the customer's marked sheet and money away to the Keno booth. And I sat there and thought: Two weeks ago. Same time Wendy Oliver was fired from her job at the Nevornia, which Arthur Welker also owns a piece of. And almost the same time David Burnett killed himself. There's a connection . . . what's the connection?

I waited through Game #257, watching the numbers flash on the board until fifteen had been random-selected. True to her word, Candy came back shortly after #258 opened.

I asked her again if she knew where Janine Wovoka lived. She said, "Well, she used to live over by Virginia Lake. But I don't know if she still does."

"Do you remember the address?"

"Eastshore Drive, I think. There's a bunch of apartment buildings along there—she lived in one of those."

"Alone?"

"No, she had a roommate. Let's see . . . Alice something. Sounds like one of those rifles."

"Remington? Winchester?"

"No, no . . . carbine, that's it."

"Alice Carbine?"

"No, it *sounds* like carbine. Cardeen. Alice Cardeen."

"Does Alice Cardeen work here too?"

"Not her. She sells cosmetics. You know, Avon."

"Janine has a friend named Jerry Polhemus," I said. "You know him?"

"Jerry who?"

"Polhemus. From San Francisco. She was seeing him off and on, dating him."

"Oh . . . him. Jerry." She pulled a face. "What she saw in him *I'll* never know."

"You didn't like him?"

"Well, I only met him once. Janine brought him to a party I was at. He seemed like kind of an asshole."

"Was David Burnett at the party too?"

Another Keno player was calling her. She said, "Got to hop again," and hurried off on her rounds.

So I sat and nursed my beer and watched the Keno board for another fifteen minutes, until #259 opened and Candy finally made her way back to my table.

"Now who was it you asked me about?" she said. "David somebody?"

"David Burnett. A friend of Jerry's—the same young guy who won the big jackpot."

"Big jackpot?"

"On the Megabucks progressive slot about three weeks ago. The two-hundred-thousand-dollar payoff."

"You mean here? At this club?"

"Yes."

"Gee," Candy said, "I don't think so. I don't think we've had a big slot payoff all year. Not *that* big, anyway."

". . . Are you sure?"

"Well, I'm not positive but I don't think so. Why don't you go upstairs by the Lucky Trevi and look at the wall where they advertise all the big winners? If this guy David hit one of the Megabucks slots, his picture'll be up there, you can bet on that."

"His name isn't familiar to you? David Burnett?"

"No," she said, "it sure isn't."

I gave her five bucks for her time and the information. She didn't want to take it—"Gee, I'm just glad to help"—but I insisted. Guilt money, because I'd lied to her about a thing like a missing daughter. Then I went and found the escalator and rode up to the second floor.

The Lucky Trevi, for Christ's sake, was an alabaster-and-neon abomination designed to look like the Trevi Fountain in Rome. It was where the funseekers took the freebie booklets they got from hotels and motels and travel agencies, to exchange coupons for rolls of coins and free spins on a giant "Lucky Trevi Wheel of Fortune." The way to it was marked by lighted bulbs set into the floor, and along the wall bordering the pathway were more lighted bulbs that spelled out LUCKY GLADIATORS. Under the sign was a long row of framed photographs of the club's big winners, plus names and dates and dollar amounts.

It did not take me long to determine that the last big winner, of $50,000 on a Keno ticket, was three months ago, and that the last big winner on a progressive slot was a woman from Salem, Oregon, the previous August.

Candy had been right: David Burnett hadn't hit a $200,000 Megabucks jackpot in the Coliseum Club, not three weeks ago and not ever.

AT TEN O'CLOCK Wednesday morning I put in a call to the offices of the Nevada Gaming Control Board in Carson City.

Before leaving the Coliseum Club the night before I'd got some literature from the cashier's booth on the state gaming laws. It told me that all slot-machine jackpots over $1,200 had to be reported to both the Internal Revenue Service, which then automatically withholds twenty percent of the total winnings, and the Nevada Gaming Control Board; and that on the mega-jackpots—of a $200,000 payoff, for instance—state gaming agents come to verify that the equipment hasn't been tampered with and that there are no other irregularities. The payoff is not made by the casino until the agents finish examining the machine's computer chips and any surveillance film that recorded the event through the one-way ceiling mirrors. The Gaming Control Board therefore has a record of any major jackpot won anywhere in the state, and detailed reports on any jackpot won on a machine hooked into the Megabucks computer system.

The man I spoke to was named Buford. I gave him my name, and said that I was a California private investigator working on a case, and read him the ID number from my license, and told him just what it was I wanted to know. He said it would take some time to get the information out of the Board's computer files, meaning that it would take some time to verify that I was who and what I said I was; he took down the Starburst's telephone number and my extension and said he'd try to get back to me before noon.

To kill some time, I went and bought a copy of the Reno *Gazette-Journal* from a stand in front of the family restaurant. It was five minutes past eleven and I had just finished reading the sports section when the phone rang. Buford, with the information I'd requested. It was what I had already suspected, and what I did not particularly want to hear.

David Burnett had not won a $200,000 Megabucks jackpot at any casino in Reno or the entire state of Nevada. Nor had he won that much money—or *any* large amount of money— playing another gambling game or machine. The Gaming Control Board had never heard of him.

So where did he get the money?

Where and how did a not too bright, twenty-five-year-old sports junkie get his hands on two hundred grand in cold cash?

Chapter 13

VIRGINIA LAKE was a body of water the size of a couple of city blocks, edged with little strips of park, in a residential area off South Virginia. Good neighborhood, close to downtown and a couple of big golf courses. Ringing the pond was a mix of expensive homes, middle-income homes, condos, and apartment complexes. The apartments off Eastshore Drive were a string of two-storied buildings, newish, with balconies and well-kept lawns that faced the pond.

I had looked up Alice Cardeen's name in the telephone directory. No listing. But when I'd checked the *A*'s, there she was under "Avon Representative": A. Cardeen, 4210 Eastshore Drive. The entrances to the various apartments were off one of the cross streets, and you got to them by way of a flower-bordered path that bisected the block. A bank of mailboxes under the numerals 4210 said that A. Cardeen, Avon Rep., occupied number 6.

Number 6 was a ground-floor apartment midway along. I rang the bell and waited and rang it again. Nobody home. Well, that was hardly surprising; it was almost noon and cosmetics salespersons, if they're good at their job, don't sit around waiting for customers to come to them.

I rang the bell at number 8; no response there, either. But at number 4, on the other side, I got results. The woman who opened the door was middle-aged, plump, wearing a pair of too-tight slacks that advertised her big behind. She said, "Yes, what is it?" in the vaguely annoyed way of people who have been interrupted doing something that gives them pleasure. In her case, it was probably watching a daytime soap opera. I could hear the sounds of it coming from behind her.

"I'm sorry to bother you, but I wonder if you know the people who live next door? In number six."

"Alice? The Avon girl? Yes, I know her."

"Do you also know her roommate?"

"She doesn't have a roommate."

"She did have one, though, didn't she? Until recently?"

"That's right. The Paiute girl."

"Janine Wovoka."

"Yes. Why do you ask?"

"Well, I'm trying to find Janine. You see, she's a friend of my daughter's," and I went into the missing-daughter pitch again. It worked just as well today. The woman's face softened; she said she had kids of her own and she understood what I must be going through.

I nodded, feeling guilty again, and asked, "When did Janine move out?"

"Well, it was about two weeks ago, I think. Perhaps a little longer."

"Do you know why she moved?"

"She lost her job and couldn't afford the rent. The rents here aren't cheap."

"Would you know where she moved to?"

"No, I'm afraid not. Have you talked to Alice?"

"Not yet. She's not home."

"Hardly ever is, days. She's a hard worker, that girl. Works long hours."

"So you haven't any idea where Janine might have gone?"

"Well . . . back to the reservation, I suppose."

"Reservation?"

"The Indian reservation. She's a full-blooded Paiute, you know."

"Yes," I said. "Which reservation?"

"Pyramid Lake, of course."

"She has people there? A family?"

"I imagine she does," the woman said. "That's where she came from, so she must have. Don't you think?"

YOU GET TO PYRAMID LAKE by way of Highway 445 through Sparks, a small community that adjoins Reno on the northeast. I'd been out there a couple of times, the last one with Kerry a few years ago. Odd desert lake in the middle of nowhere, some thirty miles north of Sparks and entirely on Paiute land. Mostly uninhabited except for a hamlet called Sutcliffe on its western shore.

Time was, once you left Sparks proper you were in open desert, with no sign of human habitation other than a few scattered cattle and horse ranches. But now, over to the west, there are a bunch of planned communities with names like Sun Valley and Golden Valley and Panther Valley; and Sparks itself is growing in the same sprawling, unappealing way as Reno. For almost ten miles beyond its former boundaries I drove through housing tracts that were completed, partially completed, or about to be built on reclaimed desert land. They were all of such a monotonous sameness, without a single tree to relieve their bleak appearance, that I began to feel mildly depressed. One day this entire area—the whole damned face of the country, for that matter—would be covered with clone housing and clone shopping centers and clone people with all the individuality bled out of them. Sheep in identical pens. The pioneer spirit turned into the American dream turned into an Orwellian nightmare vision of total conformity. I was glad I would not be alive to see it happen.

Once I got past the last of the tracts under construction, and into what was left of the desert, my depression lifted. Stark landscape here, whole vistas opening up ahead where there was nothing but brown rocky hills and sagebrush flats. The desert colors were distinctive and sharp: browns, dark greens, dark reds. Puffy clouds, pushed by a high wind, made shifting shadow patterns on the barren hills. Heat shimmered faintly on the two-lane blacktop and out across the flats—but it was nothing like the heat that would blister the area in the middle of summer. After the clone tracts, the desolation had an elemental beauty that was somehow reassuring. The developers and their political cronies couldn't get all of the wilderness land—not *all* of it, surely.

There wasn't much traffic, so I could drive pretty much on automatic pilot. And that gave me the chance to reflect on the implications of what I'd found out this morning from the Gaming Control Board.

So David Burnett hadn't won the two hundred thousand gambling. All right, then, how *did* he lay hands on that much cash? Had to be by some illegal or extralegal means or else there was no reason for him to make up the story about the Megabucks jackpot. Had to involve organized crime in some way, too; and at least peripherally, Jerry Polhemus and Wendy Oliver and Janine Wovoka were mixed up in it as well.

Drugs? That was the first consideration nowadays when large sums of illegal cash turned up. But Burnett had no history of involvement with drugs beyond the smoking of a little grass; Harry Craddock had scoffed when I'd broached the possibility to him. And while the Mob has its fingers deep in the national drug trade, its operations in Nevada are more or less restricted to gambling and prostitution. The Bay Area is a hotbed of drugs and drug deals, so why come up to Tahoe or Reno to buy or sell? And why would anyone connected with organized crime deal with a young amateur in the first place? In a time when multimillion-dollar drug transactions are commonplace, two hundred thousand is strictly small potatoes.

Some other kind of contraband? But what sort was there around here except drugs? I'd heard of a resurgence of high-profile gold mining in northeastern Nevada, in the area around Elko; but neither the Mob nor David Burnett were likely candidates to trade in contraband gold.

Stolen cash? Hell, that made even less sense. Two hundred thousand dollars was a big score for a *professional* thief—and not even a professional would hit a Mob-run operation. The idea of Burnett planning and executing a big caper was ludicrous. From all I'd learned about him, his idea of high adventure was to perpetuate a trite little double life spiced with small-time gambling and casual sex. Polhemus was in the same category. Wendy Oliver was a bimbo and Janine Wovoka probably wasn't much better.

Found money? Every now and then you read about people stumbling on large sums of cash on buses or in taxicabs or the like. But not in Nevada, not when it almost has to be Mob money. Their employees do not leave two hundred thousand lying around for somebody to play finders-keepers with. That sort of mistake makes you dead in a hurry.

Four unlikely possibilities. And I was fresh out of ideas for a fifth, even an unlikely fifth.

One thing seemed evident now, at least: Burnett hadn't lost what was left of the two hundred thousand gambling with Reno and Vegas sports books. That had been another lie concocted for the benefit of his sister and fiancée. The probable scenario was that the Mob had come around demanding money, as a payback for a debt owed. Thus Burnett's frantic scramble to sell off his new Corvette and the presents he'd bought, and to raise an additional thirty-five thousand. And when he couldn't raise the money, Mob pressure or fear of Mob reprisal prodded him into doing the Dutch.

Pretty story. Allyn Burnett and Karen Salter would be so pleased to hear me tell it.

I thought about Polhemus. Something had happened in that cabin of his yesterday, some sort of violent act—to him or by him to someone else. Was that Mob-connected too? The easy answer was yes, but it didn't stand up under scrutiny. It had been more than a week since Burnett's suicide; if the Mob was after Polhemus, they'd had plenty of time and opportunity to take him out. I could see no reason for them to wait this long. Or to want him dead in the first place. It was possible he'd done something stupid enough in the past few days to turn himself into a target, but it seemed out of character for him to buck the Mob in any lethal way. They kill their own often enough, but when it comes to outsiders, average citizens, they'll order a hit only as a last resort. All that stuff you see on TV about Mr. Average being chased all over the country by Mob assassins is so much crap. Besides which, when those people take somebody out, they clean up after themselves—all nice and tidy, with no loose ends. They don't remove dead bodies and leave bloodstains and the victim's personal belongings and automobile behind.

Well, then? Was yesterday's violent act tied in *any* way to the Burnett case? I had a feeling it was. Coincidences happen —I'd run across them before in my work—but I couldn't see that explanation here. Polhemus had been running scared; if he'd contacted anybody after he arrived at Fallen Leaf Lake, it figured to be Janine Wovoka. Or maybe Wendy Oliver, because she lived nearby. Either way, there was a connection— and the connection made whatever had happened my business. . . .

A big wooden sign appeared ahead, marking the border of the Paiute reservation and advertising Pyramid Lake as a paradise for fishermen after cutthroat trout. The terrain here was even more barren and rocky, a sere landscape capable of supporting life only with great effort. Which figured. When the government handed out land to the Indian tribes late last century, it was almost always poor land nobody else wanted. And at that they'd expected the Indians to lick their boots in gratitude, and been surprised, outraged, quick to revoke rights and privileges, when instead there were complaints and sometimes open rebellion. Must be hell, I thought, to be born with a skin color different than that of the men who run your country, particularly when the country had belonged to you in the first place.

I came around a curve and into a long downslope, and Pyramid Lake was there ahead—so suddenly that the effect was almost startling. It was as I remembered it: pale blue, glass smooth, somehow unreal, so that in the first moment you saw it, it struck you as a desert mirage; surrounded by more of the stark brown hills, with a bare pyramid-shaped island and a bunch of little islets jutting up off the east shore. The last time

I'd been here it had been summer and those islands were alive with thousands of gray and white birds—migratory waterfowl, mostly pelicans. Pyramid Lake was a nesting ground for them in the summer months. Now the islands were deserted, and so was the lake itself except for a handful of widely scattered boats.

As I came down to the shoreline I could see the buildings of Sutcliffe along the west shore—but that first impression of strangeness lingered in my mind. There was something prehistoric about this whole area, as if in some elemental way it had been untouched by the passage of time and the rise of civilization, like the mountaintop in *Lost Horizon.* I would not have been very surprised to see a Tyrannosaurus rex pop up from behind one of the low brown hills.

At the bottom of the downslope, 445 joined another road that ran both ways along the rim of the lake. I turned left, toward Sutcliffe. It seemed even warmer here than on the drive out; the thin, dry desert wind blowing in through the open window smelled of sage and held the promise of a blazing summer. The sky looked more white than blue, not with clouds but with a milky sun-glare, like an alkali flat turned upside down.

The village was small, maybe a hundred buildings clustered on flatland extending back from the water's edge. Most of the buildings looked to be private housing, with an air of newness about them that was enhanced by several big satellite TV dishes. On the near side was a public boat-launching facility and fishing access. I passed a structure that housed the Pyramid Lake Tribal Enterprises, dispenser of fishing licenses; then there was a road leading down into the village proper—an oasis of trees, a small trailer park, a public campground. And a weathered, clapboard building with a roof sign—DENHAM'S—and a lot of small signs plastered across its face: *Slots. Pool. Video Arcade. Groceries. Liquor. Fishing Tackle and Marine Supplies.*

I parked and went into the store. The interior was cut into two halves: the left half a saloon with dance floor, the advertised pool tables and video arcade, and a short bar at which two Indians were deep in conversation with an Anglo bartender; the right half, beyond a wall covered with photos of fishermen and their catches, contained the groceries and marine supplies. The only person in the grocery half was a gaunt, gray-haired woman behind the checkout counter. Not an Indian, unless she was of lightly mixed blood.

I got a can of diet Coke out of the cold case and took it to the counter. The woman said, "That be all?" as she rang up the sale.

"Except for some information." I paid her for the Coke. "I'm looking for a young woman named Janine Wovoka. Do you know her?"

I expected the woman to ask why and I was ready to trot out the missing-daughter ploy one more time. But she was the bored and talkative kind, without much curiosity; the kind who likes to hear the sound of her own voice. She said in tones of wry spread with relish, "I know her. But she don't live on the reservation anymore, nor ever likely to again."

"Why do you say that?"

"When she left here she left for good. Her words, not mine. A rebel, that's Janine. Nothing tame about that girl."

"How do you mean?"

"How you think I mean?"

"I'm not very good at guessing."

"Life in the fast lane. Hundred miles an hour."

"Why did she leave? Specifically, I mean."

"Couldn't stand it here, she said. Whole world out there and she wanted to see some of it. But that wasn't the real reason."

"No? What was?"

"She wants to be white," the woman said.

I had no comment on that.

"It's a fact," the woman said. "Hates being an Indian, wishes she'd been born white like you and me. If you know her, you know that's the way she is."

"Her folks still live here?"

"Her father does. John Wovoka. Mother's dead."

"Can you tell me where John Wovoka lives?"

"Trailer just south of Pelican Point. Might be there now, might not. Wednesday's one of his days off—he works for the government, fish and game commission. Goes fishing, mostly, on his days off."

"How do I find his trailer?"

"Can't miss it," she said. "Silver thing, green trim, on the lake side of the road. Nothing much around it. If he's not there, try Popcorn Rock."

"Where's that?"

"South shore. How'd you come in? Sparks road?"

"Yes."

"Take the other fork, the one says 'Nixon.' Which wasn't named after the president, we got more sense than that," she said, and laughed. Local joke.

"That's where John Wovoka goes fishing?"

"That's where. Caught a fifteen-pound cutthroat trout off that rock a few years back. Won't go anywhere else since."

I thanked her and went out to my car. But I didn't leave right away; I sat long enough to slake my thirst with the diet Coke.

She wants to be white.

Well, that told me some things about Janine Wovoka. Not the desire to be white, if that *was* her desire. The fact that she wanted something different and better for herself, and getting it had been an uphill battle all the way because of white people like that woman in there.

Chapter **14**

_____

JOHN WOVOKA'S TRAILER, silver with green shutters and a green skirt, rested on a flat-topped hump of land equidistant between the road and the lake and at least a quarter of a mile from its nearest neighbor. A rutted lane led to it across rocky ground that was more or less level. Behind the trailer, beyond a small shedlike building, the terrain dropped off sharply to the water's edge and an empty dock not much larger than a platform on stilts.

I turned off onto the lane. Parked near the trailer was a beat-up, olive-drab pickup, and when I drew in next to it I saw that the driver's door wore an official seal and the words *U.S. Fish and Wildlife Commission.* I beeped the horn before I got out, but nobody appeared in the trailer's doorway. The place looked and felt deserted.

Quiet here, the kind of stillness that is so complete, you can hear the beat of your heart. Out on the lake, the only boats I could see sat motionless like cardboard cutouts. The lake itself was clean, free of algae. No eutrophication here. There weren't enough trees or vegetation and hardly any development. But that wasn't the only reason. The Paiutes were poor, and the poor don't create major havoc with the environment;

that seems to be the right and privilege of the wealthy and ruling classes. Money and power not only corrupt, they pollute, too.

I knocked on the trailer door. No answer. There was a window in one side of it, uncurtained, but it was above the level of my vision even when I stood on tiptoe. I considered hunting up something to stand on, decided that sort of prying was uncalled-for, and moved around to the rear. The shed was just about big enough to house a small boat; alongside it was a boat trailer and an accumulation of things that looked like junk but were so tidily arranged that each may have been gathered for a specific purpose. There was no other vehicle, no indication of anyone's presence other than John Wovoka's.

I returned to my car and drove back to the main road and down past Sutcliffe to the south-shore junction. A sign on the left fork said that it was thirteen miles to Nixon and twenty-nine miles to Wadsworth. I went that way, following the southern curve of the lake.

Popcorn Rock was easy enough to spot, even without the sign that identified it; it looked exactly like a huge brownstone replica of a popcorn kernel. Beyond it was a rutted track that took me down to an equally rutted, rocky parking area and a narrow dirt-and-sand beach. Two cars were parked there, each one with an attached boat trailer. They were both empty and so was the beach.

I found a place to park where I could turn around without damaging shocks, springs, axles, or tires on the rough ground. Nearby was a big sign that said WARNING and told you Pyramid Lake could be dangerous to boaters in high desert winds and that small craft should not be operated when whitecap conditions prevailed. I walked past that and down to the water's edge. There weren't any fishermen in boats lying off this section of shoreline, and I was thinking that maybe John Wovoka had decided to do something else today when I spied the boat and the man upshore in the shadow of Popcorn Rock.

The boat was drawn up on the beach and the man was

sitting motionless in a cleft of the rock; at this distance I couldn't tell if he was asleep or just watching the lake.

I moved that way, following the shoreline. The boat was a twelve-foot outboard runabout at least twenty years old and in good repair; a homemade canvas sun awning shaded its deck. I didn't get a good look at the man until I was within a few paces of him. He was my age, or maybe a few years younger— a man big and lean at the same time, all hard edges and flat planes, with a weathered face so heavily and sharply creased, it reminded me of an adobe brick left too long to cure in the sun. Longish black hair and high cheekbones and the dark bronze color of his skin identified him as an Indian, and when I got closer I thought I detected a resemblance between him and the photographic image of Janine Wovoka. He wore khaki trousers and a faded blue chambray shirt and a San Francisco Giants baseball cap.

He was awake, maybe watching the lake, maybe lost in thought. He paid no attention to me, did not even seem to notice my approach, until I neared him and stopped and asked, "Are you John Wovoka?" Then he looked at me, slowly, without surprise or particular interest. His face was expressionless.

"Yes," he said. And after he'd studied me for a few seconds, "I don't know you."

"We've never met."

"How'd you know where to find me?"

"The woman at Denham's."

"Her. Mrs. Denham. She talks too much."

"I thought so too."

"What is it you want?"

"To ask you some questions. About your daughter."

"Janine?" Now his face and eyes showed animation, and an emotion I took to be pain. "What about her? Something happen to her?"

"No," I said, "it's nothing like that."

"She's my only child," he said.

"Can you tell me where she is?"

"No," he said. He frowned slightly, so that the facial creases looked even sharper, deeper. "Why? Who're you?"

I did not lie to him; you don't tell an elaborate lie about a missing daughter to a man whose own daughter may be missing. I gave him my right name, and said that I was a private investigator from San Francisco, and offered to let him look at my ID.

He shook his head. "Why are you looking for Janine?"

"I think she knows something about the case I'm working on."

"What case?"

"A young man in San Francisco committed suicide two weeks ago. His sister hired me to find out what drove him to it. Janine knew him."

"What young man?"

"David Burnett."

He shook his head again, to indicate that the name meant nothing to him.

"Burnett and Jerry Polhemus were buddies," I said. "Do you know Polhemus?"

There was a silence before he said, "Janine's . . . friend."

"You've met him?"

"You don't have to meet his kind to know them."

"What kind is that, Mr. Wovoka?"

"John," he said.

"Pardon?"

"I prefer John. I don't like to be reminded of the false prophet."

"I'm sorry, I don't . . ."

"Wovoka was a Paiute messiah," he said. "Disciple of Wodziwob the visionary. I'm descended from him."

I didn't know what to say so I didn't say anything.

His gaze was on the lake again. "You ever hear of the Ghost Dance? Hundred years ago?"

"No," I said.

"Wodziwob had a vision. Big train was supposed to bring back our dead ancestors, heralded by some kind of natural disaster, and when that happened all the whites would be destroyed and Indians would own the land again. What would make these miracles happen, he said, was ceremonial dancing around a pole—the Ghost Dance—and singing magic songs he'd learned in his vision. His disciple had visions, too, even grander ones. So when Wodziwob grew weak with age, it was Wovoka who led the ghost cult, spread its message. The Paiutes danced and other tribes danced along with them—the Cheyenne, the Arapaho, the Sioux. Sitting Bull danced and made war against the whites. He and his braves wore ghost shirts, supposed to protect them in battle, but they were massacred anyway. At Wounded Knee in 1890." He paused and his lips moved in what might have been a brief, bitter smile. "Wodziwob and the other false prophet were fools," he said. "There is no magic. There aren't any miracles."

I wondered if he was trying to tell me something, or if he was being deliberately obscure, or if this was some sort of outpouring of cultural self-pity. I said, "I don't think I understand."

"There's nothing to understand." He stirred himself, got slowly to his feet. He was taller than he'd seemed sitting down, six-two or -three. "Don't mind me. I like to tell stories."

"We were talking about Jerry Polhemus," I said.

"A man-child who takes and gives nothing in return."

"How do you mean?"

"Janine should have better than him. A better man, red or white. I told her so but she wouldn't listen. She hasn't listened to me since she was a little girl."

"When did you last see her, John?"

His only answer to that was a shrug.

I said, "Was she with Jerry Polhemus then?"

Another shrug.

"Where did you see her? In Reno?"

"She won't come out here anymore," he said. "She hates it here, her birthplace. She doesn't see the beauty—her eyes have gone blind."

"Where was it in Reno that you—"

I broke off because he was moving away from me, toward where the boat was tied to an outcrop. He stopped before he got to it, and pointed lakeward and said without turning, "You see the islands there? The big one, Anaho, has been a national wildlife refuge since 1913. More than seven thousand pelicans nest there every summer. Other species, too—gulls and cormorants, Caspian terns, blue herons." I came up beside him and he said then, "Janine never saw them, even when she was young and her eyes were clear."

"Can you give me any idea where to find her, John?"

"No," he said.

"Any friends she might have confided in or gone to stay with?"

"I don't know her friends. I don't want to."

"She lived with Alice Cardeen for a while, on Eastshore Drive in Reno. Do you know her?"

"I've spoken to her on the phone. She has no respect for me."

"Why not?"

No response.

"Janine moved out when she lost her job at the Coliseum Club, two weeks ago. Were you aware of that?"

"Yes. Alice Cardeen told me that much."

"Do you know why she lost her job?"

"No."

"I think it has to do with a lot of money David Burnett got his hands on a little over three weeks ago," I said. "The money is the root cause of his suicide and I think Janine knows where he got it."

"How much money?"

"Two hundred thousand dollars. He said he won it gambling—a big slot-machine payoff. But he didn't. I have an idea it was Mob money."

He stared at me. "The Mafia?"

"Organized crime, yes."

"Janine and those people?"

"No. Not the way you mean."

"But Burnett was mixed up with them?"

"In some way."

"Polhemus?"

"I'm not so sure about him. He's missing too, now. Something may have happened to him."

Silence for a time; he was digesting what I'd told him. Then he said, "Is Janine in danger?"

"No," I said. "Not from the Mob, at least. If something did happen to Polhemus, it isn't likely they were responsible."

More silence, not quite as long this time. "You intend to keep looking for her?"

"Until I find her."

"Let me know when you do. She won't call, she doesn't want anything to do with me anymore, but I'm her father. You understand?"

"I understand."

"Then let me know. That she's all right, if nothing else. Will you do that?"

"Yes," I said.

He nodded, said, "My number is listed," and then turned and untied his boat and pushed it out into the lake and swung his big lean body aboard. He started the engine, backed and turned into deeper water, then sent the craft skimming away to the north.

Strange man, John Wovoka. And a strange conversation I'd had with him, on the shore of this strange lake. But then, if I had been born an Indian, a stranger in my own land, I would likely be pretty odd myself. His daughter may not have had an easy time of it, but he had lived more than twice as long and so his time of it must have been more than twice as difficult.

There is no magic. There aren't any miracles.

His meaning didn't seem so obscure after all.

Chapter 15

THEY WERE WAITING FOR ME when I got back to the motel.

Two of them, in a white Cadillac limousine with smoke-tinted windows. The limo was parked three slots down from my unit, but because of the smoky glass I couldn't see them sitting inside and so I didn't pay much attention to the car. I parked in front of my unit, went to the door. I had just keyed it open when I heard them behind me, but they were so slick and professional that I did not even have time to turn. One of them caught my arm and together they crowded me inside. The other one flipped the light switch, then shut the door to close us in.

When the one let go of my arm I moved ahead a couple of steps, over next to the bed, to keep a distance between us and so I could get a better look at them when I turned. Young, beefy, casually dressed; cut from the same blank-faced mold as the pair at Ekhern Manufacturing, only bigger. Ex-football players, maybe—guys with no necks. Both brown-haired, brown-eyed, the only appreciable difference between them being that one wore a mustache and the other was clean-shaven. They weren't showing guns; may not even have been armed, though I couldn't tell for sure from the cut of their jackets.

But that didn't mean anything one way or another. They were here; that was what meant something.

The mustached one said through a flat smile, "How you doing, sport? All right?"

I didn't say anything. It was not the kind of question you can respond to in circumstances like these without sounding defensive. That was one reason. The other reason was that I did not trust myself to speak just yet. The edge was back, sharp, and along with it the now familiar bleak rage.

The mustache came over to where I was. The bed was on one side of me, a chair on the other, and the wall a few inches beyond my back; I had nowhere to go, even if I'd been inclined to give in to the rage and do something stupid. I stood stiffly until he said, "Turn around, let me see what you're carrying." Then I turned around.

Quick, expert frisk. The only thing he found that interested him was my wallet. He backed up with it, and when I turned again he was studying the photostat of my investigator's license. He looked at my credit cards, too; he even looked at the photos of Kerry. All without blinking or changing expression.

The clean-shaven one was checking through my suitcase. Not rummaging, not making a mess—just looking. He didn't take anything; and he closed the case again when he was done.

The mustache finished with my wallet, held it toward me without moving so that I had to come forward to get it. I put it away inside my coat with a hand that was steadier than I felt inside. Afterward I stayed where I was: no more backing off.

"Now what?" I said.

"Now we go for a drive."

"Where to?"

"You'll see. Nice day for a long drive."

"How long?"

"Don't worry, we'll get you back in time for supper."

"Arthur Welker," I said. "That who buys your time?"

The two of them glanced at each other, then back at me. Neither one answered. They'd been programmed to do certain things and telling me where they were taking me and who employed them wasn't included.

I said, "All right. But I'm going to make a call first."

"What for?"

"My own protection."

"You don't need protection, sport."

"I do if we're going to keep this peaceable and friendly."

They looked at each other again. "Hassling with us would be a mistake," the mustache said to me. "You know that."

"I know it," I said. "But I'm still going to make the call."

He thought about it. "Nobody official?"

"Nobody official."

"Go ahead then."

But I didn't head straight for the telephone; I walked to the window first, pulled the drapes aside. They didn't try to stop me. After a few seconds I went back around the bed to where the phone sat on the far nightstand, tapped 8 to get long-distance, and then dialed the number of my flat in San Francisco. The answering machine cut in on the third ring. When my own voice finished telling me I wasn't available and the beep sounded, I said, "I'm at the Starburst Motel in Reno. It's four-twenty, Wednesday afternoon, May twenty-first. I'm going with a couple of guys in a Cadillac limousine, California license number one-GDJ-three-two-six, probably to see Arthur Welker."

I put the receiver down. The two of them were grinning at me, the way you'd grin at a circus clown who had just squirted himself with a fake flower. The mustache said, "You ready now?"

"Yeah," I said. "I'm ready now."

WE DROVE SOUTH out of Reno on 395, through Carson City and then into the mountains. Heading for Lake Tahoe. The hired help sat in front, the clean-shaven one driving; I had the rear seat to myself. Back there was a telephone and a combination radio and tape deck and miniature TV and a little portable bar, but I didn't touch any of them. I just sat, waiting it out with the tension so acute that my skin felt too tight, as if it were slowly shrinking. None of us said anything

—not a word the whole time. We'd said all we had to say to each other in the motel room.

We rode south along the lake, toward the Stateline casinos. But long before we got there—a few miles outside Zephyr Cove—we turned off on Lobo Point Road and wound through timber and past expensive summer homes. A third of a mile beyond the last of the homes was a private road with a chain across it and a sign attached to the chain that told you it was a private road and warned you to keep out. We swung in there, stopped, and the driver got out and unlocked the chain and then drove us through and stopped again and put the chain back in place before we went on.

The road curled in through more woods to where a pair of closed wrought-iron gates set in a high stone wall barred the way. Spikes and pieces of broken glass were cemented into the top of the wall. The gates were electronically operated; the driver used a remote-control device to open them so we could pass through.

On a rise up ahead was a huge house made of light-colored wood, roughly circular in shape and modernistic in design: odd jutting angles and lots of glass. Across the front was a cleared area with fountains and wildlife statuary, ornate but not ostentatious, and half a dozen cars, the least expensive of which was a Mercedes. We pulled in next to a silver-gray Aston-Martin and the driver released the rear-door locks so I could get out.

I stood flexing my shoulder muscles to ease some of the stress-lock. Sounds of minor merrymaking drifted up from the rear of the house; otherwise it was quiet here. Steps led to a front entrance but we didn't go that way. We angled off on another set of steps that ended in a path made of broad stone flags; the flags skirted the north wall and brought us around back.

Three long, wide terraces back there, each on a different level overlooking Lake Tahoe. A vast black-stone swimming pool took up half of the uppermost level, the one we were on; half a dozen people, all but one of them women, were lounging around it. None of them paid any attention to me or the two hirelings. The second terrace was a jungly garden of ferns and bushes and bright tropical flowers, all in tubs so they could be moved indoors during the winter. The third level was a redwood deck on which were several pieces of wrought-iron outdoor furniture. Below that I could see a brush-tangled slope with wooded arms jutting into the lake on either side, forming a cove where there was a fringe of beach thinly slimed with algae, a big boathouse, and a dock with a good-sized cabin cruiser tied at the end of it. Stairs led down to the cove, but if you weren't in a mood to climb them, you could always ride the chair lift that was strung on an adjacent cable.

Two men sat at one of the tables on the third level, drinks in front of them; their attention was on the lake, ablaze now with silvery orange light from the westering sun. The mustache conducted me down to where they were, leaving his partner to wait topside. Neither of the seated men looked our way as we approached, or at us when we stopped. The mustache said, "Here he is," and then moved away without waiting for a reply, to stand watch at a respectful distance.

Most people seem to think all Mob bosses are either full-blooded Italians or Sicilians, communicate in grunts and broken English, and act like Marlon Brando in *The Godfather*. False perception on all counts. Some of the Mob underbosses are part Italian, part Sicilian, or WASPs who have been accepted into the Families by virtue of marriage or favor; and image is everything nowadays, especially for those who are responsible for the operation of multimillion-dollar gambling combines. The new breed of crime boss, no matter what his nationality, looks and talks and acts like a successful corporate businessman; cultivates the businessman's air of quiet but forceful respectability. It is only when you slice through the veneer that the corruption oozes out to where you can see and smell it.

These two were no exception, even at their leisure. Both were in their forties; one thin, almost skinny, with a prominent Adam's apple and carefully barbered dark hair, dressed in fawn-colored slacks and a blue silk shirt; the other of medium height and fair complexion, well-rounded without being fat, apple-cheeked, with flaxen hair and a bow-shaped mouth, wearing a polo shirt and white shorts and amber-tinted sunglasses. If I'd had to guess which one was Arthur Welker, I would have said the well-rounded one—and I'd have been right. The skinny one looked as if he belonged in a place like this; the round man looked as though he owned it.

Welker let me stand there for fifteen or twenty seconds before he raised his head, casually, and looked at me. He used up another fifteen or twenty seconds taking my measure, with the impersonal insolence of a banker studying an inner-city loan applicant. He said at length, "So you're the private eye."

"And you're Welker."

"Mr. Welker to you. You're about what I expected. Older than fifty-seven, though—closer to sixty-five. Close to retirement age."

I didn't say anything.

"What do you make a year?" Welker asked. "Thirty, forty thousand in a good year? You don't have much in the bank. A few thousand, is all. You'll be living off social security when you do retire."

I didn't say anything.

"This house cost three million, not counting the land," he said. "That was another million and a half. The furniture inside the house is all antique, mostly Early American, worth approximately two hundred thousand. I also have a collection of antique gambling devices worth about the same. All of it is protected by a sophisticated security system that set me back a hundred thousand. You, on the other hand, live in a five-room flat; good neighborhood but you couldn't afford the rent if you hadn't been there thirty years and didn't have a generous landlord. Your furniture is cheap—all of it, including the secretary desk you incorrectly consider to be an antique. You have no security system. You neither carry nor own a handgun. Your office on O'Farrell Street is rather shabby and contains no modern investigative equipment. Your partner, Eberhardt, owns a .38-caliber Smith & Wesson revolver but doesn't carry it; he keeps it in his house, in the bottom drawer of his desk."

The rage was in my throat now, like a swelling on the edge of my windpipe. I was having difficulty breathing.

"Don't you want to know how I know all of that?"

"No," I said.

"Or how I found out where you were staying in Reno?"

"No." He had ways; men like him have even more ways to find out things than men like me and we both knew it.

"Did you notice the swimming pool on your way in?" he said. "All the beautiful women? One of them is my wife, the young blonde who looks like Shelley Long. I can have the others anytime I want them, only I don't want them. I'm a faithful husband."

I didn't say anything.

"How about you?" he said. "Are you faithful to Kerry Wade?"

The rage was gagging me. I had to cough, clear my throat, to keep from strangling on it.

Welker got to his feet, yawned, stretched, and then waved a casual hand toward the lake. The thin man didn't move; he hadn't moved or looked at me the whole time I'd been there. He might have been dozing, except that I'd seen him take a sip from his drink.

"That boat down there," Welker said, "the *Arthur III*, is the baby of the little fleet I own. One of the other two is an oceangoing yacht. I own five cars, including a Rolls. The car you drive is a cheap domestic model, fifteen years old. And you don't own so much as a rowboat."

I managed to say, "Am I supposed to be impressed?"

"I would be if I were you. Yes I would. I'd be particularly impressed by this fact: I have three hundred people working for me in one capacity or another, among them another half-dozen who perform duties similar to Jimmy and Carl, the two who brought you here. I pay my gardener, my chef, my masseur, my wife's couturier, *and* Jimmy and Carl more than you make in any given year. You have no one working for you. Just you and your partner—two little fish in a sea full of sharks."

"Is that why you brought me here? To tell me what a little fish I am?"

"Partly. And to let you know what a big fish *I* am."

I didn't say anything.

"Now then," he said. "I understand you've been asking questions about matters that don't concern you. For instance, you were asking about someone named Manny at Ekhern Manufacturing last Saturday. Have you found out who Manny is?"

"No."

"I'll tell you then. It's no secret; I want you to know. Manny is Manny Atwood, one of my assistants. That's him sitting right there."

The thin man looked my way for the first time, for about two seconds and with an expression of utter disdain. Then he put his gaze back on the lake and took another pull at his drink.

I had my hands in my pockets now, to keep them from shaking, maybe twitching toward Welker's throat. "All right," I said, "you've answered a meaningless question. How about answering one that isn't meaningless?"

"And that is?"

"How did David Burnett get hold of two hundred thousand dollars of your money?"

It didn't faze him. You don't catch men like Welker off guard, not on their home turf. "You see?" he said. "Just what I've been saying—matters that don't concern you. Questions like that are how little fishes get swallowed up by big fishes."

"Little fishes like Burnett."

"And you."

"So you're not going to answer the question."

"Of course not. It's a dead issue, and none of your business in any case. Don't you listen? Do you really need any more convincing?"

I didn't say anything.

"You strike me as a moderately intelligent man," he said. "Certainly not a dummy. You *do* understand what we've been talking about here, the crux of this whole conversation?"

"Yeah. I understand."

"Well, then, let me finish up with a piece of excellent advice. Tonight, or first thing tomorrow morning, go back home to San Francisco and forget about David Burnett and those friends of his you've been asking about. Forget about me, too, and I'll forget about you. Then you'll go on swimming in your little corner of the ocean and I'll go on swimming in my big one and we'll both live happily ever after. How does that sound to you?"

I said between my teeth, "It sounds like what it is—a threat."

"Good. Will you take the advice?"

"I don't seem to have much choice, do I."

"No," he said. "No, you don't."

"Then I'd *be* a dummy not to take it."

He liked that answer. He nodded and smiled and said, "Good, good," and patted my arm the way you'd pat a dog on the head. And then he moved away, around the table and around me so that I was looking at his back, and called, "Jimmy."

The mustache came hurrying over.

Without looking at me, Welker made a thumb gesture over his shoulder. "Take this back where you found it," he said.

Jimmy came my way and cupped a hand around my elbow, not too hard or tight, and nudged me gently toward the stairs. It took all the willpower I possessed not to pull loose and break his arm if I could, knock him on his ass if I could, and then go after Welker. There was sweat all over me; I could feel it trickling down my cheeks and under my arms. I was shaking too. Jimmy saw the sweat and felt the tremors and grinned at me the way he had back in Reno. He thought I was afraid.

We went over to the stairs. I did not look back at Welker and Manny Atwood, because if I looked back, it was still possible I would lose control. Up the stairs, through the garden, up more stairs to where the other muscle, Carl, was waiting. Laughter from over at the swimming pool; laughter from behind me, down where Welker and Atwood were. My step faltered. Jimmy said, "Careful there, sport, you don't want to hurt yourself," and tightened his grip on my elbow.

Around to the front, down to the Caddy limousine, me into the back and Jimmy and Carl into the front. And we began to move, and I sat there sweating and shaking, feeling as humiliated as I was supposed to and thinking what I wasn't supposed to—thinking that I was not going home to San Francisco, I was not going to forget about David Burnett and the two hundred thousand, my involvement in this business was a long way from being finished and to hell with Arthur Welker and his intimidation and his threats.

I was a dummy after all.

But I was *my* kind of dummy, not his.

Chapter **16**

IT WAS NEARLY SEVEN-THIRTY when they let me off in front of my room at the Starburst. None of us said anything; dead, brooding silence all the way back from Tahoe. Carl unlocked the rear door, I got out, they drove away, and that was the end of it. For now. And for now, I was alone and in command of my life again.

I went inside and into the bathroom and washed my face and hands. I felt dirty and I needed to be clean. Then I sat on the edge of the bed, with the room close around me, and did a series of slow stretching exercises to try to relieve the knots of tension in my upper body. All the while, I kept seeing Welker's smug, contemptuous face and hearing the things he had said to me in his mocking voice. Calm, rational, dehumanizing—sugarcoated evil. Sitting up there in his three-million-dollar fortress, looking down on the rest of us, looking down on the law; as guilty of killing David Burnett as if he had personally forced those pills down the kid's throat, and yet immune, secure, untouchable. I hated him as much, right now, as I'd hated the man who had imprisoned me for those three months last winter.

But it was an impotent hate, an impotent rage. What could

I do against a man like Welker, with all his power and all his "people"? Go after him like Mike Hammer in *Vengeance Is Mine* . . . the same sort of crazy vendetta I had embarked on last winter? I knew better than that, now more than ever. It was a fool's game, even when the stakes were intensely personal—and I had no personal stake here, nothing to avenge except a small injustice and a few hours of humiliation. You don't fight the Arthur Welkers of the world with righteous anger, a gun, and a prayer. You can't beat them that way.

Maybe you can't beat them *any* way, I thought bitterly. They're a system within a system, and everybody knows you can't beat the system.

So what was I going to do about Welker? Nothing. Except to keep on swimming in his waters, and try not to let myself get swallowed while I was there.

The exercises helped a little, not much. When I quit doing them the room felt even closer; if I stayed here much longer, I would become claustrophobic. I needed space around me, people, but I didn't feel like driving any distance, not after the long ride to and from Tahoe and not through unfamiliar territory. Someplace close by, someplace crowded—

The telephone rang.

The sudden eruption of the bell made me jump. Christ, my nerves were scraped raw. I looked at the phone, listened to it ring a second time—and I was not going to answer it. Then I thought: Come on, that's childish. On the third ring I reached over and picked up.

"Hi," Kerry's voice said cheerfully. "I wasn't sure if you'd be in or not. How's it going?"

I was glad to hear from her, I truly was—she was a bright light in the dark places of my life—but I was not ready to talk to her or anyone else. I tried to make my voice as cheerful as hers when I said, "Fine, fine," but I couldn't hide the strain. She had known me too long; she knew me too well.

"Something's the matter," she said. "What is it? Are you all right?"

"Yes. I had a bad afternoon, that's all."

"Anxiety attack?"

"Not exactly. I'm okay now. Getting there, anyway."

"Do you want to talk about it?"

"No. Not right now."

". . . All right. Can I ask if you found Jerry Polhemus?"

"Not yet. He's still among the missing."

"Then you haven't learned anything more?"

"Not much. A little."

"I wouldn't ask but Allyn has been after me. She says she hasn't heard from you since Saturday."

"I should have called her, I guess. But I don't know enough yet. And what I do know she's not going to want to hear."

"Bad?"

"Bad enough. Her brother wasn't what she thinks he was, not by a long shot."

"I was afraid of that," Kerry said. "She's so fragile right now . . . I hate the idea of her being hurt even more."

"So do I. Karen Salter, too. I shouldn't have taken this thing on. They'd both be better off not knowing the truth."

"Is it too late for you to call it off?"

"Yes." I was on my feet, pacing in a tight little circle, feeling damp and twitchy. The room was very close now. "Babe, listen, I've got to hang up. There's something I have to do. I'll call you tomorrow, okay? In the morning?"

"Okay. You sure you're all right?"

"I will be."

"I love you," she said.

I said, "I love you too," and when I put the receiver down the palms of my hands were wet.

Immediately I went outside and walked around in the cool night, taking deep, slow breaths, until the sweat dried and the closed-in feeling was gone and I felt able to drive. Then I got into the car and took myself up to Bally's, the closest place where there would be plenty of people, plenty of distractions.

It was a floodlit, neoned island in a sea of parking spaces: casino, resort hotel, two-thousand-seat theater, convention facilities, even a bowling center. The casino was the only one left in Reno that catered to a wealthy, exclusive clientele. Crystal chandeliers, fancy decor, plenty of glitz and glitter—

all of which added up to high prices and five-dollar minimum bets on most of the gaming tables.

Crowded tonight; noisy, festive, thick with smoke and the smell of money. Just what I needed. I walked around for a while, watching some of the high rollers work the crap and baccarat tables, making myself an anonymous cell in the rippling crowd body. I bought five dollars' worth of quarters and waited until somebody vacated a twenty-five-cent slot and then fed the machine and yanked the handle in monotonous rhythm like any other sucker, winning just enough small line payoffs to play for twenty minutes before I used up the last coin. I went into one of the lounges for a beer. I found the coffee shop and forced myself to eat a sandwich.

Nine o'clock by then. And the edginess had finally dulled away. I felt in control again, able to be alone with myself again.

Out of the casino, into my car, away from Bally's. Too late to make a house call? I decided it wasn't and drove over to the Virginia Lake apartment complex where Alice Cardeen lived.

Wasted trip. Her apartment was dark and there was no answer when I rang the bell.

On the path nearby was a night-light on a pole. I stood under it and wrote on the back of one of my business cards: *Please call Starburst Motel, #8, before midnite or by 10 a.m. 5/22. Urgent.* After which I returned to Alice Cardeen's door and wedged the card into the jamb so that it covered the lock. She couldn't fail to find it there.

MIDNIGHT CAME AND WENT. No call from Alice Cardeen. I lay in the dark and waited for sleep.

I DREAMED I was running uphill with a gun in my hand, toward the big modernistic house on the rise. It was dark but there were lights all around me, flashlight beams like tracer fire crisscrossing the night. I ran and ran and finally reached the house and then ran around to the rear. Arthur Welker was there, standing on the water in the swimming pool, pointing his finger at me and saying, "Little fish, little fish." I lifted the gun but I couldn't pull the trigger, and Carl and Jimmy came out from behind two of the flashlight beams and shot me instead. I felt the bullets go into my chest, into my arms and legs and neck, but there was no pain when I fell down. I lay on cold stone and their faces floated above me, disembodied, and Welker's face said, "Take this back where you found it." Hands lifted me, carried me down and away into cold dark; laid me on something dank and clammy. I said, "This isn't where you found me." Somebody laughed, and a long way off I heard Welker say in a voice that came as a hollow echo, "How do you like it down there in my belly, Jonah?" And there was more laughter, shrill and loon-crazy, swelling and swelling until I began to swell with it like a bladder pumped too full of air—

I woke up shaking, my face hot, my mouth dry.

It was an hour before I slept again.

Chapter **17**

ALICE CARDEEN CALLED AT 9:00 A.M., just as I was thinking that maybe I ought to try calling her.

I'd been up and dressed since seven-thirty. Except for ten minutes around that time when I had called Kerry to reassure her, I had been sitting on the bed drinking coffee—there was one of those little portable coffee-makers in the room—and watching mindless early-morning TV to keep from thinking too much. I was working on my fourth cup when the phone rang—two cups too many. Combined with the dream-haunted night, the caffeine had me feeling jittery. But it wasn't the same kind of jitteriness as last night. There were none of the sharp edges in me this morning, that grating sensation as of bone splinters rubbing together just under the skin; none of the shadow shapes and no feeling of being closed in. This was not going to be one of the bad days. Not starting out, anyway.

When I picked up the receiver Alice Cardeen identified herself and then said in wary tones, "I have your card. What on earth would a private detective want with me?"

"My business doesn't concern you directly, Ms. Cardeen. It's a friend of yours I'm interested in—Janine Wovoka."

"Janine? Why? Has she done something?"

"No, it's nothing like that," I said. "Would you mind if I explained in person? Be easier that way."

"Well . . ."

"I can be at your apartment in fifteen minutes. Or you could come here or we could meet somewhere—whatever you prefer. I won't take more than a few minutes of your time."

Small silence: she was thinking it over. I didn't blame her for her caution; in fact, I admired it. She was a young woman evidently living alone now, and I was a stranger, and the way things were nowadays any young woman who wasn't leery of strange men, even in broad daylight, was begging for trouble. But I'd had to ask her. You never get as much information out of somebody over the phone as you can in person. Nor can you properly gauge just how much of what you're told is the truth.

At length she said, briskly now, "There's a coffee shop on Virginia Street not far from here—the Copper Urn. I could meet you there in fifteen minutes."

"That would be fine."

"Do you know what I look like?"

I smiled a little; she was still being wary. "No, I don't."

"What do you look like?"

"Big, graying hair, late fifties. Brown suit, no tie."

"In fifteen minutes, then," she said, very businesslike, and rang off.

THE COPPER URN was another of the neutral-decor, indifferent food-and-service "family restaurants" that proliferate under a hundred different names in every city and small town in the United States. The color scheme here was dark brown and a sort of faded tangerine; that was the only physical difference between this place and the one near the Starburst. Most of the customers wore the unmistakable stamp of coffee shop people. The kind who always eat in this type of establishment, at home or on the road; who have seldom—in some cases, never—taken a meal in a quality restaurant because the atmosphere makes them feel uncomfortable, the prices are too high, and the management won't let "kids be kids," which is to say noisy and uncontrolled; whose idea of gourmet cuisine is any dish that comes with cornbread, mashed potatoes, and country gravy; whose taste buds have been so conditioned to mediocrity that a genuine gourmet meal would elicit the comment, "This is okay, but the food's just as good where we usually eat." Walk into any coffee shop, anywhere, and you can pick them out as easily as if they were wearing signs. And that includes children under the age of twelve.

I stood in the entryway, looking around, but none of the women customers showed any interest in me. There were several empty booths in the no-smoking section; I claimed one near the entrance. And waited close to ten minutes, without being acknowledged by any of the four waitresses, before Alice Cardeen showed up.

We spotted each other at the same time. Before she approached she used up thirty seconds or so giving me the once-over—as if you can get an accurate reading of somebody across thirty feet of floor space. When she finally did come over, and we confirmed identities, she sat as far away from me in the booth as it was possible for her to get. She was edging into her late twenties, tall, dark-haired, wearing a cherry-red suit and a pale yellow blouse. Not attractive until she smiled; she had a nice smile and it softened the severe, angular lines of her face. She sat erect, eyes steady on my face—self-contained and as sensible and businesslike as she'd seemed on the phone.

A waitress finally put in an appearance. Alice Cardeen ordered a cup of herb tea. I ordered a glass of grapefruit juice; I'd had enough coffee. The waitress went away.

"Now then," Ms. Cardeen said, in what I imagined was the same tone of voice she used to sell cosmetics, "why are you investigating Janine?"

"I'm not investigating her. I'm trying to find her."

"Oh, so that's it."

"What is?"

"Her father hired you, didn't he?"

"Why do you think that?"

"He's been after her ever since she left the reservation to move back. I suppose she didn't tell him where she was moving to this time and that's why he went to you."

"Do you know where she moved to?"

"No. I wouldn't tell you if I did. Janine doesn't want to go back to Pyramid Lake. It's her life; why doesn't her father just leave her alone?"

"I suppose because he loves her."

"Love," Ms. Cardeen said, as if she were repeating an indecent word. "He wants to control her. Not that she couldn't stand to rein herself in, but that should be *her* choice."

"Have you known her long?"

"We met at the university here."

"And you've been close friends since?"

"Hardly. Janine and I have never been close."

"Then how did you happen to room together?"

"I ran into her six months ago and we got to talking. She was looking for a place to live and I . . . well, my former roommate had moved out and I wasn't doing as well professionally as I am now. We decided to share expenses." She made a rueful moue. "Frankly, it was a mistake."

"Why is that?"

"Janine and I have different life-styles."

"How would you describe hers?"

"She's a party animal," Ms. Cardeen said flatly.

"Late nights, drinking?"

"Yes. And she was always having men stay over. I'm not a prude but, my God, two and three different men in one week?"

"Was one of them Jerry Polhemus?"

The name inspired another little grimace. "Yes."

"You didn't like Polhemus, I take it."

"Not at all. Loud, crude, drunk half the time . . . that sort."

"How about David Burnett? Was he like that too?"

"Worse. Why Janine wanted to hang out with those two and that slutty friend of hers from Tahoe . . . I just don't understand the appeal of people like that."

The waitress picked that moment to deliver Ms. Cardeen's tea and my grapefruit juice. When she was gone again I said, "The friend from Tahoe—Wendy Oliver?"

"A little slut if ever there was one."

"How well do they know each other?"

"Quite well. They used to work together in one of the clubs in Carson City."

Did they now, I thought. So why did Wendy lie to me about her relationship with Janine?

Ms. Cardeen was eyeing me speculatively over the rim of her teacup. "Why are you asking so many questions about those three? Does Janine's father think she ran off with Jerry Polhemus?"

"I don't know," I said. "I'm not working for Janine's father."

"But you said—"

"No, Ms. Cardeen, *you* said it."

I told her who I was working for and why. The news of David Burnett's suicide surprised her; so did the fact that Burnett had gotten his hands on such a large sum of cash. Janine had told her nothing about any of that, she said. Nor offered any reason behind the loss of her job at the Coliseum Club.

What Janine *had* told her was that she'd come into a little money herself, not long before she was fired. "She was thinking of buying a new car," Ms. Cardeen said. "That's why she mentioned it—because she had enough for a down payment."

"Did she say how much?"

"No. But I don't think it was a great deal."

"No hints as to where she got it?"

"None. She was secretive about it."

"Have you had any contact with her since she moved out?"

"No. I told you, we weren't close."

"Or heard from Jerry Polhemus in the past few days?"

"Of course not. Why should I hear from him?"

"I just thought he might have called looking for Janine."

"Well, he didn't. If you want to know the truth, I'm glad Janine is out of my life. If she hadn't moved, I probably would have asked her to leave. I'd had all I could stand of her wild partying and men like Polhemus. I'm much better off living alone."

I had no doubt of that.

I drank my grapefruit juice in a swallow, caught up the check the waitress had left, and slid out of the booth. "Thanks for your time, Ms. Cardeen. You've been a big help."

"I have?" she said. "How?"

"I think you told me how to find Janine."

"But I don't have any idea where she is. . . ."

No, I thought, but I'll bet Wendy Oliver does. I smiled at Ms. Cardeen and left her sitting there with her businesslike reserve slightly askew. There are some people whose feathers you like to ruffle a little, for perverse reasons. Ms. Alice Cardeen was one of them.

WENDY OLIVER wasn't home.

Neither the Toyota Tercel with the dented rear fender nor the primer-patched old Porsche was parked under the carport. And nobody came to the trailer door in response to my knock.

I got back into the car and drove down to Lake Tahoe Boulevard and along it beyond the wye junction. Traffic was heavier in South Lake Tahoe today: more gamblers and fun-seekers filtering in as the weekend approached. It was cooler here than it had been in Reno—mid-seventies—and there were nonthreatening clouds piled up like meringue above the snow-draped shoulders of Mount Tallac to the west. Enough of a breeze had sprung up to invite a few sailboats out onto the lake with the power and excursion boats.

I hadn't eaten all day and my stomach was giving me hell; it was almost one o'clock. I was weary of coffee shop atmosphere, coffee shop food, and coffee shop people, but there didn't seem to be anyplace else to get lunch along the strip. And I didn't feel like driving all the way back over to the Nevada side and bucking the casino trade. So I pulled in at the next "family restaurant" I saw.

Like a lot of things, coffee shops are a lottery: every now and then you can pick a small winner, but mostly you come up empty. This one had better service than the two in Reno and lousier food than most. The booth I was given faced the lake to the north, which reminded me again that somewhere over there, hidden by distance and trees and landmass, was Arthur Welker's fortress.

Driving in earlier on Highway 50, I'd promised myself one thing where Welker was concerned. And I reaffirmed that promise again now. I was not going to stand for any more humiliation at his hands, any more of his bullshit. If he sent people after me again, I would do my damnedest to make him regret it.

I lingered in the coffee shop, killing time, so that it was two o'clock when I again pulled up in front of Wendy Oliver's trailer on Tata Lane. The wasted minutes hadn't bought me anything, though: the carport was still empty and my knock on the door still produced no response.

Now what?

I was in no mood to murder any more time, aimlessly. Canvass the neighbors, then, see if any of them knew where I could find Wendy? That was a long shot, but I couldn't think of anything better to do.

There were a dozen other trailers in relatively close proximity. Nobody was home at half of them. Three women and one man told me they didn't know Wendy or her boyfriend. Another woman said Wendy was "a bitch, she tried to put the moves on my husband once," and slammed the door in my face. A second, elderly man said he knew Wendy and Scott to talk to, not that he talked to them much; he didn't know where she might be but Scott—whose last name was McKee —worked part-time at a boat place out at Pope Beach called Adams & Conley Marine.

Bust.

I considered driving to Pope Beach, but the information I was after I wasn't likely to get from Scott McKee. So? There was only one other thing I could think of to do. More wasted time, maybe, but it was better than wandering around or staking out the trailer.

I drove to Fallen Leaf Lake, to see if anything had changed at the Polhemus cabin.

* * *

SOME THINGS HAD CHANGED, all right. For one, the dark red Cougar was gone.

I turned onto the empty parking platform. Got out and went to the far railing and peered downslope at the cabin and deck and dock beyond. From this angle, it all looked as it had on Tuesday—deserted. But I couldn't see the front entrance because of the wall and the trees.

I picked my way down to the deck. Then I could see the door, and it was shut as I had left it. No sounds from inside; and no answer when I rapped on the panel. I knocked again, with more authority. Then I tried the knob, turning it with my palm and the inside of my thumb.

That was the second thing that had changed: now the door was locked.

After a few seconds I went around onto the part of the deck that overlooked the lake. The facing windows and sliding glass door were tightly shielded by the rattan blinds inside; there wasn't even a chink for me to peer through.

Back at the door, I twisted and pulled on the knob while I squinted at the lock. Not much of a lock—the old-fashioned spring type. And the door didn't fit tightly in the jamb. Any burglar in the state could have had it open in less than a minute. It took me forty seconds, using one of the blades in my penknife. Breaking and entering, this time, not just a simple trespass. But it did not seem to matter as much as it would have once, not so long ago. I was a different man than I had been before last winter, whether I liked the idea or not: not as cautious, not as scrupulous. Among all the other things my kidnapper and jailer had done was to put a bend in the straight arrow.

Thick shadows inside; the familiar smells of dust and careless human habitation. I went in by a couple of paces, eased the door shut with my shoulder, and reached back to knuckle the light switch.

Nothing different here. The spatters of dried blood were still on the floor; the scuff-and-drag marks in the dust hadn't been altered in any way. No one had removed the roach butts from the ashtray, nor the remaining snapshots from the fire-place mantel.

I stood for a few seconds to get the feel of the place. No aura of wrongness this time; all it felt was empty. I crossed into the kitchen. Ants had gotten into the open packages of bologna and cheese; there was mold on the hardened crusts of bread. I kept on going, looked into the bathroom first. The bloodstains still darkened the sink and floor underneath. I moved on into the larger of the two bedrooms.

That was where I found the last of the changes: Jerry Polhemus's two suitcases and duffel bag were missing.

I looked in the closet, got down to peer under the bed. Nothing but dust. Back in the living room, I took one more look around without touching anything. Then I reset the lock on the door and went out and shut it behind me.

On my way up to the parking platform I thought: Either Polhemus came back and got his luggage and car himself or somebody else did. Makes more sense if it was Polhemus. It's his cabin; if he was in a hurry, distracted, he wouldn't have bothered to clean up the bloodstains. Somebody else, covering up a crime against Polhemus, *would* have cleaned things up.

That was how it figured, anyway. But it didn't have to be as cut-and-dried as that, depending on who and why and what had happened here two days ago.

Whose blood, dammit?

And was somebody dead or not?

SOME IDIOT piloting one of those oversize, cumbersome RV road hogs had misjudged the turn into the campground off Fallen Leaf Lake Road and tipped the damned thing over onto its side in such a way that it completely blocked the road. The accident must have happened within the past few minutes, but already cars were starting to string out in both directions. A bunch of people, citizens and a park ranger, were standing next to the overturned RV, gesturing and making angry conversation.

Christ.

I stopped the car and shut off the engine. Wait here or back in town—what difference did it make? Or so I told myself. But this kind of enforced waiting is the worst there is, because it has no purpose and you're at the whim and mercy of too many others.

A pair of tow trucks and two county sheriff's cruisers showed up within twenty minutes. But then another twenty minutes got used up in discussion and strategy and preparation. And it took close to half an hour to maneuver the toppled RV out of the way and then to get the lines of traffic moving again. By the time I crawled out onto Highway 89 and turned back toward South Lake Tahoe, it was four-thirty and I was twitchy and wilted and out of patience. What I wanted was a cold beer in a quiet, uncrowded room. What I did was drive straight to Tata Lane to find out if Wendy Oliver had finally come home.

She had: the banged-up Tercel was angled in under the carport. There was no sign of Scott McKee's Porsche, which meant that she was probably alone. About time something went right, I thought. I walked up the drive and onto the porch and raised my hand to knock on the door.

Sounds inside froze me, put a clutch of tension across my shoulders: a groaning, a whimpering, as of somebody hurt and in pain.

I smacked the door with the heel of my hand, hard, and called out, "Wendy!"

Another groan. A garbled cry that I couldn't make out.

"Wendy!"

Another cry, the words faint, liquidy, but discernible this time. "Help . . . oh, God, help me . . ."

I caught the doorknob, twisted it. Locked. But the lock wasn't any better than the one at the Polhemus cabin. When I threw my hip and shoulder into the door, the spring catch snapped free and the door flew inward so suddenly that I almost fell into the trailer; the flimsy metal walls and floor shimmied from the impact. I caught my balance, straightened. Kitchen. She wasn't in here; the sounds were coming from a room beyond an archway. I plunged through the opening.

Living room. Overturned coffee table, smashed table lamp, other things upended and in disarray. And Wendy Oliver down on the floor, trying to drag herself onto the couch, sobbing through a bruised and bloody mouth. There was blood all over her face, spattered on her hands and torn blouse and white shorts and bare legs.

Somebody had beat the hell out of her. Not more than fifteen minutes ago, while I was driving away from the scene of that frigging accident.

Chapter 18

I RUSHED OVER TO HER, sidestepping the remains of the lamp and some kind of potted plant, and batted the table out of the way and then lifted her up onto the couch. Most of the blood seemed to have come from a gash above her left eye. That eye was swollen half shut and ringed by a nasty purpling bruise. Her blouse had been torn half off, so that both of her breasts were exposed; she wasn't wearing a bra. An afghan was draped over the back of one of the room's chairs, and I got that and shook it out and covered her to keep her warm.

She was in shock. Her one good eye stared up at me with glazed terror and no recognition. She kept saying, "Oh, God," over and over between little hiccoughing breaths, like a plea for mercy.

I left her and ran down a short hallway that bisected the rear half of the trailer lengthwise. The bathroom opened off that—little more than a cubicle with a toilet, sink, and stall shower. I ran cold water, tossed a hand towel in under the stream. No medicine cabinet in there, but under the sink I found a plastic tray that contained some first-aid supplies. I wrung the towel out, took that and the tray back to where Wendy was.

She lay trembling now, as if with a bad chill, the afghan pulled up under her chin. She looked small and very young and very badly used. If it hadn't been for that idiot driver and his RV . . . no. This was not my fault; it had nothing to do with me. Things happen, that's all. Everywhere you go, every second of your life, things happen over which you have no control.

I knelt beside Wendy, making soothing sounds, and used the wet towel to cleanse the blood off her face. She didn't resist, just lay there whimpering like a hurt puppy. The gash above her eye didn't look deep enough to require stitching. A cut on her upper lip was even shallower. She'd been knocked around quite a bit, but not enough to need hospitalization. It was the kind of beating abusive men inflict on their mates, not a professional job. When a hired slugger works somebody over, the victim needs hospital care—no question.

I daubed Mercurochrome on a piece of gauze and pressed it gently over her eye cut. She flinched and cried out at the sting, but I kept talking to her, telling her she was going to be all right, and she responded by lying still and letting me apply pressure to the wound until that and the antiseptic slowed the bleeding. Some of the shock had worn off by then and she was no longer trembling. She was aware of who was ministering to her; I could see it in her good eye.

She said thickly, as if her voice had been bruised too, "How bad is it? My face?"

"Not so bad. Just lie still."

"Will I have scars? Did he scar me?"

"I don't think so. But I'll call a doctor—"

"No! Not unless I have to have stitches. Do I have to have stitches?"

"I'm not a doctor, Wendy."

"I hate doctors," she said. It hurt her to speak through her cut and bruised lips; she winced each time she spoke, and the words came out low and clogged, so that I had to lean close to hear them. "They'll make trouble, they'll call the cops . . . please don't let anybody else see me like this, *please* . . ."

"Ssh. Lie quiet."

I saturated a fresh piece of gauze with Mercurochrome, tore off a couple of strips of adhesive from a roll, and taped a makeshift bandage over the eye gash. The cut on her lip wasn't bleeding much now, but I swabbed it anyway. I couldn't bandage it because of the location.

When I was done she said, "I'll be okay. This isn't the first time he hurt me. But he'd better not do it again. I'll fix him if he hits me again, I swear to God I will. I'll fix the dirty son of a bitch."

"Scott?"

"Who else. God, I hate him. I should have left him a long time ago."

"Why didn't you?"

"I don't know," she said, as if the fact puzzled her.

"Why did he beat you like this?"

She started to answer, then grimaced and shook her head.

"Did it have anything to do with you and David Burnett?"

"Why do you . . . no. No."

"Don't lie anymore, Wendy. I know most of it anyway."

". . . What do you know?"

"Burnett didn't win a Megabucks jackpot," I said. "It was Mob money. They found out he had it—that's why he killed himself. And that's why you and Janine lost your jobs and Polhemus is running scared."

"Oh, God," she said. She turned her head and closed her eyes and began to cry softly.

I blotted the tears with a clean corner of the towel. "I'm not one of them, Wendy. I don't work for people like that. I'm on your side."

"Yeah, sure," she said without opening her eyes.

"It's the truth. I don't want to get you into any more trouble. All I want is for you to be truthful with me."

Nothing from her this time.

"Why did Scott beat you?"

Silence.

"Why, Wendy?"

". . . Janine," she said, and her eyes popped open and she stared at me as if I had somehow forcibly extracted the word.

She wet her lips, swallowed, wet her lips again. "She told him about Dave and me . . . the four of us . . ."

"Why would she do that?"

"I don't know why. Maybe she didn't mean to . . . he said she was crying on the phone . . . he went crazy when I came home and started calling me names, accusing me of going back up to Fallen Leaf and screwing Jerry . . . I tried to tell him but he wouldn't listen, he just started hitting me . . ."

She was becoming agitated again. I soothed her with the towel and meaningless words until her body stilled.

"My mouth," she said, "it's so dry . . ."

"I'll get you some water. Don't move."

I went into the kitchen. It seemed unnaturally warm in the trailer; I was oiled with sweat. I could smell myself along with the sour odors of dirty laundry and garbage and yesterday's fried food. There was a roll of paper towels on the drainboard; I tore off a couple of sections and wiped my face. Then I found a reasonably clean glass, filled it, drained it to relieve the dryness in my own throat, and refilled it for Wendy.

She tried to sit up and take the glass. I pushed her down, tilted it up to her mouth so she could drink. The afghan had fallen away to reexpose one of her breasts; she didn't seem to notice or to care if she did, but a little modesty was all she had left right now. I drew the rough material back up under her chin.

"We'll go slow now," I said, "nice and slow. You said Scott accused you of going back up to Fallen Leaf Lake. What did you mean?"

"I was up there Monday night. Last Monday."

"To see Polhemus?"

"Yeah."

"He called and asked you to come up?"

"Yeah."

"Why?"

"Tell me about you . . . detective that had been hassling him about Dave and the money. He wanted company too. He didn't want to stay there alone."

"You mean he asked you to sleep with him?"

"Yeah."

"I thought he and Janine were lovers."

"He didn't know where Janine was. They hadn't been in touch since all the shit hit the fan."

"So he came on to you. Nice guy."

"Wasn't like it was the first time," she said.

"The first time he came on to you?"

"First time we got it on. The four of us switched off a couple of times."

"You and Jerry, Janine and Dave?"

"Just for grins. It was no big deal."

Yeah, I thought, no big deal. Just like AIDS and herpes are no big deal. Just like fidelity is no big deal.

I said, keeping my voice neutral, "Did you sleep with Polhemus Monday night?"

"No. I couldn't on account of Scott." She shivered. "Jesus, if I had . . ."

"If you had—what?"

"He would've caught us. He was there."

"Scott was? At the cabin?"

"He followed me. He didn't come in, but he would have if I'd stayed any longer . . . he said so."

"When did he say that?"

"That night. After he got back."

"Let me get this straight. Scott followed you to the cabin—why?"

"He's so goddamn jealous. He was outside when Jerry called but he was listening, I should have known he'd listen. He heard enough so he knew I wasn't going to a job interview like I told him."

"How long were you with Polhemus?"

"About half an hour."

"You came straight back here afterward?"

"Yeah."

"Did Scott follow you back?"

"No, not right away."

"How long was it before he showed up?"

"I dunno . . . a while."

"More than fifteen minutes?"

"Half an hour, I guess."

"He say what he'd been doing during that time?"

"No. Just started in on me about Jerry, what a slut I am, the same old crap."

"He hit you that night?"

"I thought he was going to but he didn't. He just warned me. One more time, he said, and he'd scar me for life. That's what he said—scar me for life." She grimaced, coughed, swallowed. "Can I have some more water?"

I held the glass up to her mouth and she drained it. Then I asked, "Did Scott know who Polhemus was before then?"

"No. I told him Jerry was a friend of Janine's and I was trying to get them back together and that's why I went up to his cabin. He didn't believe it but it was the truth. The last thing I said to Jerry before I left, I told him where Janine was living and he should call her and get back together with her." Wendy's lower lip began to tremble. "I did that for Janine and look what she did for me. Damn her, why'd she have to call tonight? Why'd she have to tell Scott about the four of us?"

"Why did she call? You have any idea?"

"No. Oh, God, my mouth hurts, my head hurts . . . I'm gonna be in bed three days this time, it'll be a week before I can go out and look for a job . . ."

I let her spew out self-pity until the little wellspring ran dry. "Do you know if Jerry got in touch with Janine?"

"No. I don't care if he did."

"You haven't talked to him since?"

"No."

"Or Janine?"

"No."

"Where's she living, Wendy?"

"Paradise Flat."

"Where's that?"

"Up past Emerald Bay."

"Alone or with someone?"

"Alone. She's house-sitting for some people that went to Europe for the summer. Year-rounders she met someplace."

"Why didn't you tell me that when I was here on Tuesday? Why did you lie about your friendship with Janine?"

"Jerry told me not to tell you anything if you ever came around. He said we had to stick together. He's scared shitless they'll do something to him."

"The Mob?"

"Yeah."

"Why is he so afraid of them?"

"Why do you think? Look what happened to Dave."

"Burnett gave Jerry ten thousand dollars. He give you and Janine money too?"

"Five thousand apiece."

"But none of you have it anymore?"

"They made us give it all back, just like they made Dave. I'd already spent some of mine. I had to go sell my grandmother's garnet ring to get the last five hundred. Then they fired me anyway. Me and Janine both."

"Who did? Who'd you pay the five thousand to?"

"Somebody I hope I never see again."

"Manny Atwood?"

". . . I'm not gonna say. I don't want them doing anything more to me. I don't want to end up like Dave."

"All right," I said. "Tell me how Burnett got the two hundred thousand."

"I thought you knew how."

"Not the details."

"I don't know the details."

"Come on, Wendy."

"Honest, I don't know. Dave wouldn't tell us . . . wouldn't even tell me when we were in bed."

"He must have said something about where the money came from."

"No, he didn't. All he said was he found some cash, fifty thousand dollars . . . a crazy piece of good luck, like hitting a Megabucks jackpot. He made us all promise not to say a word and not to bug him and he'd give us some of it. So we promised."

"He said he *found* it?"

"That's what he said."

"Did you believe that?"

"Sure, why not? How else would he get it?"

"Some kind of drug deal, maybe."

"Dave? That's a hoot. He wasn't into the drug scene. A little grass, sure, but he wouldn't even snort a line of coke."

"He told you the amount was fifty thousand?"

"Yeah. Jerry told me how much it really was, after Dave killed himself."

"Why do you think Dave lied to you?"

"Jerry said it was because he was greedy, so we wouldn't try to talk him out of bigger shares."

"Where were the rest of you when he found the money?"

"In Reno. He was supposed to drive up and meet us later that night."

"But he didn't?"

"No."

"Why didn't he go with you?"

"He said he wanted to play some blackjack."

"At the Nevornia?"

"He didn't say which club."

"When did he tell you about finding the money?"

"After we got back. Late that night."

"He show you any of it?"

"No. Just the suitcase."

"It was in a suitcase?"

"Big leather one, yeah."

"You think he knew then it was Mob money?"

"I warned him. So did Janine. You work in the clubs, you get to know about that kind of thing. All that cash in a suitcase . . . I *told* him it might be skim or payoff money. But he wouldn't listen. He just laughed and said it didn't make any difference because there was no way anybody could find out he had it." She tried a bitter laugh, but pain turned it into a groan. "Well, they found out and now he's dead. We could *all* be dead. Jesus, why do I always hook up with assholes and losers?"

I had an answer for that but I didn't offer it. I said, "Did anyone tell you how the Mob found out?"

"No."

"Dave didn't warn you or the others that they were on to him?"

"Not me or Janine. We found out the hard way."

"You get in touch with him after the Mob came down on you?"

"Bet I did. I called him right away."

"What did he say?"

"He wouldn't talk about it. Hung up on me."

"Was that the last time you talked to him?"

"Yeah. Then a week later Jerry got in touch and told me he was dead. You know something? I didn't feel a thing. It was like some stranger was dead . . . just like some stranger . . ."

She was tiring; her eyelids were heavy and her words came more slowly. Subject the body to physical abuse, and once the shock wears off completely and the pain eases, it craves sleep to begin the healing process.

"Wendy, where can I find Scott?"

"Scott? Fuck him."

"Where does he go when he's all worked up? A bar he hangs out in, maybe?"

"He doesn't drink."

"One of the casinos? A movie, a friend's place?"

"Maybe back to work on the boat he's building," she said. "Boats . . . that's all he cares about."

"Where is he building this boat?"

"Where he works. Pope Beach."

"Adams and Conley Marine?"

"Yeah."

"Just one more question. The house Janine is living in— what's the address?"

"You going to see her?"

"Yes."

"Tell her I said thanks a lot. Tell her she can go to hell for all I care."

"The address, Wendy."

"Sweetwater Drive in Paradise Flat. I dunno the number. Last house at the end, right on the lake."

I got to my feet. My knees and joints were stiff from kneeling for so long. I flexed both legs before I asked, "You have a friend who lives close by, someplace you can spend the night?"

"No. Why?"

"You can't stay here alone—"

"Don't worry, he won't hurt me anymore. He'll be all sweet and sorry when he comes home. He always is."

"Just the same, I'd feel better if you'd let me take you somewhere."

"Where? There's no place."

"No friends, relatives?"

"Nobody," she said. "I don't have anyplace to go."

I stood looking down at her for a few seconds. I did not want to leave her alone, but the only other choice was to take her with me and that was out of the question. Finally I said, "At least let me help you into bed."

"No, I'll be okay here. If I'm in bed when he gets home, he'll try to get in with me."

Her eyes were almost shut now. The lines of strain and pain had smoothed out of her face, leaving it in pale repose beneath the marks of her beating. She looked so young . . . and at the same time, so old. One of those people already battered by life in their mid-twenties, like a doll in the hands of an indifferent and malicious child—a doll destined for more abuse, until she was used up and tossed away.

I backed off a couple of steps, being quiet about it, but she wasn't asleep yet. Without opening her eyes she said, as much to herself as to me, "I guess that's why I haven't left him. I guess that's why I never will."

I didn't say anything. There was nothing more for me to say to her.

"I just don't have anyplace to go," she said.

Chapter **19**

POPE BEACH was out off Highway 89, not all that far from the turnoff to Fallen Leaf Lake. When I saw the sign I turned and followed the road down along the Tahoe shore. After what Wendy had told me, and after what Scott McKee had done to her, I wanted a talk with McKee as much as I wanted one with Janine Wovoka and Jerry Polhemus. If he was at Pope Beach, fine; otherwise I would drive up to Paradise Flat from here and track him down later.

The road ran between a long stretch of beach and boating facilities and the Truckee Marsh, down toward Tahoe Keys. Adams & Conley Marine was near the end, on the lake side— a biggish complex composed of a retail store, a fenced-in boat-yard, a warehouse-type building, and a row of boat slips. The retail store was closed and there was nobody out and about in the yard. Both halves of the yard gate were shut but they weren't locked. And parked inside, near a sailboat up on davits, was McKee's primer-patched Porsche.

I parked to one side of the gate. It was cool here, this close to the lake; would have been chilly if the wind hadn't died down. After six o'clock now, and most of the pleasure-boaters had brought their craft in for the day. But there were still a few boats moving here and there, smoke-dark specks on a surface as bright and shiny as sheet metal.

Inside the yard, I picked my way through a clutter of small boats and trailers, hoists and other equipment. When I got near the closed doors to the big building I could hear the soft buzzing whine of a power tool being used inside. Metal handles were mounted vertically on both door halves; I tugged on one and the half bumped open. I walked in.

Gloomy interior, lit by shielded lights on long dropcords suspended from ceiling beams. Pleasant, mingled smells of sawdust and paint and linseed oil and turpentine. Most of the concrete floor was occupied: stacks of board lumber and plywood sheets and wooden forms; rows of shelving laden with marine supplies; lathes and drill presses and table saws and workbenches; a pair of skeletal shapes on davits that would one day be boats. And just one man in the midst of it all, hunched over one of the lathes, shaping something that I took to be a spar. He was wearing a pair of protective goggles but there was no mistaking his size or his blond curls.

He was half turned away from me and the noise of the lathe kept him from hearing my approach. I was within thirty feet of him when he finished shaping the spar and switched off the machine. In the sudden silence that followed, my shoe made a small scraping sound on the concrete; it brought him around in a jerky, startled movement. He must not have been able to see me clearly through the goggles because he yanked them up on his forehead. Even then it took five seconds of narrow-eyed staring for him to place me—and while he was staring I kept walking until I was close enough to him to smell the sour odor of his sweat. And to see the scrapes across the knuckles of his right hand, the scratches on his forearm where Wendy had marked him.

"What the hell you doing here?" he said.

"Looking for you."

"This is private property, man. You're trespassing."

"You want to try throwing me out?"

Either the words or my tone made him nervous. He tried to

cover it by glaring at me and saying in a hard voice, "What you want, huh?"

"You, Scotty."

"I got nothing for you."

"Sure you have. You've got plenty for me."

"The hell," he said. Then he said, "You're no goddamn trailer repairman."

"That's right, I'm not."

"What are you, then? Another of that bitch's lovers?"

"What would you do if I was? Try to beat me up like you beat her up tonight?"

Now he was more than nervous; now he was anxious. He licked his lips, ran his hands up and down the legs of his jeans as if they had gone damp. He didn't say anything.

"How about Jerry Polhemus?" I said. "You beat him up too? Hurt him real bad, maybe?"

"I dunno what you're talking about."

"Sure you do. Monday night, remember? You followed Wendy to Polhemus's cabin at Fallen Leaf Lake. You sat around outside for half an hour, while she was in there with him, and when she left you went in and confronted Polhemus. Isn't that the way it was?"

"No. She tell you that?"

"She told me a lot of things. Not that it was easy for her to talk with her mouth all bruised and bloody."

"She had it coming. She's a fuckin' whore."

"And what are you, Scotty? A tough guy? Beating up on girls and cowards makes you tough?"

No response.

"How'd you like to try beating up on me?" I said.

No response.

"Come on, give it a try. I'm more than twice your age. You ought to be able to kick the crap out of an old guy like me."

"What are you, crazy?" I had him good and worried now. He backed up a step, as if he thought I might jump him—or maybe pull a gun or a knife.

"Tell me about Polhemus."

"I already told you, I don't—"

"Did you kill him?"

"What? Jesus, what—"

"Beat him to death? That what you did?"

"No!"

"Knocked him around, though, didn't you? Drew some blood?"

"What if I did? What the hell business is it of—"

"How bad did you hurt him?"

He shook his head, backed up another step.

"How bad, Scotty?"

"Leave me alone. You get out of here and leave me alone or—"

"Or what? You'll call the cops? Why don't you go ahead and do that? Then I'll tell them what you did to Polhemus Monday night and what you did to Wendy tonight."

His eyes flicked left, right, left, right—looking for a way out.

I said, "Where's Polhemus now? Where's he been the past three days?"

Headshake. Eyeflicks.

"What'd you do with his body? Dump it in the lake?"

"I never killed nobody!"

"Tell me what you did do, then."

"You're crazy, man!"

"Maybe it was self-defense. He pulled that Saturday night special of his, you took it away from him, there was a struggle, the gun went off with him in the way. That how it was?"

"No!"

"How, then? What happened between you and Polhemus?"

I took a step his way, sudden and quick. It broke him: he lunged sideways to the lathe, going after the spar. I got there first and swiped it away from his clutching fingers, sent it clattering to the floor. He reeled back the other way, stumbling, heading for the nearest of the workbenches. I went after him, reached him just as he fumbled up a wooden mallet and started to swing around with it. I took it away from him without much effort, hurled it down, then caught a handful of his shirtfront and leaned into him, hard. Our faces were inches apart; his breath came out ragged and sour, spraying a mist of spittle. He tried to wrench loose, and when that didn't work he punched at my rib cage with his right fist, not getting much force behind the blows. I put a stop to the slugging by jamming him farther backward over the bench with the weight of my body, pinning both of his arms. He twisted, struggled, made little noises of mixed terror and rage, but I had him locked down, exerting pressure all along his spine. He wasn't going anywhere until I let him go.

"You're hurting me . . . Jesus . . ."

"Like you hurt Polhemus and Wendy, huh?"

"They had it coming, they both had it coming—"

I let up on him just enough so that I could slap his face with my free hand. Not too hard—just hard enough to sting. He struggled again, and I slapped him a second time, and he quit squirming. I slapped him a third time anyway. And a fourth for good measure. His eyes had gone wet; it's degrading to be smacked openhanded that way.

"Let me go!"

I slapped him again instead. "Tell me about Polhemus. What did you do to him?"

". . . Hit on him a few times, that's all, I swear that's *all*."

"Because you thought Wendy had been seeing him on the sly."

"Yeah. A whiny little bugger like him . . ."

"Did he pull his gun on you?"

"Gun? I never saw no gun—"

"How bad did you hurt him?"

"Busted his nose, maybe . . . he was bleeding . . ."

"What'd you do then? After you finished hitting him?"

"Left him there . . . went home . . . Jesus, let me loose, you're breaking my back!"

"Where was he when you left the cabin?"

"On the floor, lying on the floor."

"Conscious?"

"Yeah, conscious. Bawling like a woman."

"You see anybody else around when you left?"

"No."

"You been back to his cabin since?"

"No. Why would I go back there?"

"See Polhemus since? Have anything to do with him?"

"No. No!"

"So you don't know where he is now?"

"I swear I don't. Ahh, shit, let me *up* . . ."

"Not yet. When Janine called tonight, did she say anything about Polhemus?"

"Janine . . . what?"

"You heard me. Wendy's friend, Janine. She called tonight and you answered the phone. That's why you beat up on Wendy, because of what Janine told you."

"Yeah, yeah, Janine . . ."

"She say anything about Polhemus?"

"No."

"Didn't mention his name?"

"Once . . . maybe twice . . ."

"What did she say?"

"She was crying her head off . . . I couldn't understand half of what she was saying."

"What did she want? Why was she calling Wendy?"

"Wouldn't tell me. Only Wendy. Didn't have nobody . . . nobody else she could talk to. That's what she said."

"She say what happened, why she was upset?"

"Nothing that made sense."

"What'd she say that did make sense?"

"She wished they'd never met Dave and Jerry . . . her and Wendy . . . never spent so much time with them. Everything was Dave's fault . . . something about money and a suitcase . . . stuff that didn't mean nothing to me."

"Is that all?"

"All I remember. I was crazy mad by then . . . I heard Wendy's car, I hung up quick. Her and some dude named Dave, fuckin' around while I was down in San Pedro working my ass off . . . when she came in I lost my head, I just laid into her. . . ."

"Where was Janine calling from?"

"Dunno. She never said."

"You're sure?"

"I'm sure . . . unnh, my back . . . chrissake, *please* . . ."

I held him a couple of seconds longer, but there was nothing to be gained in hurting him any more; he was talked out and so was I. I released my grip on his shirt and shoved back off of him. He rolled over sideways, grimacing, moaning a little, and then slid down onto one knee and knelt there with one arm crooked behind him, massaging his spine.

"You damn near busted my back," he said, but there was more self-pity than anything else in his voice and he wouldn't look at me as he spoke. He'd had enough of me.

I said, "You're not hurt half as bad as Wendy. But I can fix it so you're hurt twice as bad if you lay a hand on her again. You understand me?"

Headshake. But it was a reflexive movement, not a denial.

"I mean it, Scott. Hurt her again, I'll find out about it and I'll come back and kick the hell out of you."

". . . Who are you, man? What you get out of all of this? A piece of Wendy?"

"Say that again and I'll break your arm. Right now."

Silence.

I said, "I'm somebody you don't want to mess with, sonny boy. You believe it?"

Still nothing.

"I asked you a question."

"Yeah. Yeah, I believe it."

"Good. Here's one more thing for you to think about: Treat Wendy right from now on, she won't run around on you."

"She won't want nothing more to do with me, not after tonight."

"You're wrong about that. She's not going anywhere and neither are you; you're stuck with each other, for better or worse. Treat her right, she'll treat you right. You believe that?"

"Sure. Yeah, sure."

"So long, Scotty. I hope we don't see each other again—for your sake."

"We won't," McKee said. He still hadn't looked at me since I'd turned him loose.

I went away from him, taking my time about it, glancing back once to see if he was going to try anything. He wasn't; he stayed on one knee, rubbing his back and looking at the floor. Waiting for me to be gone.

Outside, I stood for half a minute to let what was left of the wind dry my sweat. I felt dirty, the way I had when Carl and Jimmy brought me back from Arthur Welker's place. Some men, some detectives, thrive on the rough stuff; I'm not one of them. I don't like hurting or humiliating people—even when they're the kind who deserve it, and especially not after I've been humiliated myself. But sometimes it's necessary; sometimes there is no other way to get information or accomplish an objective. Sometimes life is a sewer. You don't have to spend all your time in the sewer, though, or enjoy yourself when you're forced to wade through it.

Across the yard, into my car. Back up to Highway 89, north. With all the windows down, I felt the bite of the wind-rush as I drove, smelled the good clean scent of mountain pine and mountain water.

I still felt dirty.

Chapter 20

THE DRIVE UP AROUND EMERALD BAY made my palms damp and my fingers clamp tight around the wheel. The two-lane highway climbed to several hundred feet above the deep inlet and hugged its inner rim, so that you had a fine vista of the bay, its one verdant island and long wooded arms, and the sweep of Tahoe beyond; but I couldn't even look at the view because the road ran smack along the edges of a number of sheer drop-offs and there were no guardrails to create an illusion of safety. This kind of road always makes me edgy because I suffer from acrophobia—just one more in a long line of anxieties. Detectives are supposed to be a version of Superman; not me. I'm Clark Kent, with a pocketful of my own private brand of kryptonite.

On the north side of the bay, the highway dropped back down close to lake level on its way through Bliss State Park. The tightness in me eased, and I was able to turn a part of my mind to what I'd learned from Wendy and Scott McKee.

I knew most of it now—all but a few key links in the chain of events stretching back to the night three weeks ago when David Burnett turned up a suitcase full of Mob money. And the ones I didn't know yet I ought to be able to learn tonight, at the end of Sweetwater Drive in Paradise Flat. If anybody aside from Arthur Welker and Manny Atwood knew how Burnett had come into possession of the two hundred thousand, it was Jerry Polhemus. Polhemus could also fill me in on the aftermath of his fight with McKee on Monday night, though I didn't really need him to supply the details. They were easy enough to figure: He didn't want to spend another night in the cabin because he was afraid McKee might come back, and somebody else—me, for one—might show up; but he was too shaken and too banged up to drive anywhere. Wendy had given him Janine's Paradise Flat number, so he called her and told her what had happened and she came and picked him up and took him back to the house she was sitting. Neither of them was in a frame of mind to think about locking the cabin door when they left; the last one out may have pulled it closed but it hadn't been tightly latched, which was why I found the door standing wide open. Tuesday sometime, after my visit to Fallen Leaf Lake, or maybe Wednesday, Polhemus felt well enough to go collect his car and belongings. He still didn't want to stay at the cabin, so he followed Janine back to Paradise Flat. And that was where he'd been ever since.

Simple.

Most of it was simple, really. I had no doubt now that the explanation of how Burnett had gotten the money would turn out to be simple too, whether or not he'd actually found it. It was only the lies and deceptions that had made it all seem complicated. No fancy plot involving drugs or contraband or big knockovers; no sinister homicides; no surprises. Just a series of chain reactions brought about by stupidity, cowardice, and moral corruption. Plenty of people had suffered, and at least two of them—Burnett's sister and fiancée—were going to suffer even more. But hey, that's life, right? We all suffer, all of us. One way or another, to one degree or another.

As far as I was concerned, it would be over tonight or tomorrow at the latest. I would finally come face-to-face with Janine Wovoka, confront her and Polhemus, and then I would go home to San Francisco and break the news to Allyn Burnett and Karen Salter and write my report and collect the balance of my fee. And that would be the end of it. I had been hired to find out a difficult truth; I had found it out. Mission accomplished.

Never mind that Arthur Welker had been as responsible for Burnett's suicide as Burnett himself; never mind that he would continue to carry out his own special brand of evil, untouched and untouchable, ever at the ready to destroy anybody else who got in his way. Justice is blind; who says there has to be justice? This is the real world, and in the real world the bad guys win as often as the good guys. More often, these days, because they're better organized, have better resources, and operate under a much less restrictive set of rules.

But there was nothing I could do about that, and in the long run it was none of my lookout anyway. Why beat my head against a stone wall? So Welker had humiliated me, just as I had humiliated Scott McKee . . . so what? Life is full of humiliations large and small; swallow the bitter, savor the sweet. It all evens out in the last analysis.

Clichés.

Hollow truths that were no comfort at all.

This may have turned out to be a basically simple case, but it was also one that would live in my memory and stick in my craw for the rest of my days.

PARADISE FLAT was one of a dozen little communities strung out along the California rim of Lake Tahoe, at the southern end of Rubicon Bay and butted up against the wilderness and recreational acreage of Bliss State Park. Heavily forested mountain slopes extended down close to the water along this stretch, and the highway mostly hugged the irregular shoreline, running in twisty loops through trees and around massive protrusions of granite. But in Paradise Flat, as in some of the other hamlets farther north, there was enough forestland between the road and the lake to support a few score year-round and summer homes, while at the same time providing the owners with plenty of privacy.

I slowed when I came out of the park and began hunting for Sweetwater Drive. I didn't find it. When I spotted a sign announcing Rubicon, the next little enclave northward, I pulled over and got out the Tahoe map. Sweetwater Drive was on it; the reason I'd missed it was that it didn't open off Highway 89, as I'd assumed it would. Teach me to consult a map *before* I got to where I was going. I made a U-turn and drove back down the highway to an intersecting road called Sierra Flat, turned there, and three minutes later I was on Sweetwater Drive.

The narrow blacktop meandered through woods, hooked southward past widely spaced homes, then dipped closer toward the lake. I rounded a turn past somebody's perverted variation on the geodesic dome, and up ahead the road dead-ended at a wall of thick forest. At first I couldn't see another house and I thought that the perverted dome was the one I wanted; but when I'd gone a little farther, a roofline appeared among the tall pines and Douglas fir growing below the level of the road on my left. The last house on Sweetwater was half hidden in a hollow down there, just back from the waterline.

More of the house came into view, and then a driveway that cut back and down at a sharp, steep angle. I let the car drift over onto the right-hand shoulder, short of the driveway, where there was just enough room to park without blocking the roadway. Then I walked across to where I had a clear look at the house below.

It was good-sized, fashioned of cut pine logs and redwood shakes, with thick woods crowding in close on its far side. A raised redwood deck, mostly invisible from where I stood, overlooked the lake. The driveway ended in a parking area alongside the house. A path led from there to where a flat concrete pier extended into the water, a pair of short wooden floats making a broad *T* at its outer end; a small boat shelter had been built onto one of the floats. Attached to the near end of the house was a carport large enough for two cars. Only one was slotted there now: Jerry Polhemus's dark red Mercury Cougar.

I watched the place for a minute or so. It wasn't quite dusk yet so I couldn't tell if there were any lights on inside. No smoke came from the fireplace chimney.

I moved ahead to the drive, down it to a square of fern-bordered brick that served as a front stoop. There was a button inset into the doorjamb; I pushed that, listened to the distant ringing of chimes. Otherwise I was enveloped in that deep hush that settles over lakefront property at this time of day.

Nobody came to open the door. I pushed the bell again and did some more waiting, looking out over the lake. Sunset colors ran through the sky—layers of dusky rose and old gold, streaks of gray and fading orange. This part of the shore was in shadow, but the sun hadn't completely dropped behind the High Sierra peaks yet; over toward the Nevada shore, its light lay fire-hot across the surface, creating the illusion that that part of the lake was aflame.

Well, maybe they'd gone out shopping or to have an early dinner, taking Janine's car. I could sit up on the road and wait for them to return. But a natural reluctance kept me standing where I was; I dislike stakeouts at the best of times, short ones as much as long ones, and I was in no mood for passive waiting this evening. I'd thought that if I could get this interrogation over and done with soon enough, with positive results, I could start back home tonight; maybe make it out of the mountains and as far west as Auburn before I hunted up a motel.

Without thinking about it, I reached down and tried the doorknob. Locked, naturally. I turned off the bricks, but instead of heading back up the drive, I walked down to the pier and stood watching a powerboat whisk past at high speed several hundred yards offshore, half gliding and half bouncing like the flat stones we used to skip when we were kids. Insect hum came from the surrounding undergrowth; pine scent spiced the cool air. But the beauty of the evening and the lakefront was spoiled by patches of algae like green scum floating along the rim of the shore. So much pollution these days, I thought. This kind, and the human variety as practiced by the Burnetts and the Polhemuses and the Arthur Welkers.

When I turned around again I found myself looking up at the deck and a wall of glass where it joined the house. The drapes were open, I noticed, and part of a beamed ceiling was visible inside. A set of steps gave access to the deck from the dock area; on impulse I mounted them, went past some outdoor furniture to a combination picture window and sliding glass door. I put my nose close to the window, shaded my eyes to get a clear look through it.

Spacious living room: beige-brick fireplace, furniture and paneling in muted earth tones, beige-and-brown-tile floor, oval throw rugs the color of autumn leaves. Most of the surfaces were littered with glasses, dishes, overflowing ashtrays, paperback books, sections of newspaper, articles of clothing; Janine was a lousy housekeeper. At the rear was an open bar area, and beyond that a modern kitchen done in the same color scheme. To the left of the bar was what I took to be a hallway—

—and an arm, an outflung man's arm with the fingers hooked into a misshapen fist.

Somebody was lying sprawled on the hallway floor.

The hair pulled along my neck. I pressed closer to the glass, staring at the arm; it didn't move. I took a few steps to my right, to try to get a better viewing angle, but there was furniture in the way. All I could see was that bare arm.

I tugged on the sliding door; it wouldn't budge. My mouth was dry as I hurried across the deck and down the steps and back up alongside the house. Two windows flanked the front door, both made of opaque glass and both locked. A third window toward the carport was also locked. I moved under the carport, past the Cougar, around to the far side where the trees pushed in close and there were thick, fragrant shadows.

A small window midway along was open a couple of inches.

There was a screen over the window; it didn't take me long to pry it loose and lift it down. I slid the window open as far as it would go, then caught hold of the high sill and hoisted myself up and got my shoulders into the narrow opening. Tight fit, but I managed to wiggle through. Bathroom. Toilet on my right, stall shower on my left. I laid one hand on the shower door to brace myself and climbed down by using the toilet as a step. Went out of there into a wildly disarrayed bedroom and then into the hallway.

The arm belonged to Jerry Polhemus. He was naked except

for a pair of boxer shorts, lying on his side with his knees
drawn up, his other arm bent in under his body. One look at
him was enough to tell me he was dead—bloodily dead. Clot-
ted blood covered his midsection and stained his shorts and
filled the cracks in the tile floor under him. Shot in the stomach, up under the breastbone. The gun was there, too, down
by his feet—his own gun, the Saturday night special he'd
threatened me with in San Francisco.

I did not touch him or the gun. But I moved close enough
to see that healing bruises discolored his face, a pair of crude
bandages covered his broken nose and an area over his left
temple; and to determine that the blood hadn't completely
dried yet. Dead only a few hours. Since sometime around five
o'clock.

Now I knew why Janine had called Wendy, and why Mc-
Kee had said she'd been crying her head off.

But I should have suspected it long before this. Would
have, if I'd let myself think about it driving here. Denial: I
had not wanted to confront any more violence, any ugly twists
or surprises, so I had refused to consider the possibility. I'd
wanted it all to stay simple.

But nothing is ever quite as simple as it seems. I should
have remembered that, too.

Training and an old desire to create order out of chaos
drove me back into the bedroom. But there was nothing there
to tell me what had happened at five o'clock. All I found were
two sets of luggage: Polhemus's two suitcases and duffel bag,
and a pair of women's bags that I took to be Janine's. So she
hadn't packed anything to take with her when she left. Just
ran—ran scared—after the abortive phone call to Wendy.

Nothing of interest in the bathroom or the other two bedrooms. Back in the hall, I stepped over Polhemus's corpse,
taking care to avoid the blood, and made passes through the
living area and kitchen. Nothing in those rooms, either. And
no indication that anybody other than Janine and Polhemus
had been here recently.

There was a telephone on the kitchen wall. I stopped in
front of it, stood there for several seconds without lifting the

receiver. Every instinct urged me to call the county sheriff's department, report what I'd found; give my right name and then wait like a good citizen for the officers to arrive. I had had the misfortune to stumble across murder victims before, and each time I had done the correct and responsible thing. But this time . . . this time I felt disinclined to play it by the book. The waiting, the questions, the too familiar and seemingly endless routine—I had no stomach for all of that tonight. But that was not the only reason. There were answers I wanted now more than at any time since I'd begun this investigation, and as quickly as I could get them. In the past I had always been willing to wait and bide my time. Not anymore.

What I'd thought at Polhemus's cabin earlier today was true: I was not the same person I had been before last winter. I was still learning things about this new man I'd become, some good and some unsettling. And one of the things I had learned these past few minutes was that—professionally, at least—I no longer had the virtue of patience. My kidnapper had robbed me of that, too.

I told myself I would notify the authorities later tonight or tomorrow morning, after I had my answers; that my intention was only to delay my duty, not to shirk it. Then I went to the front door, threw the dead bolt, and left the house that way.

Long drive coming up; maybe a wild-goose chase, though I would have bet against that. I don't mind long drives if there is a purpose to them. And I wasn't tired, not anymore. In my business you learn to trust your hunches, and the one prodding me now was as sharp and certain as any I'd ever had.

Where does a young woman go when she's in serious trouble and has nobody else to turn to? Where does she go for help and comfort and a feeling of safety? Where does she go even if she's vowed over and over never to return there again?

Yeah.

She goes home.

Chapter 21

BY NIGHT, Pyramid Lake had an even stranger aspect than during the daylight hours. There was a harvest moon tonight, an intricate webwork of stars; their combined light dusted the lake and its barren islands and the surrounding desert in an eerie radiance that was almost spectral. Ghost lake in a ghost landscape. As if it might all disappear at any second, in the blink of an eye, the way apparitions generally do.

I glanced at my watch as I came down the long hill to the lakefront fork. A little past nine-thirty. I'd made good time from Paradise Flat, taking 89 to Interstate 80 and then 80 through Reno and onto 445. Minor slowdowns in Tahoe City and Sparks; otherwise the traffic had been light enough so that I could drive at a steady sixty-five. Fatigue had begun to gather at the edges of my mind, despite the sense of urgency. My neck and shoulders were stiff with tension.

I turned along the western shore toward the clustered lights of Sutcliffe. One lake to another the past few days—Tahoe to Fallen Leaf to Tahoe to Virginia to Pyramid to Tahoe to Virginia to Tahoe to Fallen Leaf to Tahoe to Pyramid. Linkage. Another chain that stretched back to David Burnett and his suitcase full of money. But in any chain there is a final

link. Pyramid Lake would be one, if I was lucky, and Janine
Wovoka would be another.

Past Sutcliffe, on up toward Pelican Point. Isolated lights
ahead, lakeward: John Wovoka's trailer. I slowed, looking for
the access road; saw it and made the turn and bumped along
toward the flat-topped rise ahead. In the silvery moonshine I
could see the trailer and its frontage clearly. The U.S. Wildlife
Commission pickup wasn't parked there, nor was any other
vehicle. And yet lights were on inside the trailer, showing
behind drawn blinds over front and side windows.

I coasted to a stop thirty feet from the door. Shut off engine
and headlamps and got out into a hush that matched the
ghostly aspect of the lake. No sounds came from inside the
trailer. I stood for a few seconds, stretching cramped muscles,
watching the blinds on the near window. I thought I saw
movement at one corner: someone watching me through a
canted slat.

Slowly I moved over that way. But instead of going to the
door or window, I continued around the far corner to the rear.
Car parked back there, all right. Small, pudgy foreign job—
Yugo?—drawn in close against the trailer's back wall and nose
up to the accumulation of junk overflowing the shed.

I retraced my steps to the front, went to the door. Knocked
and called out my name. "Open up, Janine. We need to talk."

No response, no sound.

"Come on, Janine. I know you're in there. And you know
who I am. You can't hide anymore."

Silence.

"I've just come from Paradise Flat," I said. "I found Jerry. I
haven't called the sheriff yet but I will right now if you don't
open the door. I've got a phone in my car. I'll give you thirty
seconds; then you can watch me make the call."

Silence for half that time. Then there were hesitant footfalls; a scraping and rattling as she released the door lock.
Muffled voice: "All right, come in."

I opened the door and entered a neat, Spartan room that
was half living area and half kitchen and dinette. Its lone
occupant was backed up against the far wall, braced there with

her feet apart. That was my first look at Janine Wovoka in the flesh: scared young woman in stone-washed denims and a loose blue sweater, crouched against a trailer wall and pointing a long-barreled revolver at me with both hands.

I closed the door behind me, doing it slowly. "Put the gun down, Janine."

"No. You stay away from me."

"You don't want to shoot me. I'm on your side."

"My side?" Her laugh was edged with hysteria. "My God, if it wasn't for you, Jerry . . . Jerry might still be alive."

Yeah, I thought. If it wasn't for me and you and Burnett and Wendy and Scott McKee and Jerry's own lust and greed. And Arthur Welker—let's not forget Arthur Welker.

"Don't make things any worse than they are," I said. "Put the gun down."

"No."

"You want to kill two people in one night? Shoot two men down in cold blood?"

"What? No . . . no!"

"You shot Jerry. Why?"

She shook her head. Kept shaking it, brokenly, so that her black hair swirled around her face in damp, tangled strands. She had been strikingly attractive in the snapshots I'd found, but she wasn't attractive now. Haggard, pinch-faced; the sweat of fear dampening skin gone pale and blotchy and stretched so tight over the high cheekbones, it seemed ready to split. Big dark eyes alight with something more than terror, as if she had gazed through a crack and seen the landscape of hell.

"I didn't shoot him," she said, "I didn't, I didn't!"

"No? There wasn't anyone else in the house."

"I tell you, I didn't!"

"Then who did?"

"*He* did. He . . . Jerry . . . he did it himself."

"Suicide? I don't buy it, Janine. Not him, not in the stomach like that. He didn't have the courage."

"You don't understand . . . it was an *accident.* He was out of his head . . . he went crazy, he just . . . went crazy . . ."

"Drugs? Was he high on something?"

Another series of head wags. "He had some grass but it wasn't that. He was sick, hurt . . . he woke up with a bad headache and stayed in bed all day . . . oh, God, I was in the kitchen, I was going to make some sandwiches, and I heard him yelling . . . he just started yelling for no reason . . . I ran into the hall and he ran out of the bedroom waving that gun of his and yelling . . . he was out of his head, he said I was one of them and I wanted to kill him but he was going to kill me first and he . . . he tried . . . I grabbed for the gun and he pulled away and it . . . it went off and he screamed and fell down and thrashed around and I couldn't . . . the blood . . ."

Headshakes, violent now. She had had a glimpse of hell, all right, and she was having it again inside her head. It made her physically ill. She coughed, then gagged, then lunged over to the kitchen sink and vomited into it. She still had the revolver in one hand but she'd forgotten about it by then; forgotten about me, too, until I eased up beside her and caught her wrist and disarmed her. She turned toward me, her features pulled out of shape, her mouth streaked and stained, but then another spasm overtook her; she vomited again into the sink. And I backed up with the weapon.

When she was done puking she began to cry—great racking sobs that shook her whole body. There was a towel beside the sink; she groped that up, blindly, and wiped her mouth and then stumbled to an old two-seat mohair couch at the far wall and sank onto it with her face buried in the towel. I let her sit there and cry while I dealt with the gun. It was a Smith & Wesson .38-caliber target revolver with a six-inch barrel. John Wovoka's, probably. All the chambers were loaded. I removed the cartridge from under the hammer before I tucked the piece into my jacket pocket.

Janine's sobbing diminished, finally quit altogether. It was another minute before she raised her head and looked at me again, out of eyes that had gone dull in the ravaged plain of her face. "I wouldn't have shot you," she said in a voice as dull as her eyes. "I didn't shoot Jerry . . . I loved him. I couldn't hurt anybody. Please, you have to believe me . . ."

"I believe you," I said.

"Do you? Really?"

"Really."

It seemed to relieve her. She took a couple of deep breaths, made a vague gesture toward the dinette table. "My purse," she said. "I need a cigarette . . ."

"I'll get it. Stay where you are."

I opened the purse and looked inside before I gave it to her, to make sure she didn't have some other kind of weapon tucked away in there. A package of Marlboros was the most lethal of the contents. She fired one with shaking hands, sat dragging on it hungrily. On the wall above her was an oil painting of an Indian woman in some sort of ceremonial costume, holding a conical-shaped basket in her hands. The juxtaposition struck me as symbolic of the differences between the Indians of yesterday and the Indians of today, the sad old world and the bitter new.

Janine took another drag on her cigarette, coughed out smoke, and said, "It must have been the fight. Jerry was in a fight Monday night . . ."

"I know. With Scott McKee."

"He hit his head when he fell. His temple, it was all soft and . . . pulpy, you know? He could hardly talk when he called me. And when I got there he was so dizzy I had to help him walk."

"Why didn't you take him to a doctor?"

"He wouldn't go. He said he was all right, he just needed to rest. The next day . . . he *was* all right, except for a headache that wouldn't go away. It wasn't until this morning that the headache got so bad he couldn't get out of bed. I wanted to call a doctor then, too, but he said no. I should have called one anyway . . . I knew I should have, I *knew* it."

"Too late by then, probably."

"What do you mean?"

"Brain damage. That's what it sounds like." And I thought

but didn't say: Walking dead man since Monday night. The bullet in his guts was like pulling the plug on a cancer patient with a short time to live.

Janine said, "But then . . . *Scott* killed him. In the fight."

"Technically, yes. But he's no more guilty than Dave Burnett or your former bosses."

". . . You know about all that? The money?"

"The big jackpot. Yeah, I know. All except where and how he got hold of the suitcase."

"I wish to God I'd never met him," Janine said with sudden vehemence. She jabbed out her cigarette in a stoneware ashtray and immediately lit another. "Him or Jerry. They ruined my life . . . my life is ruined now. What am I going to do? Live here on the reservation with my father? Be somebody's squaw like my mother was? Just another fat, ugly Indian squaw. . . ."

"How did Burnett get the money, Janine?"

She blinked her swollen eyes at me. "What?"

"The suitcase, the money—how did he get it?"

"I don't know," she said.

"You must have some idea."

"No, he wouldn't tell us. Not any of us, not then."

"Meaning he told one of you later?"

"Jerry . . . he told Jerry."

"But Jerry wouldn't tell you?"

"No. He said it was better I didn't know."

"Didn't even give you a hint?"

"No."

And now he's dead, I thought. They're both dead, Burnett and Polhemus, and the only ones left who know the whole truth are Welker and Manny Atwood. Welker, Welker, Arthur goddamn Welker . . .

"But he made a tape," Janine said.

The words jerked me back out of myself. "Tape? What kind of tape?"

"Telling everything that happened, how Dave got the money and how *they* found out. He said he did anyway. To protect himself if there was any more trouble."

"What did he do with this tape?"

"I don't know."

"Hid it somewhere, gave it to somebody, put it in a safe-deposit box?"

She shook her head. "He wouldn't tell me. Honest."

Damn all the secrecy! If I could find that tape . . . if he'd named names, mentioned Welker's name just once . . .

Janine snubbed out her second cigarette, ran her hands together in her lap as if she were trying to cleanse them. Her eyes, now, were bright, shiny—like those of a trapped bird watching a cat. "What are you going to do?" she said.

"About what?"

"About me. About Jerry. You said you haven't called the sheriff yet . . ."

"Not yet, no."

"Do you have to?"

"What do you think?"

"But why? What good will it do now?"

"Not much, maybe. But Jerry's dead. You want to leave his body lying there in the house?"

She shuddered. "No. But what if they don't believe me? I don't want to go to jail."

"You won't go to jail."

"You don't know that. Please don't call them, please. If you don't, I'll . . . I'll do . . ."

"Do what, Janine?"

"Anything you want. Anything."

That made me angry. "You can't buy me with sex, little girl. Not anywhere, at any time, and especially not here in your father's house. Not even a whore screws a customer in her father's house."

She began to cry again. But it wasn't shame; it was self-pity. Everybody I had had dealings with tonight was loaded down with self-pity and I was sick of confronting it. "Please," she said between sobs, "*please* don't call anybody. You don't understand, it's not just me . . . my father . . ."

"What about your father?"

Headshake.

A belated realization, cold and crystal-sharp, opened up in my mind. "Where is he? Why isn't he here with you? Why did he leave you alone tonight?"

She swallowed, said, "He . . ." and swallowed again.

"He went to Tahoe, didn't he. To Paradise Flat."

". . . Yes."

"To do what? Tell me, Janine!"

"He . . . he said I shouldn't worry. He said he'd take care of things . . ."

Take care of things. Christ!

"He doesn't want me to go to jail for something I didn't do," she said. "He's my father, he loves me . . ."

"Yeah. And you love him, too, now that you need him. How long ago did he leave?"

"Not long before you came . . . ten or fifteen minutes."

One of the infrequent sets of headlights I'd passed on Highway 445 on my way here. That close, the two of us rushing by each other in the dark—going in opposite directions, after different links to finish off the chain. More than half an hour's lead now. Still enough time to stop him? Depended on how fast he drove, how fast I drove, exactly what his plans were once he got to the house on Sweetwater Drive.

Nothing is ever as simple as it seems . . .

I said, "I'm leaving now," and moved over to the door. "You stay here until you hear from your father or me. Understand? Don't talk to anyone, don't go anywhere, just wait."

She passed a hand over her tear-damp face; lifted the hand toward me, palm up, in a gesture of despair. "I don't have anyplace to go," she said.

Janine Wovoka and Wendy Oliver.

Sisters.

Chapter **22**

JOHN WOVOKA WAS THERE, all right. Still there.

From where I stood alongside a split-bole Douglas fir, I had a clear view of the house and parking area below. The entire property was bathed in light from the harvest moon, with only a few streaky clouds scudding past now and then to dim its hard white shine. The moonglow was so bright I could almost read the lettering and government seal on the driver's door of the pickup. There was no sign of the man himself. Likely he was inside the house; lights burned in there, making dull gold rectangles of the opaque windows flanking the entrance.

I stayed put for a time, waiting and watching to make sure I didn't blunder into anything when I went down there. I had looked at my watch just after letting the car drift, dark and silent, onto the shoulder across Sweetwater Drive. Half-hour past midnight. Coming onto the first of the night's long empty hours. Weariness lay heavily on me now: dull ache behind my eyes, muscles like ropes knotted through the upper half of my body. The last segment of the drive from Pyramid Lake—down Highway 89 along the Tahoe shore—had been a constant struggle to stay alert and to keep myself from driving too fast and inviting the attention of a county sheriff's deputy or highway patrolman.

Last link, I kept telling myself then, and I did it again now. We'll complete the chain before dawn, one way or another.

Stillness down below. Stillness all around me, except for the whisper and rattle of the wind in the tree branches. The hard moonlight glistened off the surface of the lake beyond the house, softened into a long silverish stripe out toward the middle. The rest of the water shone like polished black onyx. The only sign of life out there was the red-and-green running lights of a boat moving away to the southeast, toward the neon shimmer that marked the Stateline casinos.

Time to move.

I stepped back up onto the road, went slowly along the edge of it to the driveway turning. Paused there, didn't see anything to detain me, and descended at the same slow pace, over at the far edge where there was plenty of tree shadow. My shoes made little sliding sounds on the rough surface, but they weren't sounds that carried.

On level ground, I angled over to the carport and across in front of Polhemus's Cougar to the house wall. Listened, didn't hear anything, started out past the corner—and then backed up quick and froze because I *did* hear something: a clicking, a scraping, then heavy footfalls. I eased my head around the corner. John Wovoka had opened the door and was coming out.

He didn't look my way as he shut the door. In his left hand he carried a flashlight—a little bigger and more powerful than the one I'd unclipped from under the dash and slipped into my jacket pocket before quitting the car. I slid my left hand in on top of it; put my right on the Smith & Wesson .38 that weighted the other coat pocket. But I did not need either one yet. John Wovoka put his back to me and moved past the pickup, walking in a stiff, purposeful stride, and made his way down to the pier and then along the float arm onto which the boat shelter had been built. He disappeared inside the shelter. A few seconds later, through chinks in the rough-wood siding, I saw flickers of light from his flash.

I sidled around the corner and along the wall to the front entrance. The door wasn't locked. And he'd left the lights on inside. I opened the door without making any sound, slipped through and shut it soft behind me.

He had drawn the drapes in the living room; that was the first thing I noticed. I moved through the foyer, past the kitchen, to where I could see into the hallway. Polhemus's body had been shifted toward the far end; it lay wrapped now in a thick canvas tarpaulin, the ends tied off with pieces of brown hemp. The hallway floor where the corpse had originally lain was so clean, it glistened. There was no sign of the Saturday night special. Had John Wovoka put it with the body or kept it on his person?

I reversed direction, eased the door open again, eased myself out. He was still in the boat shelter, but now the beam from his flash was stationary: he'd propped it on something so he would have the use of both hands. There was not much doubt what he was up to down there, or what he intended to do with Polhemus's corpse.

I worked my way along the house and the raised deck, toward the pier. Muffled noises came from the shelter: a winglike flapping, as of a piece of canvas being shaken; little thumpings and clatterings. I used those to cover my run from the end of the deck to the pier. I'd gone halfway out to the T floats when the noises in the shelter stopped. I stopped too, waiting. I had the flashlight in my left hand now, the .38 out in my right.

The light inside moved, flicked bright over another part of the wall and then dulled as he turned it away and downward. More noises then, different ones, louder but only because I was so much closer to the shelter. I went ahead to the floats, walking soft, and turned along the inner edge of the left one. The sounds inside the shelter continued unchecked. When I reached the near wall I stopped again and then poked my head around the corner so I could peer inside.

Thick, murky shadows enclosed a puddle of light from his torch. The puddle was inside the shadow-shape of a boat—a small, new-looking outboard runabout—tied to iron hooks set

into a narrow walkway on this side. On the walkway where
he'd pitched it, a canvas cover lay partly folded and partly
crumpled in a shape that resembled a huge mangled bird. He
was down on one knee in the cockpit, his back to me, the flash
on the deck beside him so he could see what he was doing
under the dash. Crossing the ignition wires, probably—an easy
enough job with a boat ignition.

I stepped around the corner onto the walkway, pointed the
gun and my flashlight at him, pinned him with the flash beam,
and said, "That's enough of that, John."

He came around on his knees with such suddenness that he
sent his own torch clattering across the deck; it hit something
and canted upward at a forty-five-degree angle, so that its stab
of light picked out a cobwebbed corner of the far wall. He
threw one arm up to shield his eyes. I could see his body tense,
like an animal gathering itself to spring.

"No sudden moves, John. I'm armed."

He didn't relax any, but the coiling stopped; he was frozen
in place now. He said in a low, tight voice, "Who are you?"

"The detective from San Francisco, remember? We talked
up at Pyramid Lake."

". . . I remember."

"I just came from there. Your trailer. Janine and I had a
long talk."

He made a sound that was as close to a growl as any human
sound I've ever heard. "If you hurt her—"

"I didn't hurt her. She had a pistol of yours and I took it
away from her, that's all."

"The authorities . . . ?"

"No, I didn't call them. Not yet. I came straight here."

"Why?"

"To stop you from getting rid of Polhemus's body."

"She didn't kill him," he said. There was anguish on his
heavily seamed face, and a fierce protectiveness as well. "It
was an accident . . . he was out of his head and he tried to
hurt her . . ."

"Then why do this? Why didn't you just notify the authorities yourself?"

"You think they'd believe her?" Bitterness warped his voice, made it crack a little. "An Indian girl?"

"What did you do with Polhemus's gun?"

"Put it with his body."

"Okay. Stand up. Turn the pockets of your jacket inside out and then turn around, slow."

He did that. The jacket pockets were empty, and if he'd had the Saturday night special shoved into his belt, I'd have seen it; the old Levi jacket was short-hemmed.

"Let's go up to the house, John."

"And do what? Call the sheriff?"

"No. There's something else I want to do first."

He stared, squinting, into the flash beam without moving. Then he started to reach down for his own torch.

I said, "No, leave it there. Shut it off but leave it there." And when he'd obeyed and then climbed up onto the walkway, "Before we go, listen to this. If you've got any idea of jumping me, you'd better forget it. What would you do if you got the gun? Shoot me with it? You'd have to, you know—shoot me and then take my body out into the lake and dump it along with Polhemus's. I don't think you're capable of murder, not even to protect Janine. How about it?"

One, two, three beats. "No," he said.

"No trouble between you and me, then?"

"No trouble."

"I'll back up and you follow."

I backed around the corner, waited for him to appear, then switched off the flash. The moonlight was bright enough. I let him precede me off the pier and he went docilely enough; he was a man of his word. But bitterness and frustration were strong in him; I could see them in the set of his face, the slump of his shoulders. It was plain enough what he was thinking: He had failed his daughter. She'd finally come home, finally turned to him as he had always hoped she would—and this sacrifice he had been willing to make for her, this compromise of his honesty and his principles, had turned out to be empty, futile. He would lose Janine again, now, and this time it would be for good. There is no magic. There aren't any miracles.

As we neared his pickup I said, "Did Janine give you the key to Polhemus's car?"

"No. But I found his keys inside the house."

"You have them on you?"

"In my pocket."

"Go on ahead to the carport."

When we got there I told him to unlock the driver's door, slide in under the wheel, and unlock the passenger door for me. He obeyed without question or comment. I sat on the passenger seat, the door open so the dome light would stay on, and punched the latch button on the dash compartment. The cassettes for the Cougar's tape deck were jumbled inside—the same ones that had spilled free last Sunday when Polhemus yanked his Saturday night special out of there. I removed them one by one. The first eight were all labeled: various groups with names like Blood and Thunder that specialized in heavy-metal rock music. The ninth cassette had no label of any kind.

I said to John Wovoka, "Switch on the ignition. I want to play this tape."

"Why?"

"You'll see. Go ahead."

He switched on the ignition. I fed the cassette into the tape deck and punched the Play button. Static ripped out of the speakers; I lowered the volume. And what was recorded on the tape began to play.

It was the right tape, the one Janine had told me about. Not the safest place to keep it, here in the car with a bunch of labeled cassettes, not if Polhemus had intended it as an insurance policy. But then, he hadn't been a very smart kid. Good for me, too bad for him.

He started out—a little stiffly, as if he'd been self-conscious about speaking into a microphone even when he was alone with it—by identifying himself and saying that he was going to record what had happened since "Dave Burnett found a lot of money and screwed up his life and mine." He was making the record, he said, in case anything happened to him the way it had to Burnett. "They say he killed himself and I guess he did but I don't know it for sure. I'll never kill *myself* and if I turn up dead and it looks like I did, it's a lie, a big fucking lie."

I glanced over at John Wovoka. He was sitting rigidly, eyes front, listening to Polhemus's scratchy, nervous voice. In the pale dome light, his face was like one cast in bronze—a Charles Russell sculpture of a Sioux warrior I had seen once.

Polhemus spent a minute or so sketching in background: his and Burnett's trips to Tahoe and Reno "to gamble and party, see what kind of pussy we could find." None of the girls they picked up meant anything to them, he said. "They were just for grins. I'm a lover, not a husband." Small-boy smugness in that last; I could almost see him smirking a little, slyly, as he spoke. I looked over at John Wovoka again; he hadn't moved. But I could feel his anger and his bitterness and his pain.

Polhemus's voice droned on. A Saturday night at the end of April . . . a party in Reno . . . the girls they were shacking up with wanted to drive up early, do some shopping, catch a lounge show at Bally's . . . Burnett didn't want to go along, he felt like playing some blackjack, but maybe he'd drive up later. Then, finally, Polhemus got to the meat of it—the first link in the big chain.

Dave left Tahoe about eight o'clock. It was dark and there wasn't much traffic, he said. He was coming down the grade from Spooner Summit and this car a couple of hundred yards in front of him, all of a sudden it started weaving funny, jumped over a lane and veered onto the shoulder. Dave said it wasn't like a blowout, it was like something had happened to the driver.

He pulled off in front of the other car, this big Caddy sedan, and went to have a look. That was Dave, always poking his nose where it didn't belong. The other driver was slumped over the wheel, gasping for breath, and when Dave opened the door the guy, an old guy in his sixties, he said something about having a heart attack. Dave didn't know what to do, he was no paramedic, but

*he thought maybe the old guy had pills or something so
he fumbled around in his pockets looking but he didn't
find any pills. Then he saw this suitcase, it was lying on
the passenger seat, and he thought maybe there was pills
in there. He got in on that side and started to open the
suitcase. The old guy had a fit, tried to stop him. Then he
grabbed his chest and slumped over the wheel again.*

*Dave thought he was dead. But he opened the suitcase
anyway, still looking for pills, and it was full of money.
Dave said he nearly crapped in his pants when he saw it
—fifty-dollar bills, hundred-dollar bills, all stacked inside
that suitcase.*

*So he took it. Who wouldn't take it? He thought the
old guy was dead, there was nobody else around except
cars on the highway and none of them was stopping, and
all that money just sitting there. So he waited until the
highway was empty and then he put the suitcase in his
car and got the hell out of there.*

*He didn't keep on going to Reno. He turned around
and drove back to my cabin at Fallen Leaf. It was the
safest place to count the money, he said. Turned out there
was two hundred thousand bucks in that suitcase. Two
hundred thousand big ones. He got a hard-on sitting
there with all that money. That's what he said when he
finally told me about it. Biggest hard-on he ever had in
his life. Bet he jerked off, too, right into all that cash.*

*Me and the girls got back late that night. He was still
up, half stoned on grass. He told us he found some
money but not how or how much there really was. He
wanted it all for himself, the greedy prick. He said there
was only fifty thousand. He said he'd give me ten—ten
out of two hundred. Big shot, big pal. I should of known
when he wouldn't show us the money, just the suitcase.
He kept that suitcase locked in the trunk of his car until
we were back in San Francisco. Then he told me how
much there really was. He had to because he was gonna
tell Karen, his main squeeze, that he'd won one of the
Megabucks jackpots and he wanted me to back him up. I*

*told him go fuck himself but he said he wouldn't give me
the ten thousand if I didn't back him up. So I had to do
it.*

Outrage tightened Polhemus's voice as he spoke those last
several sentences. He had begun to hate his best buddy when
he learned the true amount of the stolen money: the price of
friendship to Jerry Polhemus had been one hundred and fifty
thousand dollars. And his hatred really blossomed a few days
later, when the whole thing blew up in Burnett's face and the
backlash caught him, too.

*They grabbed Dave when he was leaving work. Two guys
—Mob guys, enforcers. The girls warned him, they said it
might be Mob money. Nobody has that much cash in a
suitcase in Nevada except the Mob, they said, and they
thought it was only fifty thousand then. But Dave, big
smart Davey, he wouldn't listen. He said there was no
way anybody could know he took the suitcase. No way, he
said. Well, he was wrong, God damn him. The two guys
that grabbed him, they took him to this place on De Haro
Street, some manufacturing company, and they pushed
him around and told him how wrong he was.*

*That old guy in the Caddy, he wasn't dead when Dave
took the suitcase. He didn't die until a week later. Dave's
car was in front of the Caddy, the Caddy's lights were on,
and the old guy raised up before Dave drove off and he
got Dave's license number. He was in a coma or something for a few days but he came out of it long enough
before he went belly-up to give the number to his bosses.
Then Dave, and me too, we were in deep shit.*

*The enforcers told him he had to give the money back,
all of it, every penny. And ten thousand more as a pen-
alty. He said he'd already spent some, bought a new car
and a bunch of other stuff, blew a couple thousand gambling, gave the ten thousand to me. He said there was no
way he could come up with so much cash, not in a hurry
like they wanted it. They didn't care. They gave him a*

*week. If he didn't have it by then they said they'd kill
him, and Karen and his sister too.*

*But he couldn't do it. And he couldn't get them to give
him any more time. So he went and killed himself—took
a whole bottle of pills, for chrissake. But before he did
that he came around and told me the whole story and
said I had to give the ten thousand back. I told him to
piss off, it was my money now and his problem. So the
son of a bitch sicced those enforcers on my ass. Jesus, I
was never so scared in my life. I gave them the money—I
had to. What else could I do? They said they'd kill me
and they meant it. They might still kill me. How do I
know they didn't murder Dave when he couldn't come up
with the rest of what he owed them? Maybe they did.
Those guys, those Mob guys, they'll do anything to get
what they want.*

There was more, but most of it was self-pitying maunder-
ings. And one nasty aside: He'd almost told Karen the truth
after the funeral, he said, "to get back at Dave for siccing
those enforcers on me," but decided it was smarter to keep his
mouth shut. The tape had been made before Allyn hired me,
so there was nothing about his reactions to my reopening the
whole can of worms.

He had been wrong about Burnett's death; there was no
question in my mind that David Burnett had died by his own
hand. Terrified kid no brighter than Polhemus, with a warped
sense of loyalties, in way over his head with people who had a
reputation for making good on their threats. The pressure had
been too much for him, and so he'd taken the easy way out. I
could just see him rationalizing it: He was sacrificing himself
for Allyn and Karen, the two people in his life he had actually
cared for. If he was dead, the Mob would just write off the
balance owed and that would be the end of it. All very noble
—the last act of a coward and a fool. He'd made the right
guess about Arthur Welker's decision, but he could just as
easily have been wrong. He could have put Allyn's and Karen's

lives in even more jeopardy than if he'd stayed around and faced the consequences of his greed.

No loss, David Burnett. No loss, either, Jerry Polhemus.

I let the tape run for a full minute after Polhemus's voice stopped, to make sure he hadn't recorded anything else; then I pushed the rewind button. I had closed the car door midway through the cassette and John Wovoka and I were sitting there in the dark. I still had the .38 resting on my lap but I might as well have tossed it into the backseat. Or given it back to John Wovoka.

So here we were, at the end of it, with the last link in place. Nothing much left to do now except to call the sheriff's department and explain the whole sorry business to the authorities. Tell them about Arthur Welker, too—sure. Let them listen to the tape. Only problem was, Polhemus hadn't mentioned Welker's name. Likely never knew it because it had never been given to him or to Burnett. Welker had let Manny Atwood handle things and kept himself hidden in the background. There was nothing to tie him to Burnett or Polhemus, no evidence of any wrongdoing on his part.

WELKER WINS. Like a gleeful headline in Satan's newspaper. WELKER WINS.

The recorder made a low clicking sound and switched off. I retrieved the tape, put it into my pocket. I was aware, then, that John Wovoka had turned his head and was looking at me for the first time since we'd got into the Cougar. I met his gaze in the faint glow from the tape deck's red indicator light.

He said, low, "Pigs—rutting pigs. I'm glad they're dead, both of them."

"You have a right to feel that way. But they were victims too, John. Just like Janine. The real villain is the owner of that two hundred thousand dollars."

"The Mob," he said, nodding. "Scum of the earth."

"Just one man. His name is Arthur Welker."

"You know him?"

"I know him," I said. I explained about Welker, with the name bitter in my mouth. I even confessed my humiliation at Welker's hands on Lobo Point.

"He won't pay," John Wovoka said, "not in this life. His kind never pays. They're above the law."

"Not always. This time . . . yes."

He was silent for a clutch of seconds. Then he said, " 'When your loved ones die or are hurt you must not cry or do harm to anyone in return. You must not fight. You must do right always. It will give you satisfaction in life and rewards in the afterlife.' " He laughed, a short sharp humorless bark. "The words of the false prophet Wovoka, disciple of Wodziwob."

"They're good words," I said, "for the most part."

"I believed in them once. No more."

"What do you believe in now? That sometimes you have to fight? Maybe even fight evil with evil?"

"Would I have come here tonight if I didn't?"

"No. No, you wouldn't. Let's go into the house, John."

He switched off the ignition and we went on into the house. From the foyer, you could see the phone on the kitchen wall. John Wovoka stopped, looked over at it, looked at me.

"No," I said, "I'm not going to make the call. Not now, maybe not at all."

A puzzled frown added creases to his deeply lined face. He stood watching me.

There was a thickness in my chest; I felt sweaty, hot and cold at the same time. A voice in my head said: Don't do this, you're as big a fool as David Burnett if you do. But I had been thinking about it for some time now, off and on. I had started thinking about it on the drive down from Pyramid Lake.

John Wovoka said, without emotion, "What, then? Will you help me, help Janine?"

"Not by dumping Polhemus's body in the lake, no."

"Then—?"

Don't do this!

"There's another way," I said.

Chapter **23**

IT WAS JUST 2:00 A.M. when we slipped out of the boat shelter onto the lake.

The boat that had been tied in there was a twelve-foot Chris-Craft powered by a 3.0-litre MerCruiser—an open-cockpit four-seater with plenty of deck space. John Wovoka had had no difficulty hot-wiring the ignition. The engine hadn't been fired in some time and it was balky at first, but once it caught and held, it purred along soft, throaty, with no hitches. The exhaust was quiet, too, at least at idle and at crawling speed.

John Wovoka did the piloting. He knew boats better than I did. And he knew Lake Tahoe as well. Thanks to his job as a game warden, he kept government navigational charts and topographical maps of the area in his pickup. That made our task a little easier. So did the fact that the Chris-Craft was outfitted with a compass.

I sat next to him in the left-hand forward seat. Oddly, now that we were under way, I felt very calm, almost detached. Not thinking ahead, not thinking about much of anything. The apprehension had all been in making the decision myself and then laying it out for John Wovoka. If he had balked at

the idea, there might have been more anxiety for me, more
soul-searching; but he hadn't. Just listened to what I had to
say, asked a few pertinent questions, thought it all out for a
couple of minutes, and then agreed in a flat, determined voice.
His emotionless acceptance, the machinelike precision with
which he set about making the necessary preparations, had
had a catalytic effect on me. It allowed me to function in the
same way, to approach what we were about to do as if it were a
military operation: two soldiers, linked by purpose and disci-
pline, feelings screwed down under tight lids, with the mission
and its success outweighing every other consideration.

When we were a hundred yards out, he opened the throttle
to quarter-speed, then to half, to three-quarters, to full. The
engine stayed quiet at low speeds, which was all that mattered,
and there was no backfiring through the exhaust. Good boat;
we couldn't have found a better one, it seemed, if we'd set out
with a list of requirements.

He set a southeasterly course at full throttle. The distance
we had to cover was about a dozen miles all together. The
lights of South Lake Tahoe and the Stateline casinos made a
long stationary curve on our right; car headlights ran through
them now and then like pinballs on a neon-lit board. More
clouds had gathered but a high wind kept them moving, so
that when one of them obscured the moon it was only for a
few seconds at a time. Out here on open water, the night wind
was chilly enough to make me glad I'd thought to get my
topcoat out of the car. The droplets of spray that came over
and around the windshield were icy on my cheeks.

There were no other boats anywhere that I could see. Us
alone on all that silver and black, with the stars like firepoints
strewn among the clouds and the surrounding mountains lifting huge black and white-crowned goblin shapes against the
sky. It was supposed to make you feel small and insignificant,
all that dark immensity, but that was not the way I felt. Instead I felt a part of both the immensity and the darkness, like
a cell within a vast body—integral, vital to the whole.

For a while we seemed to be making no real headway, as if
we were suspended in time and space between two points.

Then, all at once, it seemed, the Nevada shore grew from a wall of shapeless black, broken only by a sprinkling of lights, into individual landmasses, houses, trees. Off on our right, the cluster of high-rise casino-hotels took on definition as well, burning varicolored holes in the darkness less than two miles away. The outjut of land that appeared directly ahead of us would be Zephyr Point. It was the landmark John Wovoka had chosen, the easiest to spot from a distance on this part of the shoreline.

He took us to within a few hundred yards of the point before he changed direction, northward. When we cleared Zephyr Cove he angled in closer to land and cut back to three-quarter throttle. A little less than three miles to go. The passive waiting had drawn me taut, made me aware of the dragging weight of fatigue; but I could feel the tightness easing again as we closed in. I leaned forward, my hands on the dash, peering ahead over the top of the windshield.

A short dark peninsula loomed ahead, lightless, heavily furred with trees. That ought to be it, I thought—and when John Wovoka throttled down to quarter-speed and shut off our running lights, I knew it was. Lobo Point. I stared up at the rise of land beyond, inshore. We were within a hundred yards of the point before I could make out the roofline of Arthur Welker's house; the rest of it was obscured by the trees.

John Wovoka chopped down to crawling speed as we came past the tip. No clouds covered the moon now; I could see the cove and the rest of the property clearly. Strip of beach, dock and boathouse, the *Arthur III* tied up at the end of the dock; brushy slope bisected by stairs and chair lift; three terraces and the house above, dark and monolithic from this perspective. None of the facing windows was lighted. There were a pair of night-lights in ornate lantern-type casings mounted one on either end of the house at the ground-floor level, but neither one gave off much illumination. The terraces and slope and beach area were all dark except for dustings of moonshine. Everywhere I looked there was stillness. The entire place had a somnolent aspect, turned in on itself for the night.

We glided on past, beyond the land finger on the north side

of the cove, until the house and grounds disappeared from view. Ahead the shoreline was barren and lightless for at least a mile, thick with timber close by. John Wovoka made a tight turn, came back on the north end of the finger; we were twenty yards offshore when he shut the throttle all the way down to idle. The boat settled into a faint rocking drift. The throb of the engine and exhaust was pitched so low, I could hear the rise and fall of insect noise filtering out of the woods.

The shore along the finger here was a low rocky cutbank, overgrown with ferns and brush and the tangled roots of pine and fir trees. John Wovoka had gotten out of his seat as soon as he shut down the throttle and was up on the bow; he held us off with the boat's emergency oar. I was on my feet too, by then, shedding my topcoat and jacket.

I said in a whisper, "Just the way it was yesterday. And no night guards or dogs." It was the first time either of us had spoken since a few minutes before we'd left Paradise Flat.

"Better hurry, then."

He let the boat ease in sideways until the port side was tight against the cutbank. There did not seem to be any underwater snags here; he felt safe in letting the Chris-Craft lie in close like this. It would have been easy enough for me to climb ashore, make my way through the woods and around to the beach. But that was the fool's way. You can't walk through woods and brush at night without making noise that might carry; and there was no way to get from the trees to the dock without coming right out into the open. More importantly, I remembered Welker bragging that his house and property was protected by an expensive security system. It was likely he'd installed safeguards out here as well—photoelectric cells, pressure-sensitive alarm devices. Men like him make enemies among their own kind, deadly enemies, and they don't like to leave themselves vulnerable to attack from any direction.

But not even the Arthur Welkers can think of everything, safeguard every possible contingency. The one thing he apparently wasn't concerned about was the one spot in which he was vulnerable—his Achilles' heel.

I stripped down to my shorts. The night wind burned cold

against my bare skin. But the water would be worse; mountain lakes are always bitter cold, even in the middle of summer and especially at night. If we'd had more time to prepare, I'd have gotten a wetsuit. As it was . . .

Even though I braced myself, set my teeth and jaw as I lowered my body over the side, the first shock almost took my breath away. I submerged to the neck, hanging on to the gunwale with one hand, enduring the chill until my body temperature could adjust. I have always been a good swimmer, and I'm a better one now that I've slimmed down and gotten myself in condition, but I had to swim several hundred yards in this icy water; starting out prematurely would only make me tire sooner.

John Wovoka's head and upper body leaned out above me. He said, "If anything goes wrong, swim straight this way. I'll pick you up."

"Will do."

He seemed to want to say something else, turned away instead.

I hung on to the gunwale for another minute or so. Dangerous business coming up, but I felt no apprehension. Seemed to feel even more detached, now, as if I were observing all of this at the same time I was taking part in it. Stray thought: *I really don't know myself anymore.* Then I quit thinking and shoved away from the boat and began to swim.

I used a steady crawl out around the tip of the finger and into the cove. Trod water long enough to get my bearings and to make sure that nothing had altered the quiescent aspect of the house, then struck out again toward the dock. I made sure to keep my arms and legs moving in a smooth, even tempo, so that I cleaved the water without sound. I no longer felt the cold. The muscles in my legs and shoulders were tight when I neared the dock but without any immediate danger of cramping. Exhaustion was the big worry; it was dragging at me again. There was still plenty to do, and on the swim back I would have to put forth twice the effort because of the company I would have.

The *Arthur III* was tied across the outer edge of the dock, her bow to the north. Sixteen-foot Bayliner, mostly long, sleek hull and superstructure, with a short squared-off stern; she would sleep at least four belowdecks. Baby of his fleet. Yeah. But it was also his Achilles' heel. He thought it possible somebody might try to sneak in at night to attack him or his house, but to steal one of his boats? Not many craft are stolen on Tahoe, and cruisers of this type almost never. Where would a thief take it once he got it?

You'll find out, Artie, I thought. Yes you will.

I swam along the cruiser's port side, around the stern to the dock. A scum of algae lay in the water there; when I broke through it it gave off a faint rotting-humus smell that made my throat close up. For a time I hung on to one of the pilings to rest and study the house and grounds again. Still sleeping. Clouds drifted over the moon, turning the slope and terraces into masses of inky shadow. When that happened I leaned up to where the *Arthur III*'s stern line was looped around a dock cleat, untied it, coiled it enough to push all of it up over the stern and onto the deck so it wouldn't drag loose. Then I swam back along the port side and around the bow to the north side of the dock.

The shifting clouds continued to cut off most of the moon's hard white shine as I untied the bowline from the cleat there. I coiled the rope but this time I held on to it. When I laid my shoulder against the bow and shoved, using the dock for leverage, the cruiser swung outward with a low scraping sound: starboard gunwale rubbing against a Styrofoam bumper astern. Not a carrying sound. I paddled back along that side and made my next push amidships, to get the Bayliner completely clear of the dock. Back to the bow, then, and a nudge there to swing her farther out until she was aimed past the tip of the land finger, northward.

John Wovoka was out there waiting. I could just make out the shape of the Chris-Craft in the still-clotted dark, lying a few yards offshore.

I stroked forward of the cruiser's bow, letting the rope uncoil behind me. There was just enough of it so that I could take one loop around my chest under my arms and still maintain some slack. It took me several seconds to tie it off; my fingers were starting to numb. Treading water, I glanced back toward Welker's property. Nothing had changed in the dark tableau. One, two, three deep breaths and I struck out again in the same steady crawl, not too fast, not too slow.

The strain of towing the Bayliner began to tell almost immediately. Its resisting weight threatened to cramp muscles in my legs, arms, and back; I had to stop and rest every couple of minutes. Seventy yards to where John Wovoka waited. Sixty. Not far now. Fifty. Not far, not far, almost there—

Cramp in my right calf, so sudden and savage that I had to bite my tongue to keep from crying out. I twisted around, clawed up the rope until I had hold of a bow-rail stanchion, and clung there with one hand and rubbed at the calf with the other, flexing the leg and foot, until the muscle unknotted. I was shaking with cold and weakness when I submerged again.

I wasn't sure if I had enough strength to swim those last fifty yards—but I did not have to find out. John Wovoka had seen that I was having trouble and took the risk of coming to meet me. I saw him swing out from beyond the finger, make a wide slow loop to come in along the *Arthur III* 's port side. I trod water, working my leg to keep it from cramping again, listening to the faint throb of the Chris-Craft's exhaust and looking back toward Welker's property. The damn moon was out again, silvering the house and grounds, but nobody had woken up and seen us out here and raised an alarm. Not yet, they hadn't.

John Wovoka shut the throttle down and nosed the Chris-Craft in just ahead of where I was. I had the Bayliner's bowline untied from around my chest by the time he leaned over the stern; I gave him the rope, and while he made it fast to a cleat I swam ahead along the port side. I was struggling to haul myself over the gunwale—my arms felt as if they had lead sinkers tied to them—when he caught hold of my arms and lifted me aboard.

"All right?"

". . . All right."

Immediately he went to the wheel and opened the throttle

just enough to get us moving. There was a jerk as the *Arthur III*'s bowline pulled taut, a creaking of the rope; we began to glide ahead at an angle past the finger. I encased myself in the heavy wool blanket we'd brought from the Paradise Flat house, then sat on the forward seat shivering, trying to get my wind back—watching behind us.

Except for the two night-lights, Lobo Point remained a slumbering expanse of black and silver as we passed out of sight.

WE TOWED the *Arthur III* a third of a mile north by northwest, so that we were well out into the lake before we shut down and boarded her. I was dried off and dressed by then, still a little chilled but no longer shivering. I might have a head cold tomorrow, but that was a small price to pay for a nocturnal swim in Lake Tahoe.

The first thing we did was to don gloves and transfer Jerry Polhemus's corpse from the Chris-Craft, where it had lain all the while under the canvas cover, to the short rear deck of the Bayliner. The body was wrapped in the tarp John Wovoka had provided, its end tied and affixed with some pieces of heavy scrap iron we'd found. In with it was a bundle made up of Polhemus's clothing and wallet and the cassette tape he'd recorded. His Saturday night special, the gun that had ended his life, was in the pocket of my topcoat—for now.

It took John Wovoka a little less than ten minutes to cross the *Arthur III*'s ignition wires. When he had the engine running smoothly, I got back into the Chris-Craft and cast off the lines and used the emergency oar to shove clear. He put on the cruiser's running lights, opened the throttle; the course he set was due west. I followed at a distance of a hundred yards. And after we'd gone a mile or so, I took Polhemus's revolver out of my coat and dropped it overboard.

The place we'd picked to abandon the *Arthur III* was a quarter of a mile outside the entrance to Emerald Bay. There were no private homes in the immediate vicinity, for one thing; and Emerald Bay was a popular fishing spot, for another. It was still early enough, though, so that there were no other boats around when we neared the area.

When John Wovoka cut the Bayliner's lights, I followed suit with the Chris-Craft's. He chopped the throttle at the same time, so that the *Arthur III* settled into her own wake. I moved up alongside at low speed, cut to idle, and held there for the five minutes or so it took him to undo the hot-wire on the cruiser's ignition. When he finally clambered down beside me, I let him take the wheel and us away from there.

That part of it—the worst part—was done.

THE FIRST LIGHT of dawn was in the sky, a line of salmon pink above the eastern peaks, when we reached the beachfront at Paradise Flat. John Wovoka eased the Chris-Craft into the shelter, and I tied up while he undid his second hot-wire; then we covered the boat with its fitted piece of canvas. Except for the amount of gas we'd used, there was nothing to arouse the suspicion of the owners when they returned from their European vacation. And the fuel loss was likely to pass unnoticed.

Inside the house, we packed up everything that had belonged to Polhemus. While I carried his luggage out to the Cougar, John Wovoka placed an anonymous call to the El Dorado County Sheriff's Department, claiming to be a fisherman and saying that he had spotted a boat adrift outside Emerald Bay and that there was "something funny" lying on the deck. That would bring a patrol boat out in a hurry.

With my handkerchief I smeared all the Cougar's surfaces, inside and out, that either of us might have touched. I was putting my gloves back on when he emerged from the house. He said, "No problem," and got into his pickup. I slid in under the Cougar's wheel. Neither of us wanted any part of a thirty-mile round-trip drive, as tired as we both were, but it had to be done. And done now, while it was still too early for most residents and early vacationers to have left their beds for the new day.

The Cougar had a chattery clutch and loose steering; there was sweat all over me when I finished negotiating the bad stretch of cliffside road around Emerald Bay. The radio, tuned loud to a rock station, and the open driver's window helped me stay alert the rest of the way to Fallen Leaf Lake. John Wovoka followed close behind, but when I pulled off onto the platform above the Polhemus cabin, he went on along the road to turn around somewhere farther on, even though there was no other traffic and nobody afoot in the vicinity. It was better, safer, if his truck wasn't parked next to the Cougar for even a few minutes.

I set the door locks on the car and managed to transport the three pieces of luggage down the stairs in one trip. I unlocked the cabin door with Polhemus's key, took the suitcases and duffel bag into the bedroom Polhemus had occupied; opened one of the cases on the floor, put his key ring on the dresser. In the front room I gathered up the remaining snapshots from the fireplace mantel and stowed them in my jacket; I would dispose of them later. Then I hurried out, leaving the front door unlocked this time.

John Wovoka was waiting when I came up onto the road. Still nobody around. I got in beside him and laid my head back against the seat and closed my eyes as we moved off. He didn't say anything and neither did I.

Now the frame was complete.

It was not perfect, particularly not if Welker reported the *Arthur III* missing before the California and Nevada authorities got around to bracing him. He had money and connections; he could buy a good criminal lawyer if he didn't already have one; chances were he could beat a murder charge. Still, the frame was tight enough to make things rough on him for a while. Maybe even put him in bad with the higher-ups in the Mob, because of the negative publicity. His boat, with a dead man on board all trussed up and ready for disposal into the lake; evidence on the corpse that implicated Welker as a known Mob figure and gave him a plausible motive for homicide. It would look like he'd killed Polhemus himself, or had it done by one of his hirelings, and something had happened to the guy he'd sent out to dump the body: fell overboard, maybe, and drowned. Tahoe is a deep lake; the bodies of drowning victims aren't always recovered. No key in the Bayliner's ignition—but that could have gone overboard, too, in the missing pilot's pocket. Thin, sure, but it made as much sense as any story Welker could tell to contradict it. More, because of the prima facie evidence.

Welker would figure that maybe I'd had a hand in the frame; I was a logical choice. He didn't know John Wovoka existed, nor would have any reason to suspect him if he did. He knew about Janine and Wendy, of course, but he wouldn't credit either of them with the guts or intelligence to build this kind of frame; the odds were good that he wouldn't send anyone around to hassle them, or mention their names to the authorities. He also had no reason to suspect Scott McKee of complicity, or Allyn Burnett or Karen Salter.

But he'd have doubts about me, too. He knew my reputation, my working methods; I was not a man to circumvent the law; I was neither a hardcase nor a murderer. One man couldn't have done the job alone—and who'd help me? Not Eberhardt; Welker would know that as soon as he had some checking done. And as far as he was aware, I had no personal stake in framing him in such an elaborate and violent way. Yeah, he'd have doubts, all right. Enough, maybe, to make him focus his attention on his own people—somebody who had a grudge against him, or somebody with too much ambition, who knew about Burnett and Polhemus and the stolen money.

In any case, I could expect him to do one of two things about me: put the law on me to help take the heat off himself; or send Jimmy and Carl or their equivalent to pay me a visit. I had an ace in the hole either way. In Polhemus's wallet, bundled with the other stuff inside his shroud, was one of my business cards. That card would bring the law to my door whether or not Welker gave them my name. When they came I would tell them about my investigation—just enough of what I'd found out to further implicate Welker—and about being brought to his home against my will, and about his threats; then I would hang my head and admit, ruefully, that the threats had scared me right off the job. Me want to buck heads with the Mob? No sir!

That would accomplish two purposes. First, it would give me a measure of personal security; if anything happened to me, the authorities would look right at Welker. And second, it would put one more doubt in Welker's head. If I were responsible for the frame, or mixed up in it, why would I implicate myself? Why would I make myself a target? His opinion of me was low, but not low enough so that he considered me a fool.

It was all a calculated risk—I had no illusions about that. Any number of things could go wrong; the whole crazy scheme could fall apart at any stage and I could wind up dead or in jail. So was it worth it, really, what John Wovoka and I had done? Here, looking at it rationally in the cold light of day?

I thought about Welker's evil arrogance; his contempt for people like me and John Wovoka, basically honest people who prefer to live our lives within the law and without harming others; the opulence in which he dwelt and the people he surrounded himself with and where the money had come from to pay for all of that; the things he and his kind had done to David Burnett and Jerry Polhemus and God knew how many others. And then I thought about him squirming, sweating, confused, struggling blindly to patch the leaks that had suddenly sprung up in his protective dike; and of the dike maybe collapsing and washing him right out to sea.

Was it all worth it?

Christ, yes, it was.

WHEN WE CAME UP along the rim of Emerald Bay, I had a clear look out to where we had abandoned the *Arthur III*. There was another boat alongside her now, and the ant-figures of men swarming over her polished surfaces.

It was just sunrise.

SOFT GOLDEN LIGHT on Tahoe's placid surface and in the woods surrounding the Paradise Flat house. The clouds had all blown inland and the sky was a sweep of blue with green and brown and white-tipped mountains in sharp relief against it. The wind had died and there was warmth in the air already: another nice day coming up, a harbinger of the summer to follow.

I did not want to spend any more of it in that house and I was sure John Wovoka didn't either. But we were both exhausted, badly in need of sleep, and we had no other place to go. I offered to let him have the spare bedroom, but he said he would sleep on the couch in the living room; neither of us wanted the bed Janine and Polhemus had shared.

I shed my clothes and crawled between cool sheets and slept immediately. Slept deep, without dreams—or at least without any dreams I remembered when I awoke a long while later.

One-thirty in the afternoon, by my watch. Muggy in the bedroom and the rest of the house. And John Wovoka and his pickup both gone.

Long gone, I thought. Back to Pyramid Lake, to be with his daughter. Maybe he could persuade her to stay there with him, continue to shield and protect her; for her sake and his, I hoped so. No miracles, no, but perhaps there was a little magic in his life after all. A little white magic to offset the black variety we had performed last night.

I was glad he hadn't left a note or awakened me. We had nothing more to say to each other, not even good-bye. Two strangers, with little in common, thrown together by circumstance—commandos on a raid into enemy territory. The sooner we forgot each other, the sooner we could forget what we had done together in the name of justice.

In ten minutes I was dressed and out of there and into my car. Like John Wovoka, going home.

Chapter 24

ALLYN BURNETT SAID, "I don't believe you."

"I'm sorry, Ms. Burnett, but it's the truth. You can check with the Nevada Gaming Commission yourself. Your brother didn't win that money gambling."

"But criminals . . . organized crime . . . no, not David. I just don't believe it."

"I didn't say he was mixed up with organized crime. I said the two hundred thousand was Mob money and he came into possession of it somehow."

"But you didn't find out how."

"No," I said, "I didn't find out how."

We were sitting in the living room of Kerry's apartment, Kerry and I on the couch, Allyn in the wing chair across from us. It was a little past eight Friday evening and I had been back from Lake Tahoe a couple of hours. I'd called Kerry from Tahoe City, before making the long drive back, and asked her to have Allyn meet me here at eight o'clock.

I didn't blame Allyn for balking at what I had told her. It was a hard thing to accept about a brother you loved and thought you knew so well—but not half as hard as if I'd told her everything I'd uncovered about David. The partial truth was shocking; the whole truth, if she ever got wind of it, would lay her low. Her and Karen Salter both. But they weren't going to get it from me. I was not in the business of hurting people, good people, and I would have kept my mouth shut about David's theft of money from a dying man and his double life even if I did not have a vested interest in doing so.

Allyn said, "You're not even going to try to find out? You're just going to quit?"

"I'm only one man, Ms. Burnett."

"You're afraid of them, aren't you? Those people?"

"Aren't you?"

"Not if they killed my brother."

"They didn't kill him. I told you that. I think they pressured him to give back the money, yes; I think they threatened him. But he took his own life out of fear."

She wagged her head stubbornly. "It wasn't the way you say. It *wasn't*."

"All right, then. Have it your way."

"I won't pay you any more money. Not to tell me things like this, lies."

"I don't want any more of your money," I said. "I can't do anything else for you. Nobody can. It's finished. Your brother's dead; nothing anybody does now can bring him back."

She was on her feet, frustrated and angry. There was nothing I could do about that, either. She said to Kerry, "You said he was a good detective. Well, he isn't. He's . . . he's . . ." She couldn't think of anything damning enough to say about me. So she turned abruptly and stalked away into the hall.

Kerry went after her. I heard them talking in low voices, saying things that I closed my ears to; then the door slammed and pretty soon Kerry came back. She sat on the couch again, closer to me than before.

"You didn't tell her everything, did you," she said.

"What makes you think that?"

"I know you and the way you operate. You think I don't?"

"I know you do."

"Besides," she said, "I stopped by your apartment last night and listened to the messages on your answering machine. Three times to the one you made yourself from Reno."

"Why'd you do that?"

"I thought maybe there was a call you'd want to know about right away. Do you mind?"

"No," I said, "I don't mind."

"There *is* more to it than what you told Allyn?"

"If there is, I've got a good reason for keeping it to myself."

"And for not confiding in me, either?"

"Yes."

"It's that serious?"

"It's that serious."

We were quiet for a time. The night was cold, foggy, wind tugging at the weather stripping around the windows—another fine San Francisco summer in the offing. She'd set fire to a Pres-to-Log on the hearth grate and it threw a flickery, blue-flamed light into the room. Warm. Cozy. It was good to be home.

At length she said, "Did you listen to the tape when you stopped by your flat?"

"The answering machine tape? No."

"Well, Bruce Littlejohn called three times. He's desperate to have you call him back. That was his word—desperate."

"Christ. I thought I was rid of him."

"No such luck. He said Frankie Eldorp is out and an even bigger name is in. Somebody from your generation."

"My generation. Great."

"He didn't say who it is."

"That figures."

"He also claimed to have a scriptwriter who was once nominated for an Academy Award."

"Yeah. The Lunatic Academy."

I got up to use the fireplace poker on the Pres-to-Log. To hell with Bruce Littlejohn; to hell with Frankie Eldorp and the somebody from my generation and the Academy Award nominee. To hell with La-La Land.

When I returned to the couch, Kerry said, "Eberhardt asked Bobbie Jean to marry him again."

"No surprise. She must've said no or you'd have told me before this."

"She didn't say no. She said she'd think about it. She's going to say yes."

"She tell you that?"

"She didn't have to. A woman knows when another woman is ready to say yes to a marriage proposal."

"You really think so, huh?"

"Yup."

"I hope you're right. She's good for him. He needs a good woman around."

"Yes he does."

"So do I," I said.

She didn't say anything.

"Don't worry, I won't propose to you again."

"I wasn't worried," she said.

I said, "Is there anything else you want to tell me or talk about?"

"I can't think of anything."

"Good. Then what I'd like to do now is make love."

"Oh, it is?"

"Yes. Very much."

"Just like that? Tarzan want mate with Jane, Jane obey?"

"No," I said seriously. "I missed you and I want to be with you. I want to hold you."

She looked at me for a little while, in that soft way she has. Then she said, "Tarzan follow Jane," and got up and went into the bedroom.

WE LAY IN THE DARK, holding hands. We seldom talk much in the immediate aftermath of lovemaking; it's a time for quietude, for silent sharing. Neither of us had spoken for five minutes when Kerry said, "I've been thinking about this so I might as well say it. Please don't take it wrong."

"I won't."

"You're . . . different, a different person these past couple of months. And I don't just mean the anxiety attacks. You know?"

"I know."

"The changes . . . well, they're subtle. But they're there. I'm not sure I understand you as well as I used to."

"That makes two of us."

"Do they worry you, the changes?"

"Sometimes. Do they worry *you*?"

"Yes. For your sake, but for selfish reasons too. Because I resist change and I wish you were just the way you used to be."

"Does it matter to you that I'm not?"

"Matter in how I feel about you? Of course not."

"I was afraid it might."

"Don't be afraid," she said. "Deep down, you haven't changed at all. You're still the same good, kind, gentle, caring man I fell in love with."

Am I? I thought. I'm not so sure.

But all I said was, "I hope you're right."

Special Advance Preview
from the new Nameless Detective mystery

BREAKDOWN

Available February 1991 from
Delacorte Press

I WAS LATE getting to the tavern that Monday night, because I let myself put in too much overtime on a routine skip-trace. Not that being late mattered much. After three barren weeks, this angle on the Lujack case had turned into a protracted waste of time. If it weren't for the fact that all the other angles seemed to be just as dead-ended, I would have dropped it by now.

Besides, working nights kept me from brooding too much about all the bad things that had darkened Kerry's life—and mine—during the past few months.

I parked my car near the foot of Taraval, where it ends at 48th Avenue. It was a raw late-January night, with a chill wind herding a low scudding mist in from the ocean a few hundred yards away. From where I parked, you could see no more than fifty feet beyond the Great Highway, which parallels 48th here; all of Ocean Beach was obscured behind shifting traceries of gray. The pedestrian-crossing signal at the Great Highway glowed an eerie red, like a disembodied hand caught and held in motionless warning by the mist.

At the moment there was no traffic of any kind in the vicinity, even though it was only eight-thirty. There were lights in some of the squat row houses and two-unit apartment buildings along this block of Taraval, and in the scattered few business establishments in the block back across 47th, but the people were all shut away behind closed doors and drawn curtains. Life at this western edge of the city —Out There at the Beach, San Franciscans call it —is nothing like life at its teeming inner core. It has a closed-off, clannish ambiance, a different taste and texture than any other neighborhood. Part of the reason is a heterogenous mix of conservative and funky architectural styles and lifestyles; of residents old and new, blue-collar and white-collar, Asian and Anglo, neo-hippies and newlyweds, and a large percentage of retirees. The other part is intangible. Maybe the salty air and the heavy fogs and cold winds have something to do with it; maybe living on the edge—of the city, of a great land mass, of earthquake country—has something to do with it too. The reshaping and landscaping of much of Ocean Beach and the Great Highway, part of an ongoing beachfront sewer project and the need to control the hazard of wind-blown sand, has done little to alter the strangeness.

And if anything, the devastating 7.1 quake in October has increased it. You can feel it as soon as you go Out There.

I donned the cloth cap I always wore to the tavern. Or rather, that Art Canino, shop steward for a South San Francisco plumbing contractor, always wore. Then I buttoned the collar on my overcoat and got out into that freezing wind.

Quiet here, too, on a night like this. If it weren't for the foghorns, bleating distantly like lost strays, you could imagine yourself in one of the small seacoast towns upstate. The pulsebeat of the city was faint here on clear days, and when it was muffled by the fog you couldn't hear it at all. I went at an angle across the empty street, back toward 47th. Several blocks away, the headlight of one of the big L Taraval streetcars probed dimly through the fog; but even though those LRVs make a lot of noise, and even though I could feel the vibration from this one as I crossed the tracks, I couldn't hear it yet—as if it were approaching through a different dimension.

The tavern's entrance was just a narrow storefront between a dry-cleaning establishment and one of the two-unit apartment buildings. Above the door, a blue-neon cocktail glass cast a faint glow that had no particular warmth or welcome to it. The lower two-thirds of the adjacent window was covered by heavy blue cloth suspended from a horizontal pole; you couldn't see inside through the upper third unless you happened to have a stepladder handy. The name of the place was painted on the window glass in flaky blue lettering that I couldn't read until I was just a few feet away:

I went in. Most of the regulars were there, maybe a dozen altogether tonight, all but one comfortably arranged at the cluster of tables along the right-hand wall and in the rear booths. The man seated alone at the bar was not Nick Pendarves. The regulars all looked my way as I entered, but none of them smiled or nodded or offered words of greeting. Three weeks was not enough time to make me one of them; three months might not be enough. But they knew me now, and no longer seemed to resent my presence, and they were friendly enough on an individual basis.

At the far end of the bar, where I usually sat, I hoisted myself onto a cracked leather stool. Pendarves wasn't anywhere in the long, narrow room. The door to the men's john was open, which meant that he wasn't in there either.

The bartender took his time coming my way. But that didn't mean anything; he took his time serving everybody. His name was Max. If he had another name, nobody had spoken it within my hearing. He was a pudgy little guy in his early fifties, muscular through the chest and shoulders, with an egg-shaped head covered with spiky tufts of gray-black hair that made you think of pig bristles. He wouldn't gossip or let you buy him a drink; he held himself aloof even from the regulars. And he used words sparingly and grudgingly, as if he had been given a small allotment and was afraid of using it up.

"What'll it be?"

"Usual," I said.

"Bud Light?" He had a good memory for what people drank.

"Bud Light."

He set me up with the beer and a frosty glass, then moved a plastic bowl my way. Well, well, I thought. I had finally reached the intermediate beer-nut level of acceptance.

"Nick been in yet tonight?" I asked him.

"No."

"Wonder how come. He's usually here by eight."

Max shrugged.

"Working late, maybe," I said.

Max shrugged again and went down to the other end of the plank.

I sat nursing my beer, waiting. I would give Pendarves the better part of an hour—long enough to maintain my cover as the newest of the neighborhood barflies. Ten minutes walked away dragging their heels. I was in no mood for passive sitting tonight, and there was little enough here, other than the regulars, to absorb my attention. The Hideaway had no jukebox, and the small TV over the backbar was seldom turned on except by special request; an old-fashioned dartboard was about the only standard tavern diversion. The talk was muted, an irregular background drone that I didn't feel like contributing to. I tried to keep my thoughts neutral but Kerry was there, Kerry and her mother, worrying at the edges of my mind. Finally I got up and went to the dartboard and began tossing darts at it, just to have something to do.

There are all sorts of neighborhood taverns in a

city of neighborhoods such as San Francisco is. Straight and gay, white-collar and blue, ethnic and cosmopolitan, rough-trade and genteel, pickup joints and "family" watering holes; hangouts for the literati and holding pens for the illiterati; places dripping with authentic local atmosphere, adorned with phony atmosphere for the benefit of suckers and slumming tourists, completely lacking in atmosphere of any kind. But there aren't many taverns like the Hideaway anymore, in San Francisco or anywhere else in the country. They're a dying breed, soon to enter the same extinct category as black-tie supper clubs and dime-a-dance emporiums. They'll survive only as long as circumstances permit and enough of their patrons remain above ground to make them marginally profitable.

The Hideaway was just what its name suggested: a sanctuary, a literal hideaway for the men and women who frequented it. It was as much a social club and senior-citizens center as a place for the consumption of alcohol, the drowning of sorrows, and the celebrating of small victories. Most of the clientele were over fifty and had been coming here for years, or at least had lived in the neighborhood for a long time—retirees and near-retirees, widows and widowers, loners and misfits; the disabled and the forgotten, the has-beens and the never-wases. They came for the companionship of others like themselves, and because it was a place close by where they could escape the loneliness and frustrations of their private lives. That was why outsiders, casual drop-ins, were tolerated but never encouraged: They were threats to the sanctuary's delicate balance, reminders of the uncaring world-at-large that the regulars sought to avoid.

An old tavern, the Hideaway, in business continually since just after Repeal and operating under its present name for more than forty years. It was owned now by the widow of Sam Delaney, the man who had christened it Hideaway. She was in poor health, and there was some concern among the regulars that when she died her relatives would sell the property and the new owners would shut it down. If that happened, it would be a serious tragedy in their lives. There were other bars in the neighborhood, but not in the immediate vicinity and none like the Hideaway. Without it, some of these people would be lost. More than one of them, I thought, would not survive its closing for very long.

There was not much to the place, as far as the decor went. Just an oblong, high-ceilinged room, ill-lighted and musty with the smells of alcohol and tobacco, of salt-damp and age and the flavors of all the people who had made it their second home for over half a century. Long bar on the left as you came in; half a dozen well-used tables and chairs and one long cushioned bench along the wall on the right; four low-backed booths built into the far right-hand corner, two on the back wall and two on the side wall. Ancient linoleum on the floor, worn through in several places so that you could see the dark oiled boards underneath. Walls adorned with faded black-and-white photographs of a vanished San Francisco: the original Cliff House, Ocean Beach in the thirties, this neighborhood when it was all salt grass and sand dunes, before Dolger and the other developers bought it up and covered it with "affordable" housing.

The first time I'd come here, just after the new year began, the Hideaway had struck me as a drab, cheerless bar ruled by ghosts and despair. But after three weeks, I had a different impression. This may have been a haven for the elderly and the disaffected, but they didn't come here to mourn or exchange bitternesses or sit around morosely waiting to shake hands with the Grim Reaper. Most of them were vital people; they brought their hobbies, opinions, insights, and verbal pleasures in with them, and shared them freely. There was sadness here, and a sense of tragedy, but there was laughter and joy too—and a kind of warmth and camaraderie that I found enviable.

Each of the two booths along the back wall had a green-shaded droplight over it. In one of them now, a retired civil servant named Harry Briggs was playing chess with fat, fortyish, painfully shy Douglas Mikan, the youngest of the regulars, who had inherited just enough money from an overprotective mother so that he didn't have to work. They played often and well and were very serious about their chess; they almost never spoke to each other while a match was in progress. In the other back booth, Peter Vandermeer sat reading a pamphlet with great concentration. He was nearly eighty, thin and sinewy, once a cable-car motorman and now an amateur historian who probably knew more obscure facts about California history in general and San Francisco history in particular than most college professors. A couple of nights ago he had spent twenty minutes telling me more than I ever wanted to know about the Panama-Pacific Exposition of 1915.

The only person at the bar, down at the far end, was Ed McBee, a longshoreman whose wife had died not long ago. Over at the tables, there was Charlie Neale, who had a crippled right leg as the result of some sort of industrial accident. And Kate and Bob Johnson, who belonged to different political parties and had evidently spent most of their married life arguing politics. And Annie Stanhope, constantly knitting from a huge bag of yarn while she drank vast amounts of dry sherry that never seemed to have any effect on her. And Frank Parigli, who had some kind of night watchman's job and who spent his mornings combing Ocean Beach for driftwood and shells; his hobby was making collages, which he sold to gift shops for the tourist trade. And Lyda Isherwood, big and brassy, with a loud voice and a louder laugh; she claimed to have once run a whorehouse in Nevada (nobody seemed to believe her), and told bawdy stories in a surprising variety of accents and dialects. There were others, too, some whose names I had learned and some I knew nothing about. But their faces were all familiar now, and even though I was here under a false name and false pretenses, and in another week or so my life would no longer intersect with theirs, I felt an odd sort of kinship with them. If I lived Out There at the Beach instead of in Pacific Heights, if I didn't have Kerry—and, to a lesser degree, Eberhardt—this was the kind of place and these were the kind of people I might find myself gravitating to.

Kerry. I threw another dart, too hard and a little

wildly. Thinking: I *don't* have her now, do I? And what if this thing with her mother gets worse, drags on and on?

Outside, somewhere close by, there was the sudden squeal of tires on pavement, the crescendo-and-fade of a car passing at high speed. Nice driving on a foggy night, I thought. And promptly forgot about it.

But not for long.

Just about a minute had passed when the tavern's door whacked open. I felt the night's gusty breath all the way over where I was standing by the dartboard—and I watched Nick Pendarves blow in.

Pendarves was a tallish, gangly man in his mid-fifties, a couple of years younger than me. He wore his usual gray work shirt and gray work pants and gray-and-black plaid jacket, but you didn't think of him in terms of gray; you thought of him in terms of rusty. He had rust-colored hair, the kind of voice that sounded as if it were corroded, and a slow, jerky way of moving, as if all his joints needed oiling—the Tin Man of Oz left out too long in bad weather. But there was something different about him tonight; I saw it even at a distance and it put me on instant alert. His movements were quicker and more agitated than usual, and he paid no attention to the other regulars as he came down the bar. He leaned up against it between two of the stools, clutching at the beveled edge as if for support.

I moved over to where he was. When I got close enough I could see that his craggy face was pale, that the fire of bitter anger blazed in his eyes. He paid no attention to me, either, as I claimed one of the stools near him.

"Bourbon," he said to Max. "Double shot."

Max cocked his head, as much of an expression of surprise as he was ever likely to betray. Like me, Pendarves was a beer-drinker; in three weeks I had never seen him order anything else.

"Well? What the hell you waiting for?"

I watched Max get busy, Pendarves light an unfiltered Pall Mall with unsteady hands. Then I asked, "What's up, Nick? You look kind of shook."

"Son of a bitch tried to run me down," he said without looking my way.

"Who did?"

"Tried to kill *me*, by God."

"When? Just now?"

"Come out of nowhere while I was crossing the street. Couldn't of missed me by more than a couple feet. I hadn't jumped when I did . . . Christ!"

Max put the double shot down in front of him. Pendarves threw it off as if it were water, rubbed the back of his hand across his mouth. His eyes looked as hot as the tip of his cigarette.

"Kids?" Max said.

"Kids my ass. One guy, no goddamn headlights. He done it on purpose. Swerved right at me."

I said, "Who'd do a thing like that?"

"Thomas Lujack, that's who."

". . . Guy you're testifying against?"

"Him. Yeah."

"You sure it was him?"

"Sure enough."

"So you got a good look at him this time too?"

"Too dark. But it was Lujack—who the hell else? Tried to run me down like he done his partner. Well, he won't get away with it."

Max said, "Call the cops, Nick."

"Hell with the cops."

"What if he tries it again?"

"I'll make sure he don't."

"How?"

"Never mind how. That's my business."

"Better just leave it to the cops," I said.

"Hell with the cops," Pendarves said again.

"Fix him in court then, on the witness stand. If you didn't see the driver you can't be positive who it was . . ."

Pendarves wasn't listening. His head was down, his face set so tightly it was full of spasming nerves and ridges of muscle. He smoked his Pall Mall in fast, deep drags, as if he were trying to burn it up as quickly as he could.

Pretty soon he said, talking to himself, "Rivas . . . yeah, that's it. Make damn sure the bastard leaves me alone. Him and that brother of his both."

"Who's Rivas?"

No answer. What was left of his cigarette seared his fingers; he said, "Shit!" and jabbed it out viciously.

"Nick, who's Rivas?"

The sudden pain had brought him out of himself. His head snapped around my way and his eyes focused on me for the first time. "Canino," he said. "What the hell you sucking around for?"

"Hey, I was just trying to help—"

"Keep your questions to yourself." He shook

himself, the way you'd shake off a sudden chill. "Max, give me another double."

"Sure."

Another voice, shy and halting, said, "Nick . . ."

Pendarves swung around. When I looked back I saw Douglas Mikan standing a couple of feet away, fingering the knot in his tie.

"What *you* want?"

"I just . . . make sure you're all right . . ."

"Leave me alone, you fat wimp."

Mikan backed off, staring at Pendarves like a hurt puppy. All the other regulars were staring at him, too, now. Conversation had died.

"What's everybody gawking at?" he demanded.

Down the bar Ed McBee said, "Don't take it out on us, Nick. We're on your side."

"Yeah."

"Notify the cops, that's good advice—"

"Butt out, Ed, huh? All of you just mind your business and let me take care of mine."

He swung around again as Max set him up with his second double. He put that one away as quickly as the first, then shoved away from the bar and stalked to the door in his rusty-jointed stride and was gone into the night.

I stayed where I was for about ten seconds. Then I shook my head and said, "Ah, the hell with it," as if I had lost my taste for beer and bar-lounging. I got up and went after Pendarves.

He was down the block a ways, just crossing Taraval—doing it cautiously, head twitching left, right, left, right. I went in the same direction but on this side of the street. I saw him get into his car, a beat-up Plymouth Fury with a loose rear bumper; heard the starter grind as I hurried across 47th Avenue. Thirty yards separated me from my car when he maneuvered out of the parking space; twenty yards when he made a too-fast turn out of sight on 47th, heading north.

I was on the run by then, with my keys in my hand. It took me less than fifteen seconds to get the door unlocked, the car started, and into a fast U-turn across the streetcar tracks. When I made the swing onto 47th, the Plymouth was two blocks away, approaching the Rivera Street intersection. Almost immediately its taillights flashed bloodily in the blowing fog and Pendarves turned right onto Rivera. I accelerated to close the gap—but I needn't have bothered. Two blocks east, the Plymouth had slowed again and was just turning into the weedy driveway next to a weathered yellow-brown corner house.

The house belonged to Pendarves. The way it looked, he was not going anywhere but home.

He quit his car, leaving it in the drive rather than putting it away in the sagging garage that crouched at the rear edge of his property. I drove past as he disappeared through a gate between the garage and the house. In the next block I made another U-turn and pulled in to the curb and cut my lights. From there I could see the mist-wreathed front of his house, the Plymouth sitting dark in the driveway.

Pretty soon lights went on inside the house. And stayed on. I sat there for twenty minutes: Pendarves did not come back out. Whatever he intended to do about Thomas Lujack, he apparently wasn't going to do it tonight.

Well, all right. That part of it was on hold. As for the rest of it . . .

For three weeks I had been working on Pendarves at the Hideaway, the only public place he frequented with any regularity, trying to pry some sort of useful information out of him; and now for the first time all that effort had paid some dividends. In fact, this was the first real break Eberhardt and I had had since we'd undertaken our investigation. The only trouble was, it was potentially disastrous in more ways than one. If Thomas really had tried to run Pendarves down tonight, it blew us right out of the water.

Thomas Lujack was our client.

And we were trying to prove him innocent of one hit-and-run murder charge already.